'*Bedwell-Grime* paints vivid pictures with her pen . . . by the end of the book I was left gasping for breath and eager for more' ***Infinity Plus website***

'*Stephanie Bedwell-Grime* has a fantastically engaging writing style and she has a wicked sense of humour as well . . . I can only pray that the real afterlife is something like that described by the twisted mind of Bedwell-Grime. A warm, funny and intelligently written look at what might be beyond the pearly gates. One of the funniest, yet at the same time rather touching, books I have read in a long time' ***Sci-Fi Online***

'With this angel in town, even Buffy and Anita Blake would have time on their hands. For high octane fantasy adventure, grab this book and fasten your seatbelt' **Juliet E McKenna, author of *The Tales of Einarinn***

'Fiery characters . . . hellish good fun!' **Freda Warrington, author of *A Taste of Blood Wine* and *The Jewelfire Trilogy***

FALLEN ANGEL

FALLEN ANGEL

STEPHANIE BEDWELL-GRIME

TELOS
.CO.UK

First published in England in 2004 by Telos Publishing Ltd
61 Elgar Avenue, Tolworth, Surrey KT5 9JP
www.telos.co.uk

Telos Publishing Ltd values feedback. Please e-mail us with any comments you may have about this book to: feedback@telos.co.uk

ISBN: 1-903889-69-3 (paperback)

Typeset by TTA Press
5 Martins Lane, Witcham, Ely, Cambs CB2 2LB
www.ttapress.com

Printed in India

1 2 3 4 5 6 7 8 9 10 11 12 13 14 15

British Library Cataloguing in Publication Data. A catalogue record for this book is available from the British Library.

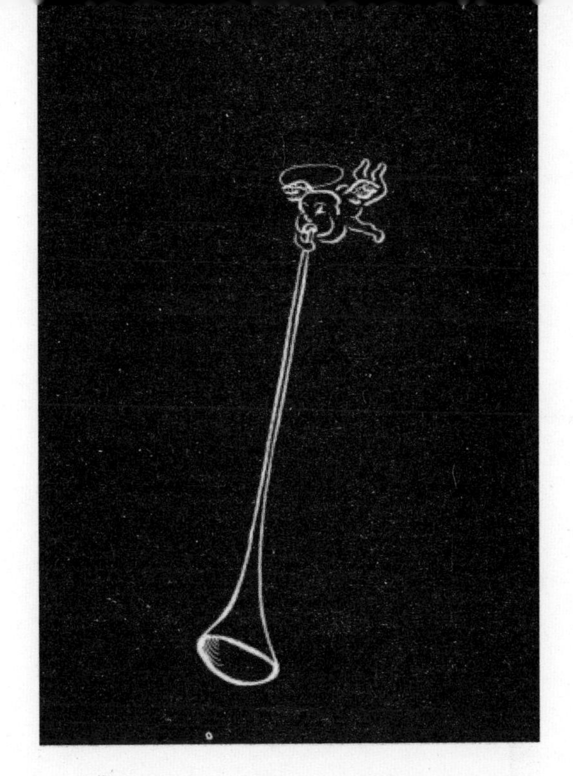

To my Auntie Marg and Uncle Alex

HOT AS HELL. IT'S NOT JUST A SAYING.

Trapped in the cloying darkness, I felt the heat, smelled the sulphur and brimstone. Iron shackles weighed my arms and legs. Every breath required effort. I glanced down to find my torso encased in a red leather corset. The outfit was designed to humiliate me, a bitter reminder of the bargain I'd made.

"Ah, there you are," said a voice out of the gloom. "We've missed you here in Hell, Porsche."

I knew that voice. It belonged to my worst nightmare, my most dire mistake. It held a claim over me. A claim currently refuted in court, but a claim nonetheless. And if I was trapped in the bowels of Devil's Mountain, then the voice could only belong to the Devil, himself.

Behind me something heavy slithered across the stone floor. I didn't need to turn to know that Lucifer snaked toward me. In his demon body, the Devil was a foreboding sight.

"Are you ignoring me, Miss Winter?" he asked in that low and compelling voice that could force me to do almost anything against my will. With the Devil it really didn't matter. In his domain I was at his mercy.

I shook my head violently. The effort rattled my chains.

"Behold then," he commanded.

My head swivelled in his direction, wrenching my neck. I tried to keep my eyes on the rocky floor at my feet. But Lucifer controlled even my vision. I just had to look, whether I wanted to or not.

The Devil towered above me in full demon face. Red eyes contrasted with pale skin stretched so thin you could see the outline of his elongated skull beneath it. His pointed ears flattened back against his skull like an angry cat. Horns sprouted from his head, bone white and razor sharp.

Cloven hooves tapped against the stone floor as he crowded in on me, not even allowing me space to breathe. His knees bent backward as he moved, unnerving me even further, if that was possible. He was naked, no missing that fact. He saw where I was looking and smiled. If you could call it that. His mouth stretched until it practically cut his face in two.

"What's the matter, Miss Winter? Miss me?"

I shook my head violently.

"Oh come now," Lucifer said. "You must miss me a little. After all that happened between us."

"Nothing happened between us," I ground out from between clenched teeth.

Lucifer shrugged. The movement rippled through his massive body. "If you say so." Insults meant nothing to Lucifer. If he wanted you badly enough, he'd have you body and soul, no matter what you called him. He'd revel in every insult as if it was a compliment.

He put his face up close to mine. I tried to back away, but the shackles held me securely. Cringing gained me only a couple of precious inches. The Devil parted his lips. Saliva dripped from his fangs. His jaw cracked, unhinging until his mouth opened far enough to engulf my head.

"What's wrong, Porsche?" The words were slurred. Hard to talk with your mouth open a couple of feet, I suppose. "No kiss for me?"

I tried to turn my head. But the Devil compelled me to look at him. Muscles wrenched as I tried to avert my gaze. I closed my eyes, but even my eyelids seemed sluggish and heavy.

"No," I whispered. It was all the speech I could muster.

Lucifer's laughter shook the cavern. When I opened my eyes, he'd shrunk back into his cover model persona. A black silk shirt clung to every muscle. He wore a pair of pleated trousers that draped exquisitely. Dark hair tumbled down over his forehead in a riot of curls, nearly hiding the pearly tips of his horns. The only remnant of his demon body was the red glint in his dark eyes.

The Devil sighed theatrically, like he really did care that I wouldn't kiss him. Not willingly anyway. And maybe he did care. His eyes skimmed over the red bustier, the figure-hugging leather trousers and the spike heels that had me weaving uncertainly even though the chains held me up. "Very well, Miss Winter. I suppose I'll be seeing you soon enough. My claim on your souls may be held up on a legal technicality, but both you and Alex Chalmers are mine. And I will recover what is mine."

Searing lips touched mine. His scorching breath stole the oxygen from my lungs.

I screamed.

But instead of being absorbed by the Devil's mouth, my cry echoed off nearby walls. To my surprise, I sucked in cool filtered air.

Vestiges of my dream overlapped reality. I looked around the bedroom seeing the shadows of furniture overlaid by the crags of Lucifer's cave. For a moment I saw demons skulking in darkened corners and minions hiding beneath the bureau. Then I blinked and the images evaporated, leaving only the hulk of a dresser and a weight bench strewn with clothes.

From beside me came a groan. "Not again." A mountain of pillows muffled the voice. An arm ringed my waist, this time one I knew.

Instead of Hell I found myself in Alex Chalmers' apartment. I sagged back against the pillows in embarrassment. "I'm sorry."

"I think you woke up half the building."

Alex's head appeared above the blankets, dark curls, tousled from sleep. "It was just a dream," he declared with certainty. But his eyes were open, wary. "Wasn't it?"

Nothing in the bedroom seemed out of place. "I don't know. It felt real."

"Dreams are like that," Alex said. "It's part of being human." He sounded so sure of that, I almost believed him. He knew far more about being human than I did. But I knew dreams were anything but innocent figments of the imagination. In The Great Beyond, dream weaving was a profession. Like a stage play or a television show, it took a multitude of people behind the scenes to make it work. Just because you couldn't see them, didn't mean they weren't there. Or that they couldn't make mistakes.

Alex knew that too. After all, I'd invaded a few of his dreams. Ones he'd rather forget.

I sat up slowly. "I think someone's trying to tell me something, Alex."

Alex reached for the lamp on the side of the bed and turned it on. I blinked in the sudden glare. "Come on, Porsche. Not *every* dream is a message from the Beyond." His eyebrows drew together. "Is it?"

"Well, not every single one." I had to admit that much. I'd worked in dream control. I knew what I was talking about. "That would be horribly labour intensive. But you can be sure the ones you remember are messages. We design them that way." I pushed blonde curls out of my eyes. "And I won't be forgetting that dream any time soon. Lucifer was in it."

"I'm sure Lucifer has more important things to worry about these days than you," Alex pointed out. "He's got a court case to prepare for."

"True. But maybe the message came from someone else."

"Who? Alex demanded. "Your buddy Cupid?"

I ran through the list of people who might want to get a word through to me on Earth. "No, nightmares aren't Cupid's style. Besides, if he wants to get in touch with me, he's more likely to send a flaming arrow. Under the union contract he can only handle erotic dreams."

Alex scowled. He didn't much like Cupid. Especially after he'd bitten him. I knew he'd wondered whether our relationship was real or one of Cupid's schemes. I wasn't worried about that. Cupid didn't like Alex, either.

"Someone in the dreams department then?" he suggested.

"I doubt it." I had no friends left in the dreams department. My former boss, the archangel Raphael, was probably still cleaning up the mess I'd made. My thoughts darkened. "Perhaps it didn't come from a friend. We were hacked by Hell once." The Devil had hijacked our computer system and sent nightmares of bogeymen across the northern hemisphere, terrifying children.

Alex let go his breath in a rush. "Porsche, this is crazy talk. It's the middle of the night!" He pulled me closer. "Go back to sleep."

He possessed the human capacity to forget the worst of experiences and go on. I didn't want to deprive him of that. Not until I knew something was definitely wrong. So I let him pull me back into his arms. I let him pull the blankets up around us to ward off the air conditioner's chill. Pressed against his warm body, I tried to go back to sleep.

Across the room stood one of Alex's sculptures. This was an angel, beautiful and serene. Alex had been creating it when we had first met. I'd moved it from his den to the bedroom because I found it soothing.

Halfway to dawn, I drifted off. And if I dreamed again, I didn't remember it.

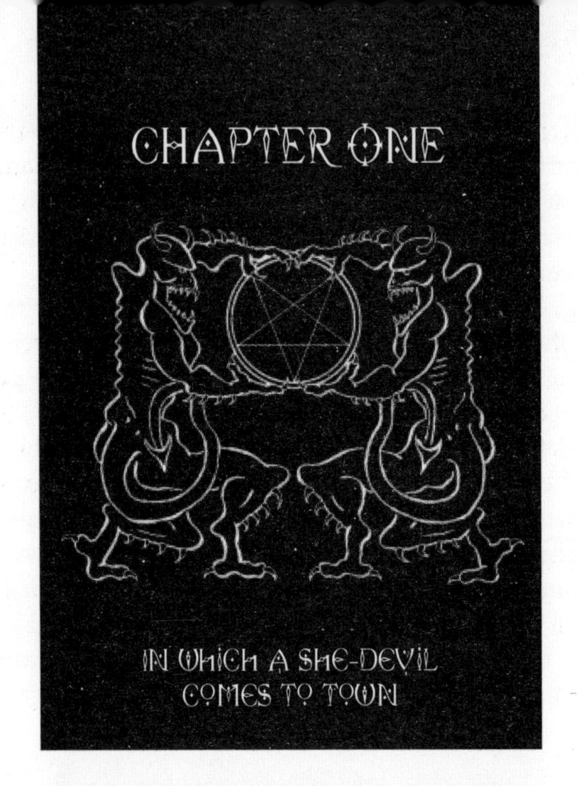

IT'S NOT EVERY DAY YOU SEE A SHE-devil in a bar on Earth. And not just any she-devil, but Naamah, Queen of Seductresses. And Lucifer's right hand.

Reclining in my chair, my face tilted toward the sunlight, that rare spectacle would have eluded me had I not picked that moment to glance up.

I squinted against the sun. I had moved the umbrella and rearranged most of the patio bar to get myself that delicious piece of sun-drenched sky. Normally, I avoided sun. I came from an environment of diffuse light and perpetually drifting clouds. I burned easily. But then I'd discovered sunscreen and decided to acquire the one thing I'd never had in my life: a tan.

As a fallen angel, I didn't have much to do these days. So as long as the weather held, a tan was a definite possibility.

Alex had taken pity on me when Heaven cast me out. We now lived together in his lakefront condo. To say this new lifestyle was a bit of an adjustment for me was the understatement of an eon.

Banished. I could barely think the word without cringing. Unemployed sounded marginally better. But then, angels are never truly unemployed. Just banished. Surely by now I'd stopped making headlines on Utopia Network's nightly news.

Or not. I was afraid to ask.

So there I was, a thin layer of sunscreen standing between me and red, itchy skin, sitting on the patio of a Harbourfront bar, watching the sun sparkle on the water and waiting for Alex to get home from work when a shadow drifted between me and the sun.

I glanced up, annoyed. I hadn't staked out this prime spot to have someone cast me in shade. That's when I noticed that this particular silhouette moved with a sashay that seemed horribly familiar. Only one type of wildlife could turn an ordinary walk into a sensuous dance. A she-devil.

I sat up slowly, trying not to draw attention to myself. The shadow passed in front of me wearing a straw hat with a large brim. Large enough to hide a pair of red horns beneath. But then, lots of people wore hats. That meant nothing. Pretending to drop my swizzle stick, I leaned over for a closer look.

As she rounded the corner, I caught a glimpse of a beaded tail beneath her scandalously short leather skirt.

"Damnation!" I whispered. And hoped The Big Guy hadn't heard me. I had to be careful now. I was mortal. I had to behave.

I watched the back of her red leather skirt swing off around the corner. I straightened, pulled the umbrella back in place to block my face and peered around the edge.

A she-devil in a Harbourfront bar. I shot another furtive glance in her direction just to be sure of my initial impression. My heart sank. Naamah, the head she-devil. I'd recognise that arrogant swagger anywhere.

Which begged the question. What was Naamah doing on Earth? I pondered for a moment. She couldn't be looking for me. Decommissioned,

I was no threat to her. Then again, perhaps Naamah hadn't heard I'd been sentenced to mortality.

A more disturbing notion occurred to me. Naamah and I had once battled over Alex's soul. Could she be hunting Alex once again?

If Naamah roamed the pier, I reasoned, it meant trouble for the entire Earthly plane. I had to find out what she was up to.

Deciding to give chase, I bolted from my chair. Metal collided with concrete, but I didn't glance back. A couple of patrons looked up from their drinks. I nearly ran down an elderly lady with a stained white poodle coming around the corner. The poodle barked. His owner glared at me with rheumy eyes.

"So sorry," I called back over my shoulder, and nearly fell into the solid form of a bouncer. Looking up into beady dark eyes, I couldn't help marvelling how taproom wildlife were shockingly similar no matter which plane of existence you were on. I grinned, slapped a ten-dollar bill into his hand as payment and rushed from the patio.

A streetcar pulled up in front of the building. Workers on summer flex hours got off. Parents and children heading for the boardwalk and the ferry docks streamed out behind them, followed by tourists with street maps. The crowd slowed my progress. And by the time it cleared, Naamah had vanished from sight.

I scanned the sidewalk, but none of the pedestrians looked like she-devils. Turning away from the traffic rushing by on Queen's Quay, I headed back toward the harbour.

A craft fair had been set up on the grass next to the pier. Canvas tents fluttered in the sluggish breeze. Any of those stalls could be harbouring a she-devil.

A trio of portly matrons bottlenecked the path through the booths. I tried to squeeze by them, but no amount of impatient sighing could distract them from their perusal of potholders bearing cutesy cats. Then disappearing between a display of silver jewellery and a table of baked goods, I caught a glimpse of red.

I crawled under the table. The proprietor squealed as I brushed past her bare legs. I clawed my way over the uneven ground, getting grass stains on my knees and emerged on the other side. The owner glared in my direction, but a question from one of the cat ladies diverted her attention. Free enterprise, I thought with a smirk and tore off down the aisle.

Up ahead a crowd had gathered beside a stall selling fresh ice cream. I could have sworn I saw the swishing tip of Naamah's tail disappear between the backsides of two men who really shouldn't have been indulging in dessert. The gap in the crowd closed, leaving me squished between two sweating ten year-olds. It was hard to compete with ice cream on a hot day. No one seemed inclined to let me pass.

The sudden shrill sound of a saxophone made me jump. I craned my neck to see through a gap in the tent. A group of swing dancers had set up a demonstration. The music blared from the overloaded speakers of a lone boom box. But the dancers in black skirts with fuchsia crinolines didn't seem to notice the distortion or the heat as they spun like coloured tops. In their midst I noticed a lithe figure in red and a straw hat. One of the male dancers caught her in a swingout and spun her off. Gaping at the swish of her tail beneath her leather skirt, he lost his step and stumbled. His partner planted her hands on her hips and glared at him.

I ducked under a flap of the tent and raced off along the grass. But by the time I reached the troupe, the dance had faltered in disarray, and Naamah had disappeared. From behind me loud voices complained about the slow service at the ice cream counter. Patrons argued over the prices in the bazaar. The ground seemed to hug the heat closer. Tempers frayed and snapped. It might be because of the heat wave, I thought trying to rationalise it all. But I knew better. A she-devil had come to town. I had to find her.

Down on the boardwalk, I heard the sound of metal impacting wood. I turned in time to see a rickshaw spilling its passengers onto the ground. Several people ran to help. I followed them.

The braying of a donkey brought me skidding to a stop. Beside the craft fair a maze of wooden pens held a petting zoo. And in the menagerie, chaos reigned. Horses stampeded their stalls, a litter of piglets had got loose and ran for freedom across the boardwalk, followed by red-faced handlers trying to round them up. Children cried. Parents proclaimed their outrage.

Across the pens, I saw a flash of red. As Naamah passed, the donkey bolted from its cubicle, scattering splinters of wood, trainers and children.

Chickens squawked in outrage and pecked at each other, trying to get away from the she-devil. I scrambled out of the way of a goat hell-bent on getting to the grass, and nearly missed being trampled by a spitting llama. When I looked back, Naamah was gone.

Then, like a fresh breeze, the atmosphere changed. The line at the ice cream stand cleared and the dance resumed. The driver loaded his passengers back in the rickshaw. A couple of confused goats gnawed at the grass.

Business on the boardwalk went on as usual. But I'd seen too much to chalk it up to a series of weird coincidences.

I searched the pier for signs of the she-devil. But no one in a leather mini or sunhat strolled there, unless she'd embarked on one of the boats lined up along the pier beside the mall. I wandered by a couple of harbour cruise boats, but the only passengers were tourists in white shorts. Heat crinkled the air above the pier, broken only by a light breeze off the lake. With all my rushing around I'd started to attract nervous looks.

I made myself walk leisurely across the boardwalk until I reached the glass doors to the waterfront mall. Wrenching the door open, I hurried inside and narrowly missed colliding with a sweating businessman in a wool suit.

The cool air was a shock after the heat outside. The smell of pizza from the food court permeated the mall.

I flitted from one glass-fronted store to another, trying not to alarm the patrons. But no she-devils perused the gift shops. That feeling of uneasiness ramped up to alarm. If Naamah wasn't in the mall, she had to have headed for the condos on the upper floors . . . and that was where our apartment was.

Darting through the crowd, I endured several angry stares. "Pardon me" and "excuse me" didn't seem to help. Finally, I reached the corridor that led to the condo elevators.

As I got there the doors were sliding closed. I looked around. The corridor was empty, the she-devil nowhere in sight. Which meant she'd probably been on that elevator. I had to stop her.

Furiously, I jabbed at the button and grimly endured the elevator's slow arrival. The doors opened, discharging a number of residents, none of them in as much of a hurry as me.

I wasn't used to these ponderously slow methods of Earthly travel. As a guardian angel one of my high-tech gadgets had been a locator, which allowed me to travel at lightning speed through planes of existence. My equipment had been recalled when I'd lost my guardian angel status. But tucked away in a bureau drawer upstairs was a locator that Cupid had given me on the sly. I never should have left it upstairs. But then, I wasn't supposed to have the thing, much less use it.

The elevator crawled upward. The doors opened on the tenth floor. I peered down the hallway. No she-devils. A well-dressed older woman got on. She pressed the button for the twelfth floor. I resisted the urge to groan out loud.

My unwanted companion's eyes skimmed over me. Her mouth turned downward in disapproval. I glanced down at the skimpy top and shorts I wore and crossed my arms. I wasn't used to the multitude of fashion options available on Earth. I'd spent most of my life in my uniform jumpsuit or dress robes. But I'd certainly seen people on the pier below wearing a lot less. I was covered, sort of. And probably red-faced from sun exposure and panting with impatience.

Whatever she thought of me, the woman got off on twelve. Another empty hallway. I couldn't shake the feeling that Naamah's visit to the waterfront had something to do with Alex and me. I punched the button for the penthouses. The elevator resumed its slow process.

I stepped out of the elevator. The odour of brimstone assaulted my senses. I bolted down the hallway. The carpet absorbed the pounding of my feet. Skidding to a halt in front of Alex's door, I stared at the wisp of smoke curling in the still air, evidence that one of the Underworld's creatures had recently been there. And had quickly departed. I fumbled the key into the lock. The door opened and I all but fell into the apartment.

Sun sparkled on the lake, framed by the two-storey windows. Alex's leather and chrome furniture stood like dark sentries between me and the glare. Nothing moved in the sunken living room, the only sound came from the hiss of the air conditioner. I peered into the kitchen, finding only the breakfast dishes where I'd left them. No Heavenly cafeteria to eat in here. On Earth it was self-serve.

Resolving to deal with the dishes later, I leapt up the steps to the hallway that led to Alex's den. His Lucite sculpting materials lay scattered across his desk where he'd left his most recent work in progress. Nothing seemed to have been tampered with.

Quietly, I crossed the last few steps to the bedroom across the hall and peered inside. The sheets were still rumpled from my restless sleep the night before. I really should make the bed before Alex got home, I thought. Seeing as I'd been the last one out of it. Everything was as I'd left it with no sign of Naamah's presence. I glanced at the clock on the bedside table. Another hour at least before Alex arrived. The angel sculpture dominated the windowsill. Alex had named it Porsche in my honour. Which was sweet, except that it reminded me painfully of all that I had lost. Sunlight caught its wings, taunting me with its brilliance. I turned away.

I *had* seen Naamah in the patio bar, hadn't I? I couldn't chalk it up to a well-used imagination, could I? No, I assured myself, I'd seen her, plain as day. And discovering a she-devil on Earth under any circumstances was legitimate cause for concern. I glanced at the phone on the bedside table and decided to call in my only Earthly ally.

I dialled. Alex's voice mail picked up.

"Alex, it's me. Come home as soon as you can." My voice sounded as lost, desperate even. And that infuriated me.

In Heaven, I'd been one of the chosen, a warrior. Adjusting to life as a mortal was tougher than I imagined. Meanwhile, Alex worked as a Bay Street stockbroker and his life went on pretty much as before. Except for the addition of a fallen angel to his bed.

That sense of impending doom wouldn't go away. Forced humanity or not, I'd learned to listen to that nagging little voice. It usually meant trouble.

But I tried to reason myself out of it nevertheless. Just because I'd seen a she-devil in the patio bar didn't mean she was after Alex.

She confessed she had the hots for him, that voice inside reminded me.

True, I conceded. *But there's plenty of other Hell on Earth Lucifer's finest could be up to.* And I no longer had the authority or the ability to stop her.

Looking around, I wondered what to do next. My eyes were drawn to the drawer where Cupid's locator was hidden. No. I had to have more to go on than chasing a she-devil across Toronto. I sighed and wandered back down the hall toward the kitchen, resigned to doing the dishes. The front door suddenly flew open with a crash.

"What the hell?" Alex demanded. He brandished his cell phone like a weapon. "What's with that message, Porsche? You scared me half to death!"

He paused, looking at me standing there.

"There is something wrong," he asked, eyes narrowing. "Isn't there?"

"I'll tell you about it inside." I pulled him out of the doorway into the apartment. He looked positively scrumptious in his dark suit, though I noted he'd loosened the tie in the heat. Respectable business attire, it hung perfectly on his muscular frame, while still managing to cling to every muscle. I caught the scent of his cologne as I squeezed past him.

"Porsche – " Alex followed me down the hallway, his hallway. The entire apartment was his. I was merely a houseguest with a long-term pass. Glancing into the bedroom, he couldn't help notice the unmade bed. Neatness wasn't among my virtues, while he was tidy by nature. Our living habits were hardly compatible. And if Alex tossed me out, I'd have to find a job.

There aren't too many opportunities for errant angels on Earth.

I'd stopped in the hallway. Alex grasped my shoulders and turned me around. By the look on his face, I could tell he was imagining the worst. And what Alex could imagine was pretty bad. He'd been to Hell and back. "What is it? What's wrong?"

I looked up into his deep brown eyes and wholeheartedly wished I hadn't gone downstairs this afternoon. "I saw Naamah today." I let that thought sink in before adding, "In the patio bar."

"*The* Naamah?" Alex asked.

"The one and only. Trust me, there isn't room in Hell for more than one Naamah."

"Are you sure it was Naamah?"

I nodded.

"One hundred percent sure?"

"Pretty sure." Vestiges of doubt took root in my mind. Okay he had me there. "I mean, the sun was in my face. That was the idea. I was trying to get a tan."

He took me by the hand and led me toward the sunken living room.

The warmth of his skin surrounded mine, slightly damp from sweat. He had to be baking under that suit. And I'd probably given him quite a scare. A veteran of the corporate battlefield, Alex was accustomed to being scared under his expensive suit and used to not letting it show. He sat me on the couch and eyed me warily. "Okay, tell me the whole story."

As I recounted the events of the morning in a way that wouldn't make me sound like a raving lunatic, Alex looked at me steadily.

"I thought she was after you," I finished weakly.

"Me? Why me?"

"Oh come on, the obvious reasons. She's had the hots for you since she saw the glimmer of your soul in Hades."

"Well, the feeling's definitely not mutual."

"Are you sure? Entirely sure? You two spent some time together. And I don't remember you objecting at the time."

Alex's eyes darkened in anger. He ran his hands through his hair, ruffling dark curls, making me wish we weren't sitting here having this conversation. Making me wish we were doing something else entirely. "I wasn't myself, Porsche."

"No," I admitted. "You sure weren't. And we don't have to get into whose fault it was, either." I scrutinised him head to toe. "Are you sure nothing weird happened today?"

"It was a horrible day on the trading floor. It wouldn't surprise me if Hell is to blame for that."

"I doubt it. Lucifer's shares have been frozen and he's been forbidden to acquire more even on Earth until his court case is resolved."

"And Lucifer is a man of his word?"

In truth the Devil could be counted on only to screw you over, I thought but I didn't say it. "No, but The Big Guy is. And right now I'm sure he's paying careful attention to Lucifer."

"Which means that whatever Lucifer wants, he's going to have to find a more creative way of doing it."

"Right." Pieces of the puzzle fell into place. "Which explains why he might send Naamah instead."

"But to do what?" Alex paced back and forth in front of the window. Behind him the sun was just starting to set over the lake. I hoped the red glow it cast into the apartment wasn't some eerie kind of foreshadowing. It reminded me of Hell. "You say she came into the building. But you came up here right after her. And nothing's out of place." He shot me a pointed look. "Well, except for the dishes all over the counter and the unmade bed."

"I meant to get to them," I said. "I thought I had lots of time, until I saw Naamah."

"The dishes aren't a personal slight, Porsche. They just need to be washed."

I sunk back into the deep leather cushions of the couch. "I know that. I just feel so . . . so useless." There, I'd said it.

He pulled me up off the couch. I leaned into him, feeling every muscle in his chest as his hard body pressed against mine. "You're not useless. You're just trying to adjust to a difficult situation."

"I'm not adjusting very well."

"You have to try harder."

I sighed. "I know."

His hot breath stirred my hair. "You think this supposed Naamah sighting has something to do with that nightmare you had last night, don't you?"

I nodded against his shoulder. "Someone's trying to warn me. Of something anyway."

He held me away from him. "It was just a nightmare." He studied my face in the dying sun. "And you've definitely got yourself a touch of sunburn." He grasped my chin and tilted my head. "You really ought to stay out of the sun, Porsche. Your skin just isn't up to it."

He was right. I could feel the first tingles as my skin tightened up.

"Don't change the subject, Alex. I know what you're doing."

"Even if Naamah was in the patio bar today, it has nothing to do with you. Or me."

"If Naamah's on Earth, it is my business."

Alex gripped my shoulders. "No, it *was* your business. Now it's someone else's responsibility."

And that rankled. To think my professional qualifications might be overlooked hurt my pride.

Pride is a sin, said that voice inside. The one I wished I could muzzle.

"But – " I said.

"Look," Alex said. "No matter what happened before, now you're supposed to live as a mortal. Which means you're supposed to behave!"

"And leave the fighting of the minions of Hell to the more capable powers that be?"

Alex nodded like I'd just uttered my first sensible words all evening.

"Well, they're not getting the picture if Naamah's on Earth, are they?"

"You don't know that."

"I saw Naamah strolling through the patio bar. And I didn't see a company of angels swoop down to deal with her."

"You don't know they didn't. Just because you didn't witness it personally."

"It's unlikely. I would notice a thing like that."

Giving up, Alex stalked a few feet away from me and stared out over the lake at the last rays of the sunset. While we'd been arguing the sky had deepened to layers of indigo and turquoise with a fiery red slash at the bottom. Pinpricks of stars started to appear above the dark shadows of the Toronto Islands.

Briefly, I marvelled at how beautiful it looked. How unlike the soft drifting clouds and diffuse light of Heaven.

And then I saw it.

A falling star gouged the heavens. It seared through the layers of colour in a sizzling ball of fire. A huge golden tail trailed behind it like a scar. It disappeared behind the dark line of the island trees. I swore I could hear it hiss as it hit the water.

I let go the gasp I'd been holding in.

Alex turned. "What?"

I pointed to the sky, so spectacularly framed in Alex's floor to ceiling windows. "Didn't you see it?"

"See what?"

I sighted down the line of my arm. But nothing in the sky betrayed the display I'd just witnessed. Above the dark green of the Toronto Islands there was only the deepening blue of the sky.

"A falling star! How could you have missed it? It cut across the entire sky."

"I was watching the Island Lady." He pointed at the pier where a crowd queued up to board a fake Mississippi river boat complete with a neon paddle wheel. "Was it a good one?"

"A good what?"

"Shooting star."

"It's a portent," I said incredulously. "A very bad one."

"It was a shooting star, Porsche. It's supposed to be good luck. You were supposed to make a wish."

I blinked. "I was supposed to what?"

No way would I ever fit in here on Earth. Not if mortals considered the skies falling good luck.

"It's just a meteorite. A piece of space junk flaming through the atmosphere. It means nothing. We get meteor showers all through the summer months." He picked up the cordless phone sitting on one of the end tables. "And I'm starving. Want pizza?"

I followed after him. "How can you even think of food at a time like this?"

"I skipped lunch. I've been thinking about food all afternoon." He punched one of the speed dial buttons. I heard the chime of the phone dialling.

The sudden rumble of thunder shook the apartment. Alex turned, the phone forgotten in his hand. The panorama behind him showed a bank of nasty clouds moving rapidly inland.

"Don't even say it," Alex warned. "It's July. Thunderstorms and shooting stars are nothing special."

I stood before the windows and stared out at the coming storm. Behind me I could hear Alex calmly placing his pizza order, complete with garlic bread and chicken wings. Special or not, that storm looked like bad news to me.

Lake Ontario, which had been flat as glass a few moments ago, suddenly churned like a giant spoon was stirring it. Black clouds blocked out the sky. The dying light had turned a sickly green. Dark waves crashed against the pier. Tourists scrambled for cover.

Out on the lake, the neon paddleboat altered course and headed back to shore, followed by a fleet of pleasure craft all with the same idea. A fat raindrop splashed against the window, followed quickly by another.

The remaining light faded to black. Rain pelted the lake and drummed against the pier. Alex put down the phone and wandered to the bedroom to change his clothes.

"Stop looking at it, Porsche," he called back over his shoulder. "A little rain isn't going to hurt the lake."

The rhythm of the rain changed pitch. The clouds split. A silver column of hail raced toward land. Lightning sizzled. Thunder shook the building again. And suddenly it didn't seem such a great idea to be perched halfway toward the sky standing before a massive plate glass window.

Hail the size of marbles drilled against the glass. Boats bobbed on the water like so many corks.

I turned back to where Alex still stood in the hall, his shirt hanging from one hand. "You were saying?" I had to shout above the hammering of hail against the glass.

He looked past me at the angry skies and the churning water. For a moment I really thought I'd won him over. But I knew from past experience that Alex Chalmers could be far too stubborn for his own good. Then he shook his head.

"No, I'm not going to do this." Striding past me, he drew the curtains, shutting the storm outside. Well, except for the crack of thunder and the persistent thump of hail.

I stood in front of him, my back to the curtains and the storm. "Trust me, a she-devil sighting, a falling star, lightning, thunder and hail all in one night does add up to one wicked portent."

"It's just a summer storm," Alex insisted. "It happens all the time." Grasping my arm, he tried to pull me away from the windows.

I went with him, hoping he was right.

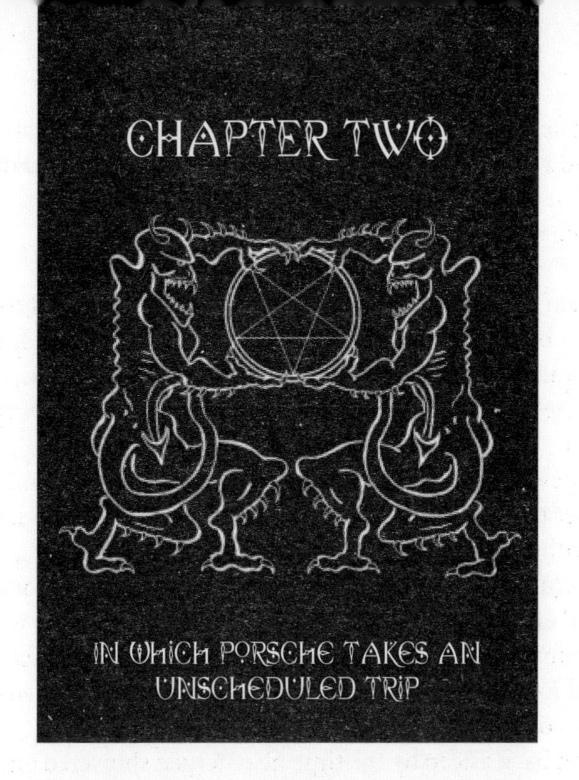

I LAY AWAKE HALF THE NIGHT LISTENing to the thump of hail against the penthouse roof and trying not to wince at every crash of thunder. That there was only the ceiling of Alex's condo between the sky's wrath and us didn't help. I found it hard enough to sleep at night. I'd spent most of my life working nights and sleeping days. And it didn't matter that I wasn't working any more or that I had nothing to get up for. I still couldn't sleep.

I knew I'd seen Naamah in the patio bar. And I knew a handful of portents in one night were nothing to ignore. Alex just didn't want to hear the bad news. He didn't want to believe that after all he'd been through, there was quite literally, more hell to pay.

And I couldn't blame him for that.

Hours later, the storm finally moved inland and the infernal drumming of hail and rain ceased. The last of the clouds blew inland off the lake and the first pink tinges of dawn stained the sky.

Morning at last, I mused. Then I finally fell asleep.

Alex's alarm went off ten minutes later. He groaned, rolled over and hit the snooze button. I dozed for what seemed like a second, only to be startled awake when the alarm shrilled again. In the kitchen, I heard the timer on the coffee maker kick in. The smell of coffee brewing filled the apartment.

Alex threw off the blankets, letting in a blast of cool air. I squirmed back under the covers. He stumbled toward the kitchen. I knew better than to bother him before he had that first gulp of coffee.

"Want coffee?" he asked, appearing in the bedroom doorway.

I peered above the covers and shook my head.

Alex grunted something noncommittal. Taking his coffee with him, he headed for the shower. I wondered idly how he managed to shower and drink coffee at the same time.

I'd fallen back asleep by the time he emerged showered and shaved. I didn't even hear him as he rummaged around the room, finding shoes, socks and another of those business suits that went so well with his model looks.

The bed creaked as he sat down beside me. I opened one eye to find him sitting there looking so gorgeous that I wished he could stay home for the day and make me forget all about Naamah and what I feared. But he only said, "Do me a favour, Porsche. Stay out of trouble today."

"Sure," I mumbled. "I'll make the bed, too."

"Right." His tone said he believed in a higher probability of Hell freezing over. He leaned over. His lips brushed mine, teasingly. And I almost grabbed him by the tie and pulled him down beside me. But then he stood up out of reach. "See you later."

I said, "Okay." I heard the jingle of his keys in the front door. Then he was gone.

Lured by the smell of coffee, I headed for the kitchen. I poured a cup and looked out over the lake. Sun sparkled on the water like last night's storm had been a figment of my imagination. Except for the puddles of water on the pier and the leaves that littered the boardwalk, you wouldn't even know a storm had blown through the area.

Picking up the TV remote, I turned to the local morning show. But the announcer made only a brief mention of the previous night's severe thunderstorm. Squinting at the fuzzy, two-dimensional picture broadcast by inferior Earthly technology strained my eyes, and after a few moments I turned it off.

I swallowed a mouthful of scalding coffee, then set the coffee mug down on the counter along with the other dishes that had collected there. With a sigh, I reached for the bottle of soap and examined the label for instructions. Other than a warning not to let children drink the product and a diagram that claimed the container was recyclable, I found no directions. Apparently on this plane of existence washing dishes was self-explanatory. Except, of course, to someone from another dimension. *You're a warrior*, I told myself sternly. *You've taken down netherworld wildlife twice your size. You can handle dishes.* I gave the bottle a healthy squeeze and started to fill the sink with warm water.

Bubbles overflowed the sink. Far more bubbles than there was water. I turned off the taps and sank the coffee mugs in the soap. But the suds reminded me of the billowing clouds of Heaven.

I stared into the sink, lost for a moment in regret. I longed for quiet, drifting clouds, for television sets that used holographic technology and everything else forsaken to me on the Heavenly plane. But it wasn't just self-pity that had me staring into a sink full of soapsuds. Morning might have dawned fresh and clear, but my instincts screamed that danger lurked just over the horizon. And I'd learned to heed that feeling of impending doom.

I needed an objective opinion. Or more correctly, an expert opinion from someone who understood how the supernatural worked. I glanced again at the suds overflowing the sink.

Only one person in Heaven was still talking to me. Cupid.

Cupid could be counted on for help, I thought, heading back down the hall to the bedroom, the dishes forgotten. Breakfast would have to wait.

Covered by a pile of neatly folded sweaters in the bureau drawer, lay the locator Cupid had given me. I'd kept it secret, even from Alex. I couldn't be caught with Heaven's contraband.

I had no idea what shift Cupid was on these days. As head of the Cherubim, his duties encompassed everything from erotic dreams and daydreams to direct hits from arrows from his ever-full quiver. I'd have to take a chance and hope he'd be home when I arrived.

My reflection in the mirror made me head for the shower first. My blonde curls stuck out at all angles, evidence of my restless night. I'd borrowed a pair of Alex's sweats and one of his old t-shirts and I looked as dishevelled as I felt. I had no job and desperately few clothes. But I couldn't let Cupid see me this way. I wanted to look like I was handling this mortality thing. Well, at least better than I actually was.

Out of respect for the dress code in Heaven, I put on a white t-shirt and a pair of white trousers. Not perfect, but better than what I'd been wearing yesterday.

Reaching under the pile of sweaters, I pulled out the palm-sized device. The screen was dark, the power off. No sense running down power cells that were impossible to replace on Earth.

Cupid shouldn't have given it to me. But Cupid, like me, had a highly developed sense of impending doom. That he'd given me his locator, meant that deep down he believed our battle with the Underworld wasn't over yet.

Which put a name to the feeling I'd been trying to smother since I arrived on Earth.

My finger hovered above the power button. Powering up the locator could hardly be considered a sin. Even a locator I wasn't supposed to have. But once I actually took a jaunt into The Great Beyond, well, that was another situation entirely.

The screen flickered to life. A topographical grid of my present location on Earth appeared. I input the coordinates for Cupid's apartment. Coordinates I knew by heart. I'd spent countless hours there. Cupid had been my best friend. I sincerely hoped that was still the case.

I'd used a locator nearly every day of my professional life. But this was a new me, a human me. Somehow scattering my atoms over half The Great Beyond didn't seem like such a great idea.

My hand shook. What if The Big Guy was waiting at the other end for me? Ready to tally up the list of my sins and put me away for good.

My thumb hovered over the send button. I took a deep breath, closed my eyes . . .

And pressed the button.

The world dropped from under me. My dissolving body felt heavier than it had before. I prayed that I'd go back together properly when I arrived at Cupid's. I prayed our reunion wouldn't involve me throwing up on his pink shag carpet when I landed.

Whump! I landed with enough force to rattle my brain. And for a moment, the only thing I could accomplish with any certainty was straining air through my bruised ribs into my lungs.

I glanced up and saw powder pink walls painted with fluffy clouds. Well, at least I'd arrived. There was no mistaking Cupid's place.

Cupid's pad was a pink fake-fur nightmare. Everything in it was fluffy and scaled to Cupid's diminutive size. Fuchsia shag carpet clashed horribly with the red velvet on the loveseat and matching chair. And the white, heart-shaped pillows certainly didn't help. Definitely not my taste. But Cupid was Cupid down to his heart-shaped bathtub and his red satin sheets. I glanced up at the miniature sofa that I'd narrowly missed and thanked The Big Guy I hadn't hit something breakable. Maybe, I thought, Cupid wasn't home yet and I'd have a few moments to compose myself.

Until a wet cherub wearing only a loincloth stomped out of his bathroom.

No such luck.

"I can explain," I said quickly.

"I certainly hope so," Cupid said. Flapping his wings in irritation, he hovered above me.

I clipped the locator to my belt and sat up.

"I gave you that thing in case of emergency," he pointed out.

"It is an emergency," I insisted.

Cupid sat on the loveseat and crossed his arms, managing to look fierce even though he was only just under two feet tall and nearly naked. "I really do hope so. It won't take Gabriel long to figure out where that locator signature came from."

I nodded grimly. "Hopefully, there's lots of traffic today and he won't notice."

Cupid didn't seem convinced. "I doubt it." Then he sighed. "Porsche, it's only been a few weeks. How could you be in trouble so soon?"

"I'm not the one in trouble here, okay?" I said, sounding crankier than I intended. I tried again. "You could give me the benefit of the doubt, you know."

Cupid looked chagrined. He patted the loveseat. "Why don't you tell me about it. Before Gabriel's seraphs bang down my door to haul you off to jail."

"Funny," I said. I practically had to fold myself in two to perch on the tiny couch. I sat gingerly down beside him. Nothing seemed broken. Next time I used the locator, I'd have to compensate for my heavier, mortal body.

Cupid glanced nervously at the door, as if he really did fear a company of archangels charging through it. When nothing happened, he relaxed and smiled. Cupid, my best buddy, was back. "So, how are you?"

"Fine," I said.

He cocked one blond eyebrow. Damp tousled curls dripped onto his forehead.

"Okay," I admitted, "fine – sort of. Earth is louder, dirtier and harsher than Heaven . . . but still kind of fun. And I really needed some time off. Not quite as much as I got – " I added.

A long silence followed while Cupid studied me closely as if he didn't really believe me. "Why is your face red?"

I offered him a sheepish smile. "I was trying to get a tan."

He doubled up laughing. Cupid has a belly laugh that ought to belong to someone twice his size. It's impossible to feel bad in his company, at least not for long.

"Fine. Laugh," I said, desperately trying to keep a straight face. "It's not like I've got anything better to do."

Cupid sobered up. He put a chubby hand on my leg. "Damnation, but I've missed you, Porsche."

"Well, you'll probably wish I'd stayed away when you hear what I have to say."

He rolled his eyes theatrically. "Okay, out with it."

I struggled for the words to explain all that I feared, and finally settled for, "Yesterday, I saw Naamah in the patio bar."

"What patio bar?"

"The one below Alex's apartment," I said.

"Okay . . ." Whatever Cupid had been expecting, this wasn't it. "That's unusual, but hardly an emergency."

"You sound like Alex."

Cupid stared at me with renewed interest. "It's Alex, now is it? What happened to Chalmers?"

He had me there. When had I started thinking of him as Alex instead of Alexander Alan Chalmers, file # 8,987,324,783? "I live with the guy, Cupid. It's only natural that I'd call him by his given name." It sounded reasonable. Even to me.

Cupid's eyes narrowed. He picked up one of the arrows lying on his tiny end table and stroked the feathered quill. "Have you met his parents?"

The question sounded innocent, I nearly answered without thinking. But the implications of Cupid's insidious query screamed loud and clear. "Of course not!"

Cupid said, "Hmm." But a wealth of meaning lay behind that one sound.

"Oh, come on. What's he going to say, *Hi Mom and Dad, meet Porsche the banished guardian angel who nearly got me damned for all eternity*?"

I reined in the urge to keep rambling, realising suddenly where Cupid was leading the conversation. "I know what you're doing." I snatched the arrow from his hands. "And you're off duty. Stop it."

Cupid held up his hands in defeat. He selected a bow from his end table arsenal and fiddled with it. "Okay, okay. I just wouldn't want you to rush into anything. Not so soon. You should allow yourself to adjust to being mortal."

"Don't think I've forgotten that you don't like Alex. Or that in your professional opinion, he's a *very bad idea*."

The air thrummed as he plucked at his bow. He snatched the arrow back from me and placed it against the string. "Suffice to say, I'm reserving judgement."

"You are?" Cupid was a buddy from way back. I didn't think it was possible for him to surprise me.

"He did take you in." He sounded embarrassed. Cupid considered himself infallible, a self-image somewhat contested by the high divorce rate. "And he does genuinely seem to care for you."

"Well, it's nice to hear you admit it."

"That doesn't mean I think he's right for you – "

He still had that arrow trained in my direction. I ducked just in case. And banged my chin on my knee. "Don't even think of shooting me. I shudder to think whom you have in mind. And mortal or not, I'll smack you."

The cherub pointedly ignored me.

"I live with Alex. So stay out of it. The last thing I need is you making a complicated situation worse."

Hurt stained his cheeks red. "Me? I hate to sound like your mother, Porsche, but you have to take some responsibility for the situation you're in."

That stung. "And Wynn Jarrett."

Evil guardian angel, Wynn Jarrett, had betrayed me. But worse, he'd betrayed Heaven by selling information to Hades. Information the Devil used against us to launch a hostile takeover.

At the sound of Wynn's name Cupid's expression hardened. Wynn's betrayal had affected us all. "Relax. Wynn is safely out of the picture for now."

Wynn had drawn even The Big Guy's wrath. I wanted to ask more, but time was pressing.

"You didn't even let me finish the story."

Guilt worked on Cupid almost as well as it did on my mom.

Cupid tossed the bow back on the end table. "Of course there's more. With you there always is."

Irked, I stood up, whacking my head on the low ceiling. Rubbing it in irritation, I looked at Cupid. "Are you going to listen? Or should I just go home?"

Damnation, had I actually called Earth home?

Cupid didn't seem to notice. "Oh, fine. Sit down. Tell me the whole sordid tale."

So I told him everything.

"Okay," he said after I'd finished. "All together, it's a little unusual . . . "

"Will you stop saying that?"

"What did Chalmers think?"

I stared at him with incredulous disbelief. "I can't believe you're asking

Alex's opinion."

He hissed in annoyance. "Just answer the question."

"He thought I should stay out of it."

"And as much as I hate to side with Chalmers, I agree with him."

I stared at Cupid's fluffy pink carpet.

"Look Porsche," Cupid said more gently. "Like you said, Earth has its charm. And Jarrett is truly out of commission."

"What did The Big Guy do to him?"

"Best not ask. I've heard some pretty scary rumours."

Maybe I really didn't want to know, I decided. After all, I'd been the one to accuse Jarrett.

"So you really don't need to worry," the cherub continued as I pondered that disturbing thought. "Everyone else in The Great Beyond knows how to do their job. You have to trust in that. And leave other people to handle it."

"Wynn Jarrett was the biggest traitor since Lucifer," I pointed out. "And no one noticed but me. No one *handled* it, Cupid."

Suddenly it became desperately important to know who sat in my chair. Who was charged with the safeguarding of Alex's soul . . . and, I supposed, mine as well, now?

"Who did they hire in my place?" I really shouldn't have asked.

"Percival Thor."

I groaned. *Thorny Percy* we'd called him in college. Not that Percy was a bad guy or anything. But I'd always thought he'd have made a better accountant than a guardian angel. He lacked imagination, and a personality.

"He's a perfectly competent guardian," Cupid said in Percy's defence.

"Every woman you've ever matched him up with has bolted in utter boredom!" It was the truth. Percy was a sore point with Cupid.

"That doesn't mean he can't do his job. The guy is meticulous to a fault."

Percy's faults were just what had me worried. "Oh yeah, I can just see Percy taking on the likes of Naamah."

I expected a sarcastic reply from the cherub, but he fell suddenly silent. I had the feeling he knew more about Percival Thor than he let on.

"Seriously, he's no match for her. He wouldn't know what to do about

Naamah. Or Lucifer. The problem with Percy is that he thinks the entire universe should behave the way he expects it to."

Cupid shot me a straight look. "Sounds like someone else I know."

"Do not," I said, "compare me to Thorny Percy."

I contemplated this new turn of events and decided I didn't like it. What was wrong with Uriel? Even after all we'd been through, he still didn't get it. Hades wanted to take over Heaven. Once cast out, Lucifer was forever looking for a way back in. And nothing would distract him from that goal. Nothing. If he couldn't buy his way into Heaven, he'd unleash Hell on Earth, for a diversion or just for the sheer spite of it.

"I really am worried, Cupid."

Something in my voice must have alerted him because he backed away, flapping his wings furiously. "Oh no, Porsche. We've been through this all before. And no good can come of it. So go home to Chalmers and listen to his advice. Stay out of it. Do not get involved in this one."

"I'm already involved."

"No you're not. Be smart, Porsche. Don't fall prey to one of Hades' schemes."

It wasn't that simple. Whatever Naamah was up to on Lucifer's behalf, someone had to stop her. Someone who understood that no matter what, Hell would play dirty.

"Look, I'm not asking you to – "

"Good," Cupid interrupted. "Because I won't."

I sighed and slumped lower on the undersized couch. "All I'm asking is for you to keep an eye on things here in Heaven. If Naamah's really up to something, it can't have escaped The Big Guy's notice. Rumours are bound to leak out."

"Nothing escapes The Big Guy's notice." He ruffled his wings in annoyance. "Especially you."

"I haven't been reduced to a pillar of salt."

It was a joke. Cupid didn't laugh. "Yet."

"Yet," I conceded.

"Okay, I'll see what I can find out," Cupid said. "And in return for this *huge* favour, I want you to stop interfering!"

"I'm not interfering!" I protested. Well, my conscience admitted, not really, not yet at least.

"This – " Cupid waved his hand at the tiny sitting room, "is interfering! As much as I'm glad to see you – you're not supposed to be here. You're supposed to be on Earth behaving yourself and learning what it is The Big Guy means for you to understand."

"But The Big Guy never tells you what it is you're supposed to learn. He leaves you to figure it out yourself."

"It's called personal growth, Porsche. And watch your tongue." He looked around like The Big Guy might be listening as we spoke, ready to swoop down and cast me into oblivion. "If anyone so much as finds out you were here. Or that I gave you what I gave you – " He cast a pointed glance at the locator.

"You'd really catch hell. I know. But what happened yesterday really concerns me."

"Stop worrying. Leave it to the people whose job it is to deal with it."

"But – "

Cupid stomped toward me along the couch. The cushions put a bounce in his step that ruffled his drying curls. I almost laughed. He looked so adorable and harmless. In reality he was neither. I let him seize my hand in both of his chubby ones. "Porsche, listen to me."

I said, "Cupid, don't lecture."

"Okay, I'll forgo the lecture. But I'm totally serious here."

He swallowed hard. "If anything happened to you, Porsche, it would kill me." He pinned me with another of those looks. "Really it would. Not to mention what it would do to your mother."

"Don't say that – " I started to protest.

He unclipped the locator from my belt and thrust it back into my hands. "So take this back to Earth and don't use it unless the Four Horsemen of the Apocalypse come galloping down your street!"

I opened my mouth to say something else, but he said, "Please."

"Okay, okay." I dialled in the coordinates and remembered to compensate for my heavier body. I didn't want to land like that on Alex's parquet floor. "I'll behave. Don't worry."

"Impossible," he protested.

I couldn't tell if he meant me behaving or not worrying.

"And by the way," he called after me. "I'll tell your mom you *are* behaving yourself and doing fine!"

"Thanks, Cupid, you're a pal," I called as I dematerialised.

I hit the floor of Alex's apartment. A marginally better landing than the last. Sitting in the middle of the sunken living room, I contemplated my lot. I'd risked everything to get a message through to Cupid. And only succeeded in worrying my best friend.

Thus far my day had been a total loss. I was sorely tempted simply to sit there feeling sorry for myself, but I'd promised Alex I'd at least make the bed and do the dishes. So I pried myself off the floor and wandered into the kitchen. I rinsed out the coffee maker and, adding more soap to the water, I washed and dried the mugs and put them back in the cupboard.

Then I headed down the hall to tackle the unmade bed. My stomach rumbled loudly, reminding me that I'd skipped both breakfast and lunch. After I straightened up the sheets and duvet, I wandered to the kitchen to see if there was anything in the fridge that could be heated up for dinner. Standing in the cold blast of the open refrigerator door, I contemplated the bare shelves.

"Hi," said a voice from the other side of the door.

I yelped and slammed the refrigerator door shut. Alex was standing behind it, still in his thousand-dollar suit. He must have come in while I was in the bedroom.

"You're home early," I said, trying to stay calm. Already I knew something was terribly wrong.

"No, I'm home for good."

I said, "What?"

Dark eyes stared back at me, more mournful than I'd ever seen them. "They found out about the money, Porsche."

I leaned against the counter. "But Alex, you told me you put the money back."

He sighed. "I did put it back. Every penny. But that doesn't change the fact that I took it. That kind of thing can be traced."

Guilt tore at my gut. On my watch as guardian angel, a demon had stolen Alex's soul. Even though I had sorted the situation out, that couldn't erase the damage that a soulless Alex had done in the meantime. Namely embezzle a lot of money. He replaced the money and I returned his soul. But computer records of the crime existed, albeit carefully concealed. Now someone besides Alex, The Big Guy and me knew what he'd done. Sins beget consequences, or so I'd told Alex many times.

"Damnation," I whispered. "I'm so sorry, Alex. I really hoped things would be okay."

Alex gave me a rueful smile. "No, actually working as a stockbroker for the rest of my life would have been eternal damnation."

"Don't say that! Never, ever joke about eternal banishment!" Mortal or not, I knew something very bad was sneaking up on us. Seeing Naamah, the sky falling and now Alex losing his job was only the beginning. I could feel it.

"I meant it's hardly the end of the world."

"Let's hope not," I said, only half joking. "What will happen now?"

"I really don't know. I guess I should call my lawyer."

Lost in thought, I wandered into the living room and stared out at the lake.

"Porsche . . . " Alex came up behind me and pulled me against him. I leaned back into his strong, muscular arms. Well, he'd have more time to work on that spectacular body, I thought, then immediately realised we were going to drive each other crazy cooped up together in his apartment. Not to mention that Alex had a mortgage and neither of us had a job.

"You're right. It could be worse," I conceded. Worse in ways I shuddered to contemplate. Late afternoon sun slanted on the water in golden waves. "Someone was bound to find out."

"Someone was," Alex agreed morosely.

Distracted, I watched the crowd disembarking from the Centre Island Ferry. And amongst the sea of faces, the parents dragging beach umbrellas and tired children, I caught a sudden flash of red.

I squinted against the afternoon sun, afraid to trust my eyes.

"There!" I yelled.

Alex jumped. "What?"

I pointed at the crowd. "Naamah, I saw her. I swear!"

Nearly knocking Alex off his feet, I tore down the hallway to the bedroom. Scattering clothes, I pulled the locator from its hiding place. The floor shook as Alex ran down the hall after me.

"Hold on!" I commanded and seized his arm. Alex's eyes widened as he realised what I held in my hand.

"Oh no – " He started to say something else, but his words were stolen by a rush of air as the floor fell from under us.

I hoped I'd compensated well enough for the both of us.

We hit the ground behind one of the potted topiary on the boardwalk. A better landing than my earlier two. I sincerely hoped whoever was watching the scope today in The Great Beyond wouldn't notice an Earth-bound locator beam.

Alex stumbled, but managed to keep his feet under him. I narrowly avoided colliding with the potted tree.

"Tell me you're supposed to have that thing," Alex said, still trying to catch his breath.

"Actually, I'm not supposed to have it," I said. Clasping his hand, I pulled him after me along the boardwalk toward the ferry docks.

"I don't suppose I want to know how you got it, do I?"

I glanced back at him. "No, you don't."

Only seconds had passed since we'd left the apartment. But it was enough time for the crowd to have thinned out.

Working against the stream of people toting picnic baskets and children in strollers, we earned more than our share of nasty looks. We nearly tripped over a woman with twin blond toddlers.

"Sorry!" I blurted absently, scanning the mob for another glimpse of red leather. Alex pulled me out of the path of a woman walking a bicycle. Her belongings overflowed from a basket drooping from the handlebars. A couple of teenagers, with multiple facial piercings and wearing black leather despite the oppressive heat, swore at us as we squeezed by.

Finally, the ferry emptied and the crowd dispersed, heading for the Terminal Building and Queen's Quay. And still no sight of Naamah. The ferry blew its whistle. The gates opened to let the crowds departing for Centre Island board the ferry.

None of them wore red. No one sported a wide-brimmed hat or walked with Naamah's sinuous grace. The crowd embarked and the ferry cast off.

Out of breath and sweating in the summer sun, we stood alone on the ferry docks.

Leaving a locator trail that could be just as easily traced as Alex's embezzled funds.

ONE OF US NEEDED A JOB. FINDING A job couldn't be that hard – could it? The next morning, I opened the local paper and tried to ignore the blurry pictures and ink that rubbed off on my hands. Scanning the want ads, I looked for anything I might be remotely qualified for. Set in bold type, the words *Network Specialist* leapt out at me. Being no stranger to high-tech gadgetry, I read further.

Troubleshooting and maintenance topped the list of responsibilities, no sweat there, I'd done both. But the advert continued with a laundry list of unfamiliar software. Even the hardware would be a challenge, I thought dejectedly. In theory I knew how most Earthly machines worked. But there was a world of difference between knowing in theory and being able to put that knowledge into practice. It would be like a twenty-first century person trying to use a spinning wheel or a blacksmith's forge. I decided that something a little less high-tech might be in order.

Continuing down the page, I focussed my attention on the hospitality section. After all, I had mastered dishwashing yesterday. Sure enough a few restaurants in town were hiring. But even the ads for dishwashers specified two years experience. I doubted washing dishes once would suffice.

"It's hopeless." Folding up the paper, I put it down on the bed. "I'm hopeless."

"Porsche," Alex said. "You gotta get a grip!"

He lay on his weight bench, two hundred pounds poised above his head. In the old days I could lift that thing with one hand. As I recalled, Alex had been impressed.

"Let me have a go at that," I said, and swapped places with Alex on the bench.

Alex divested the bar of one hundred and twenty-five pounds and I tried to lift seventy-five.

I tried to stop my face from turning red. Definitely un-sexy. I got the bar two inches above the rest.

So far so good, I thought. Then my muscles gave out. I watched helplessly as the weight came crashing toward my face. Alex grabbed it with both hands, rescuing me from a broken nose, and laid it back on the rest. I groaned in frustration.

"You couldn't just try fifty-five, could you?" Annoyance crept into his tone. Not just because of my near miss with the weights. The two of us had been stuck in his apartment all day with nothing better to do than get on each other's nerves. And last night I'd led him on a wild chase after Naamah. An unwelcome adventure that only reminded him of things he'd rather forget. Like Hell.

I deflected his irritation. "It's not a macho thing. I miss having strength."

"Well, you're not going to get it by breaking your nose or putting another hole in my floor." He shot a pointed glance at the dent in his parquet floor, a souvenir of the first time we'd met. "Here, try sixty." He stripped off twenty-five pounds and added ten.

"That's better," I said trying to hide the lie. But he saw through it easily. My trembling arms were a dead giveaway. He snatched the weight back and put it on the rest. I sat up. My muscles tingled with overexertion. But I'd lifted sixty. It was a slight improvement, if nothing else.

"You're mad at me, aren't you?" If we were going to fight, it might as well be now.

Alex sat down beside me. "No."

"Yes you are, I can tell." Guardian angels were trained to pick up such nuances. It didn't matter that I wasn't an angel anymore, Alex practically bristled with aggravation. I sighed. "And I can't blame you. I lost your soul, got you dragged to Hell and back. Now I'm living in your apartment and you just lost your job and the last thing you need is another mouth to feed – "

"It's not that."

"Okay . . . so what is it?"

His eyes blazed with repressed anger. I didn't care much for that look. It reminded me of the person he'd become under Lucifer's influence. It also meant he was about to say something unpleasant.

"Whatever Naamah's up to, I don't want any part of it." He got up and paced the floor between the bed and the weight bench. "And I want you to stay out of it, too."

I stood in his path. "I can't do that, Alex. Something bad is brewing out there."

He grasped me by the shoulders, forcing me to look up at him. "It doesn't matter. You're off the project, Porsche. Get over it! You need to stop thinking about Heaven and Hell and concentrate on living – here on Earth."

I'd hardly call mortality living, but I couldn't tell him that. I sagged against him. "Fine for you to say. I don't have the slightest idea where to start. I never thought adjusting to being human would be so hard."

"You haven't given it much of a chance." He traced the side of my face with one finger. "It isn't so bad being mortal, is it?"

What could I say? Alex had never been anything but mortal. He couldn't begin to comprehend what I'd lost. "No."

By his triumphant look, I could tell he thought he'd won. And maybe that wasn't such a bad idea. I decided to switch tactics.

"Maybe I should go for a run, get my mind off Naamah." Snoop around was more like it, but instead I said, "I need some fresh air."

"There's none outside," Alex remarked. "They've declared another pollution warning."

I scoffed. "I've been to Hell, remember. If I can breathe sulphur and brimstone, a little smog's not going to bother me."

He glanced at my sunburned face. Plucking the bottle of sunscreen from the bureau, he handed it to me. "Don't forget the sun block."

A breeze blew in off the lake, freshening the heavy air somewhat. I sniffed the humidity-laden wind and frowned. Beneath the odours of ozone and smog was a fetid smell. I glanced back at the lake, dismayed to see a school of dead fish floating belly up in the harbour. Their white underbellies sparkled in the sun as the current deposited more of them against the shore. Groundskeepers scoured the boardwalk, trying to scoop them out of the water before the tourists noticed.

The heat wave raised the lake temperature, we'd suffered through a violent storm, and it was no secret the lake was polluted. But the scene troubled me. The lake hadn't been full of dead fish before Naamah's arrival.

But I was out in the open air, with no one looking over my shoulder. If Naamah was up to something in my city, I intended to find out what it was.

I ran along the lakeside path until it met Yonge Street. Afternoon heat reflected back at me from the pavement as I headed up from the lake into downtown. The combination sucked the energy from me. I stopped in the feeble shade offered by twin trees that flanked the entrance to an office building. The poor things stood in terracotta pots in a cement courtyard. They looked as wilted as I felt. I took a sip of bottled water and thought again about the dead fish in the harbour. The city's tap water came from the lake. It was no wonder that Alex preferred to drink something from a bottle.

I lifted the hair off the back of my neck and fanned myself. Why Alex enjoyed living in a city that was nearly as hot as Hades in the summer and as cold as the Arctic in the winter, was beyond me. I shoved the water bottle back into its holder in my belt pack, ready to resume running.

My human muscles protested violently. I clenched my teeth against the discomfort and kept going, determined to pound some resiliency into my body.

Office buildings began to empty themselves of people. Men and women in business suits juggled briefcases as they tried to strip out of their suit jackets. I glanced down at the bicycle shorts and sports bra that I wore and was glad I'd forgone a t-shirt.

The sidewalks grew progressively more crowded as the working population headed home. I took refuge in a small park, which contained a weather-beaten bandstand and several trees. Lying flat out on the grass, I looked up through the branches at the clouds that drifted sluggishly past. I shut my eyes, enjoying the barest hint of a breeze.

A loud whirring sound made me sit up. It sounded like the buzz of a million insects. I looked around the park. A couple of teenagers sitting on the bandstand obliviously sucked on each other's faces. On one of the picnic tables, a trio of businessmen smoked and drank coffee and looked grim. No helicopters hovered above the park. Everything seemed fine. Except for the sound, which came closer. I spun, looked out over the other side of the park.

That's when I noticed that the tree behind me was shuddering in a manic dance.

Standing up, I drew closer. No one else seemed to notice anything unusual. But the entire tree vibrated like every leaf had suddenly sprung to life. I squinted against the sun. No, the tree was covered with something. Something that whirred and buzzed.

People streamed through the park, heading for the nearby subway station. Not one of them glanced at the tree. I stood beneath the branches and looked up.

Insects covered the tree. Thousands of them, all engaged in devouring every leaf, every morsel of greenery. They spilled down the trunk and onto the grass, continuing to eat. I backed up quickly.

More insects swarmed off the tree and onto the grass. I bent for a closer look. Grasshoppers? Crickets? One jumped onto my running shoe. I flicked it away.

With a sinking heart, I studied the insect calmly chomping on the grass at my feet. Definitely not crickets.

Locusts.

Far as I knew, a plague of locusts was a rarity in downtown Toronto. Which meant that along with the dead fish in the harbour, something in the natural order of things was way out of whack.

In horror I watched as the locusts finished chowing down on the maple tree. As one, they swarmed to its nearby companion, devouring the grass in between. The dour-faced businessmen still drank their coffee and sucked on their cigarettes. But the hiss of thousands of locust wings had finally attracted the attention of the teenagers on the bandstand.

A locust landed on the girl's knee, momentarily distracting her from her beau. "Ew!" She scrambled to her feet and fled into the glass atrium of a nearby building, leaving her neglected boyfriend to rush after her.

The plague continued across the park. Briefly they detoured into a planter of red geraniums, quickly leaving only dusty soil in their wake. They beat their wings against the glass windows of the atrium, desperately trying to get at a fake ficus inside. Like a dark cloud, they hovered over the park.

A trail of devastation lay in their wake. Maple trees, stripped of their leaves, looked like the dead of winter. Where sickly grass had once covered most of the park, now only sand remained. The locusts headed for the last remaining tree.

One of the businessmen ground his cigarette butt into the grass. A locust splashed into his Styrofoam coffee cup, splattering his white shirt with coffee. He stared into his cup, and then stared in disbelief at the maple tree being defoliated nearby. His companions glanced up from their conversation. They stared around at the ruin of the park, and then bolted for the atrium, trampling locusts underfoot.

The stream of office workers continued through the park to the subway as if nothing had happened.

Locusts abandoned the tree. As one they took to the air and disappeared behind the monolith of a nearby building.

I stared down at the locusts squished into the dirt. I knelt in the sand and considered the insects. Locusts. No doubt about it.

And swarms of locusts along with falling stars, she-devil sightings, dead fish, hail and thunder could only mean one thing.

Apocalypse.

Alex and Cupid were wrong. This was no coincidence. The signs were clear. I picked up a squished locust and put it in my belt pouch.

Hurrying against the tide of people heading into the subway station, I started to make my way home. A flash of red caught my eye. I stopped abruptly, colliding with a middle-aged businessman who cursed under his breath and brandished his laptop like a weapon.

I stepped out of his way, bumping into someone else, trying to keep that glint of bright fabric in view. Giving up on being polite, I shoved my way through the crowd, earning more curses and a well-aimed elbow to the ribs.

Ahead, almost hidden in the sea of pinstripe, I caught another glimpse of crimson leather. I struggled toward it and almost got hit in the face by a glass door. I dodged the door and let the crowd carry me down the stairs into the subway tunnel. The stairway spilled me onto the platform with the rest of the commuters.

The train was packed. No way could that mob squeeze through the train's narrow doors. But as the chimes signalled the train's imminent departure, I spotted Naamah sensually wriggling her way onto the train as a businessman beside her cast an appreciative glance down her cleavage.

I looked around for ideas, knowing I had to behave myself in view of the surveillance camera trained on the platform. Something moved in the periphery of my vision. I turned just in time to catch the twisted body of a minion scrambling down into the darkness at the end of the platform. A pair of red eyes glinted at me. In the shadows it was likely neither would show up on the video cameras, but at least it confirmed my suspicions as to how a plague of locusts had got loose in downtown Toronto.

Naamah! I knew it. And apparently, she had help.

The doors to the train began closing. With no way to squish myself into the car, and knowing I couldn't let Naamah get away, I took the only option left to me.

I reached out and snagged her by her beaded tail, and hauled her back onto the platform.

Naamah roared with outrage. She swung her tail with such force, it nearly ripped my arm from its socket. But I hung on. Baring her teeth, she showed her true face. Passengers tripped over themselves trying to get out of her way. She swiped at me with her long nails. I ducked. Her nails grated against the closing doors. But I'd stopped her from getting onto the train.

I let go of her tail, noting with perverse curiosity that today she'd decorated it with blood-red beads. I shouldn't have looked because I barely had time to sidestep the spike heel aimed for my throat.

The train glided away into the tunnel. Panting, we faced each other on the platform, surrounded by bemused commuters. I noticed I was breathing a lot harder than Naamah, and that irked me. When it came to dealing with the netherworld, none of the running and pumping iron made much difference. In a human body, I was badly under-muscled.

We circled each other warily in clear view of the video camera. Somehow I had to get Naamah somewhere we could have a private conversation. But she didn't look likely to oblige.

I turned, and, keeping an eye on my nemesis, moved out of the brightness cast by the overhead lights into a shadowed tunnel leading from the platform out of the camera's area of surveillance and free of commuters. Naamah followed with the grace of a snake. Every muscle in her body tensed to spring at me.

"Well, if it isn't the fallen angel," she sniped.

Her hand shot out. Two-inch nails lashed at my throat. I darted out of reach, just in time.

But my slow reflexes alerted Naamah. Dismayed, I watched the realization cross her face. Now she knew I wasn't just a fallen angel. I was human.

Tasting impending victory, Naamah pursued me deeper into the passage.

Mortal or not, I refused to back down. Even if she killed me, I'd get a piece of her first. But as my mother often reminded me, that kind of thinking lay behind most of my rash acts. The ill conceived plans that led to her perpetual embarrassment.

Like clobbering Naamah, even though that was a very seductive thought. So, I choked down the impulse and stared her down. "Well, if it isn't Naamah, Demoness of Seductresses and Head of Lucifer's Administrative Staff."

Naamah beamed in response. She loved to hear her official titles spoken aloud. There were several more I could have added, but it wouldn't have been polite.

"Enjoying life here on Earth, *mortal*?" Naamah asked with sickly sweetness. She was testing me, daring me to deny it. Damned if I'd give her the satisfaction.

I felt the grip I held on my temper unravel. But I managed to force my lips into a smile. "Matter of fact I am enjoying life on the Earthly plane."

"And how is Alex?"

"He's –" The question sounded so innocent, I almost answered. Almost. How could she have known I lived with Alex? But then, she'd always suspected more was going on between us than a professional guardian angel and subject relationship. And I couldn't forget that Naamah had wanted Alex for herself. She'd wanted him enough to steal his soul, even after I'd rescued him from Lucifer. The grip on my temper loosened further. "Oh, cut the crap, Naamah. You don't give a sweet damn how I am. And Alex Chalmers is none of your business. So why don't you just tell me what you're doing here on Earth. Where, I might add, you shouldn't be."

She snapped her tail in annoyance. Deadly barbs clove the air. I tried to leap out of the way. But I no longer had the agility I used to. The tip of her tail caught me across the thigh. A she-devil's tail could raise a welt as nasty as a whip. I felt the sting, then the hot rush of blood.

Naamah smiled. "Aren't we feisty for a disgraced angel. Would have thought dishonour might teach you a little humility."

I swung at her and missed as she danced sinuously out of the way. I ground my teeth, audibly. But said nothing. No sense letting her beat me senseless before I found out what I wanted to know.

Naamah studied me, much the way I'd studied the dead fish in the lake. "Well, I have to give you points for attitude, however misplaced. Don't even think of threatening me, little human. I could brush you off like a fly."

"Don't be so sure of that," I bluffed. I couldn't help adding, "Don't you mean, like a locust?"

Naamah's eyes narrowed. Her tail struck out again. I jumped out of the way. "I have no idea what you're talking about."

"And I'm St. Peter."

"I'm sure your mother wishes you were."

Ah, the saint jibe, it never went away. I was going to have to hit her, I decided. But people had started to look inquisitively down the passage after us. So I wiped the blood off my leg and said, "Out with it, Naamah, what is it this time? Death, destruction . . . Armageddon?"

Naamah's multifaceted eyes stared down at me. I saw myself reflected a million times, looking as insubstantial as I felt. I thrust my fists against my waist to make myself look tougher.

It didn't help.

"Like I'd tell you, Heaven's disgrace."

I did throw a punch at her then. But the movement caught the eye of one of the passengers. I pulled the punch and clenched my fist so hard I felt the bite of my nails into my palm.

"I will find out," I snarled back.

"And do what?" Naamah asked. Knowing for certain I was pretty much helpless against her, she couldn't help launching another barb. "Zap me with your discourager?"

Good question. Pummel you with my insubstantial human fists, I wanted to shout at her.

Another train pulled into the station. People surged toward the doors. "Nice talking to you, Porsche, but as you can see my train is here."

With that she stepped past me and back onto the platform, neatly sliding into the subway car that opened in front of her with annoying precision. My body coiled tightly to spring, I considered my dilemma. I could jump in there after her and pound her until I felt better or she killed me, whichever came first. And the police would probably throw the bloody remnants of me in jail. They'd have all the evidence they needed to convict me on the video cameras.

So I let her go and stepped back as the doors closed. Naamah waved cheerfully from inside. "Say hi to Alex for me."

As if.

"Tell Lucifer I will stop him," I called after her.

Somehow, I added silently.

Alex was hunched over his desk sculpting when I arrived back at the apartment. I tried not to drip blood on his carpet.

Finally noticing me, his face clouded with anger. "God, Porsche can't I let you out of my sight for a moment?"

"Apparently not," I said. "And kindly don't use The Big Guy's name. We really don't want to attract His notice."

He got up from the desk and pulled me after him into the bathroom to get a damp towel. Gently, he wiped the blood from my thigh and examined the wound underneath.

"How's it look?"

"Not good," he admitted. "Should I even ask how this happened?"

I sighed. "I had a conversation with Naamah." He opened his mouth, I held up my hand. "And yes, it was Naamah. Of that I have no doubt."

Alex whistled. "Some conversation." He rinsed the towel with cold water and held it to my leg.

"Naamah says hi."

He had the good sense to shudder.

I reached into my pouch and pulled out the squashed remnants of the locust. "Do you know what this is?"

Alex stared at the mashed bug in my hand. "A grasshopper?" he asked in the kind of hushed tones reserved for conversing with lunatics.

I shook my head.

He gave up pretending to understand. "You brought home a dead insect? Gross!"

"It's not a grasshopper, it's a locust."

"A what?" He answered his question with another question. "How do you know?"

"I saw him . . ." I held up the locust for closer inspection and Alex took a step backward. ". . . and a few thousand of his buddies demolish an entire park."

"Demolish?" Alex looked from the gash on my thigh back to the dead bug in my hand. From the expression on his face I suspected he wished I would just take all the weirdness I'd brought into his life and vanish.

I tossed the locust into the toilet and flushed it. "Devoured. As in stripping an entire park of vegetation in a matter of minutes." I watched the remains of the insect disappear around the u-bend. "And the strange thing was, no one seemed to care much."

Alex stared at me in horror. I don't think it was the locusts that bothered him, I think it was me. I imagine it suddenly occurred to him that as long as I lived with him, he'd never be free of the weird problems I brought into his life. I saw things from a totally different perspective. I saw things beyond mortal perception. "Are you sure it was a plague of locusts? They could have been some other kind of insect."

I pointed at the empty toilet. "That was definitely a locust. And yes, I'm absolutely sure. I wasn't the only witness."

"Maybe there's something on the news," Alex said hopefully. "Like a rational explanation that doesn't involve the paranormal."

"Paranormal phenomena are completely rational if you understand enough about them," I pointed out. "And I'm sure the explanation involves Lucifer somehow."

"I thought your Big Guy had it all under control."

"Shh!" I held a finger to my mouth. "Will you stop doing that?"

"Doing what?"

"Mentioning His name."

Alex said, "Oh."

"The courts seized Lucifer's shares in Utopia, Inc. But don't think that this prevents Lucifer from causing havoc on Earth."

I took the cloth from him and dabbed at the gash on my thigh.

"That won't heal the way it used to," Alex commented. "You've got to learn to keep yourself out of trouble."

I sat on the side of the bathtub. "I know. But when I saw Naamah I just couldn't ignore it. Trust me, Alex, this is bad."

"Bad doesn't necessarily mean it's your business, Porsche."

I tossed the towel on the floor and rested my head in my hands. "True enough. But something's up, and it's not good. And my conscience just won't let me sit by and pretend I didn't see it. I have to tell someone. Someone who *can* do something about it!"

"Now hold on – " He might not be a stockbroker anymore. He might have lost his job, but Alex sounded every bit the Bay Street mover and shaker. "Some weird weather and seeing one of Lucifer's chosen on Earth doesn't necessarily mean Hell is plotting against us."

"Hell is always plotting against us. And don't forget the locusts," I pointed out. "Locusts are definitely an ominous portent."

"Okay . . ." He ran a hand through his dark curls. I wished we were sitting in the patio bar downstairs having a romantic evening and watching the sun set over the lake. I wished we were doing anything except discussing Naamah, Lucifer or any of his minions. "I'll admit, locusts aren't usually seen in downtown Toronto."

"Alex, locusts are *never* seen downtown. They ate an entire park!"

"But that doesn't necessarily mean – "

I threw up my hands in frustration. "You sound like Cupid – " I started to say, then realised what I'd just revealed.

Alex regarded me shrewdly. "When exactly were you talking to Cupid?"

Too late to take it back, I figured I might as well just tell him everything. "Yesterday."

Dark brows drew together. I watched him put the pieces of the puzzle together. "You used that locator, didn't you? Before we made that speedy jaunt down there to the ferry docks." He pointed downward, as if we could see through the many floors between us and the pier.

I studied the tiles between my feet.

"Don't tell me you've got *him* involved in this thing." Alex and Cupid were never going to get along. I'd given up hoping. "He calls me the bad idea."

"Very bad idea," I corrected.

"Thanks."

"Look," I stood up. "I wanted an objective opinion."

"Cupid is hardly an objective opinion. He's not big enough to give an objective opinion."

"Now that's just mean."

"He bit me."

"And you provoked him. I was there, remember?" I looked in the mirror. A sweaty, bedraggled human looked back at me. I said, "Ugh."

Alex sat beside me on the edge of the bathtub and put his arms around me. "Porsche, I just don't want you to get hurt."

"Too late," I said with a bitter laugh. "And don't worry, whatever your opinion of Cupid, he didn't believe me any more than you do. And that's not all. Somehow Naamah knows we live together. She made a veiled threat at you."

"You said she said hi."

I stifled a groan. Alex had been to Hell and back and had managed to learn very little from the experience. "From Naamah that *is* a threat."

He grinned. "Maybe she just has a thing for me."

"Trust me, you don't want to go there. Naamah is Lucifer's right hand for a reason. That reason being, she's every bit as evil as he is. If Naamah has a thing for you, you should run screaming in the other direction."

"Trust me, I would."

But would he? I'd got Alex's soul back, but not entirely in pristine condition. With his soul in Lucifer's keeping, Alex had been all too easily tempted by the underworld. That he'd stay on the straight and narrow this time was too much of a risk. I still worried that he'd been irrevocably corrupted. Naamah's appearance just might be the thing that sent him over the edge. And this time I might lose him to Hades for good. My conscience couldn't stand it.

"Whatever Naamah's planning, I've already stepped in it. But I shouldn't be involving you."

His smile faded. "No, Porsche, you should stay out of the Devil's schemes!"

"But if Naamah – and ultimately Lucifer – is behind all this weirdness, it's unconscionable for me to let them get away with it." I pressed two fingers to his lips, cutting off the rest of his protests. "But my conscience is my concern. You have another chance, Alex. I don't want to ruin it for you."

He moved my hand out of the way and pulled me closer. Warm lips covered mine, teasing me to think of things other than Naamah and the locusts. "You've been given another chance too," he said, raising his head.

True enough. The Big Guy had given me another chance. And I was about to blow it, quite literally, to Hell.

EVENING STRETCHED INTO NIGHT with no further supernatural phenomenon. Even the weather seemed to cooperate. The night passed without thunderstorms or hail. But morning dawned hot and humid. Violent storms seemed a definite possibility.

Alex left early in the morning for an appointment with his lawyer. That he'd been under Lucifer's influence when he *borrowed* money from his clients' accounts wouldn't wash with the authorities on Earth. He needed to find a way to stem the tide of destruction caused by the discovery of his theft and his ultimate dismissal. Damage control seemed the order of the day. On all fronts, I thought grimly. If Naamah really intended to unleash Armageddon on Lucifer's behalf, it wouldn't matter what Alex's lawyer said.

But I didn't tell Alex that. Instead, I promised to stay close to home while he was gone and not to fight with any passing she-devils.

Roaming the downtown core qualified as being close to home. I decided I wasn't breaking any promises. Hidden in the pouch around my waist was Cupid's locator. I tried to convince myself that just carrying it didn't violate any oaths, either.

Heat still held the city in its oppressive grasp. Relentless sun had scorched the grass yellow. And what the sun hadn't burned to a crisp the plague of locusts had eaten. Reports of the infestation dominated the local news, along with weather reports lamenting the unseasonably high temperatures and severe thunderstorms.

Streets of concrete and tarmac hugged the heat close. I'd only walked a few blocks and already my hair stuck to the back of my neck in a sweaty mass. A humidity-laden wind rippled down the street, bringing with it the hint of faraway music. Barely audible above the rush of traffic, I wandered toward it.

Despite the heat and the lack of shade, a concert was underway in the square in front of city hall. The line of ice cream trucks at the curb seemed to be doing a brisk business. I stood on the outskirts of the square, listening to the rock band's pounding beat. A subway train rumbled by underneath the street. For a moment its vibration warred with the thud of the music, then the bass player won out.

A crowd of barely-clothed teens crammed the square. Oblivious to the heat, they writhed in time to the beat. Mounted riot police were posted at strategic points, sweltering in their black uniforms and visored helmets. Their horses had to be feeling doubly hot underneath thick saddles and protective faceplates. But aside from some overly enthusiastic youths shaking their long hair in the mosh pit, there didn't seem to be anything unusual taking place.

I headed for the walkway that led behind city hall. Dodging the edge of the surging crowd, I passed in front of a small group of riot police. One of the horses snorted.

I glanced up. If not for that small, animal sound I would have missed the spectacle. Instead, I took a closer look at the mounted policemen.

Behind their black helmets and transparent faceplates, they could have been any other riot police. Their black uniforms matched those of the others clustered around the square. Red lights blinked on the stirrups and at the backs of their saddles, giving them a futuristic and dangerous look. Except for the insignia on their shoulders, I might have been fooled.

On second glance, the horses were all wrong, too. All the other riot police rode dark brown horses. Except for the four gathered on this side of the square.

The first rider sat astride a horse so white that its coat blazed in the sun. I stared at the shoulder of his black uniform where the crest of the local police should have been plainly visible. Instead, it bore an emblem with a bow and a golden crown.

Conquest. The First Horseman of the Apocalypse. No, it couldn't be. Squinting against the sun, I studied him. A hint of blond curls escaped the severe black helmet. With his square jaw and sparkling blue eyes he looked every bit the conqueror. He levelled a regal stare back at me. Coincidence, I thought. There had to be at least one blue-eyed, square-jawed cop on the police force. But the effect he had on his surroundings was unmistakeable. The consummate commander, not even the blazing sun could vanquish him. He didn't so much as cast a sliver of shadow in the sunlight.

My gaze moved to the rider beside him. Seated on a reddish-brown horse, his uniform was identical to his handsome colleague's. Except for the insignia of a silver sword that stretched from shoulder to elbow. Dark eyes scrutinised me from under black brows. Heavier set than his co-worker Conquest, he was built for the nastier work.

A few locusts swarmed around him, attacking each other in buzzing waves.

War. Oh no.

The red horse sniffed me and snorted again. Conquest's white horse echoed the assessment. Like recognised like. Even if I wasn't a supernatural creature any longer, the warhorse realised I was no ordinary mortal. I couldn't decide whether to be relieved or insulted.

If Conquest and War came dressed as riot police in a city plagued with locusts, falling stars and freak storms, then that meant the other two could only be: *Famine* and *Death*.

Famine was astride a horse as black as a moonless night. Behind his visor, his gaunt face was barely discernable. But his eyes followed my movement as I shifted for a look at the insignia on his shoulder. A pair of black scales stood out against a silver background. Behind him, the leafless branches of a tree the locusts had defoliated, drooped in submission.

Their gathering made sense in a twisted kind of way. The lust for conquest brought war, which in turn caused famine, pestilence and plagues, which resulted in death.

With a sinking heart, I looked at the last of the four. With the sun glaring on his visor, most people wouldn't notice the skull's head under the black helmet. Or the bony frame beneath the bulletproof vest. Black leather gloves hid his skeletal hands. The crest on his shoulder though, screamed danger. A skull and crossbones. His horse looked like someone had taken a healthy animal and bleached it an unhealthy shade of cream. Ribs showed plainly through its hide.

Death's path stood out clearly against the city street. Everywhere Death's horse had trod, the soil and even the concrete was scorched black.

The four horsemen stared back at me. Plainly, I had their attention. Their interest followed my every breath as they waited for me to make the first move. I glanced back at the concert still in progress and wondered how the crowd could dance in the blazing sun while the Four Horsemen of the Apocalypse and a fallen angel held a conference on the pavement. The ability to be completely oblivious of the events around them seemed to be a human trait. Devoutly, I wish I possessed it.

I stared up at the four shadows against the sun. For a moment we watched each other. Then, I said, "Gentlemen."

As one, they nodded in greeting.

Okay, so they weren't being rude, but they weren't being entirely helpful, either.

I tried again. "What brings you to Toronto?"

Death, Famine and War glanced at Conquest. As head of the department, he spoke for the lot of them.

"Heard there might be work here." Every bit the commander, he barely had to raise his voice to be heard above the din.

I said, "Really?"

Another one of those abbreviated nods. Like that was any kind of answer.

"Who said there was work here?"

Again the crew looked to Conquest. After a second's pause, he said, "Heard a rumour."

"Through the office grapevine," War added. Conquest shot him a dangerous look and he fell silent.

Already rumours had begun to circulate. That certainly didn't bode well.

"So . . ." I had to ask. "Is there work here?"

"Perhaps," Conquest said enigmatically.

"Perhaps not," Famine countered.

I opened my mouth to probe further. But the concrete beneath me rumbled ominously. For a second I felt as if the ground twisted, trying to throw me from its back. There was a groan of complaint from deep below me which reverberated bone-deep.

An earthquake, I realised, deciphering the unfamiliar sensation. Added to plagues, hail, falling stars, she-devil sightings, that boded ill indeed. And now The Four were sniffing around, looking for work in *my* city.

Then just as swiftly as it started, the Earth's rumbling fell silent. Traffic roared by on Queen Street. The band kept playing and the teens in the mosh pit gyrated to the beat. Except for me and the Four Horsemen of the Apocalypse, no one else seemed to notice.

For a moment none of us spoke. Death shrugged. I heard the hollow sound of his bones rubbing together. "Maybe there is work here, after all."

Conquest answered him with a non-committal grunt.

A cloud obscured the sun, casting The Four suddenly into shadow. I glanced skyward to see a bank of threatening storm clouds blowing inland from the waterfront. Under cover of the unexpected darkness, The Four shimmered and vanished.

"Wait!" I called after them. But my voice was lost in the music. As an ex-colleague they hardly owed me an explanation, I reflected.

If The Four were on reconnaissance, they had to have a reason. One backed by future plans and budget allocations. And if rumours of something afoot in Toronto had reached levels of management that high, every other minor player had to be skulking around as well.

Anger bristled through me. Another raw, human emotion.

"Not in my city, you don't," I whispered after the glittering departure of The Four.

One of the ice cream vendors caught sight of me talking to myself on the sidewalk and looked quickly away. Great, now I was scaring the locals.

"Naamah," I muttered, not caring whether I frightened people or not. I began walking down Queen Street, away from the concert and the ice cream trucks. "This all started with Naamah."

And while I'd been conferring with The Four, Naamah was probably roaming the city, carrying out more of Lucifer's evil deeds.

I reached into my pouch, feeling the locator's weight. I might be mortal, but I was hardly without resources. If Naamah and other underworld wildlife still lurked in my city, I intended to find out. And chase them out of town.

Ducking into a nearby mall, I headed for the restrooms. Enough supernatural activity had taken place in the downtown. I didn't want to frighten anyone with a sudden disappearance. Especially a tourist toting a video camera.

Barricaded in a stall in the women's washroom, I took out Cupid's locator and dialled coordinates. A topical map of the downtown appeared on the tiny screen. I keyed settings for the immediate area. Lights blinked green. Blips moved across the screen. Something inhuman prowled the downtown. I pressed the button to sample the life form.

The screen produced its verdict. Horsemen.

"The Four," I said under my breath. So The Four Horsemen had found sufficient activity to justify further investigation. But so far, their activities had been limited to reconnaissance, so I kept scanning.

I widened the grid to include all of downtown. A red blip appeared on the screen, heading rapidly south toward the lake.

I pressed the sample button again. The screen spat out another verdict. She-devil.

Naamah. Or one of her staff. Who else could it be? For a moment I stared at the blinking light on the locator's grid. Matching up the coordinates, I cursed softly under my breath. Naamah was making good on her threat and heading straight for Alex's apartment.

Perhaps Alex was still with his lawyer. Or maybe he hadn't gone straight home. No, I thought with a sinking heart. My luck just wasn't that good.

I hefted the locator in my hand, debating. Damnation, I'd promised Cupid I wouldn't use the thing. But if Naamah's destination truly was Alex's condo, then this qualified as an emergency.

Aiming for a secluded patch of ground behind the bandstand in the park, I input coordinates. Hidden by the stage, at least I'd be blocked from view by anyone strolling by on the boardwalk. Uttering a silent prayer, I activated the locator.

My feet left the bathroom's tiled floor. For a moment I hovered weightlessly, then my feet hit ground. Hard.

In my haste I'd forgotten to adjust the settings. I hit the sandy soil, pitching forward onto my hands and knees. Briefly, I regretted not putting on a pair of blue jeans this morning. Then, I was picking myself up, brushing the tiny stones and dirt that had got into my grazed palms. I glanced quickly around.

Luckily I'd landed behind the stage as I'd planned. Tourists passed by on the boardwalk, but most of them were more interested in the hot dog stand and chip wagon parked nearby. Unfortunately, I'd left a locator signature as big as the exhaust from a jet engine. One of these days Gabriel was going to look over the log. And then I'd be really sorry. Hopefully, it wouldn't be today.

Tucking the locator back in my pouch, I brushed the last of the sand from my knees and tried to look nonchalant as I headed toward the condo entrance.

Laughter cut through the din of a dozen conversations emanating from the patio bar. Husky feminine laughter. I turned in the direction of the sound and saw Naamah smiling oh-so-sweetly at a square-shouldered bouncer with no neck. No customary red leather for the head she-devil today. Instead, she wore a skin-tight black denim jumpsuit, its front zip open to her chest revealing her cleavage, a sight the bouncer clearly enjoyed. He said something that Naamah plainly found hilarious. Her laughter echoed out over the water. She slapped a red-nailed hand playfully against his back and then sauntered off toward the mall entrance. The bouncer stared after her departing silhouette. That jumpsuit left nothing to the imagination. I wondered where she'd hidden her tail, then decided I didn't want to know.

Giving the bouncer a wide berth, I took off after her.

But Naamah was adept at using unsuspecting humans as camouflage. The crowd closed around her. Within seconds she had disappeared into the mass of hot dog and candyfloss eating tourists strolling the boardwalk.

I bolted through the mall doors, nearly knocking over a woman teetering on high heels and carrying two fruity drinks with pink umbrellas. She cursed me as I rounded the corner and disappeared into the air-conditioned gloom of the mall. It took my eyes a moment to adjust to the relative darkness. Naamah's denim-clad body was nowhere to be seen.

A glance at the elevators showed the numbers steadily climbing on both lifts. I groaned. Even if I waited for one of the elevators to come back down, Naamah would have several minutes to unleash whatever hell she had in mind on Alex.

Unfortunately, it took very little time to strip a soul from a body and send it to Hell.

With a sinking heart, I watched the elevators climb another couple of floors. Out of options, I slid the locator from my pouch. I'd already broken my promise to Cupid by using it, I thought with a pang of guilt. Every use of the thing meant another promise broken, and brought me closer to the eventuality of Gabriel finding out. If I involved Gabriel, it had better be for a good reason. I had to get on one of those lifts before they reached the penthouse.

But which elevator was Naamah on? My head turned right, then left, trying to decide. The sun shone brightly through the mall doors, blinding me to everything outside. I was alone in the foyer, shielded by the sun. I pointed the locator, dialled coordinates, closed my eyes and prayed.

Hitting a moving target with a locator is no small feat. I didn't want to become corporeal within the walls of the elevator. On top or below wouldn't be a good idea, either. I'd tried to compensate for velocity, but I wouldn't know until I landed if I'd been successful

My feet hit the floor awkwardly. I bent my knees. It took my body a second to adjust to the movement, but at least I'd landed *in* the elevator. Opening my eyes, I realised I'd guessed wrong.

Instead of Naamah, an empty lift greeted me. The passenger had obviously got off, and it had started its descent to the ground floor. I groaned. Sincerely hoping the elevator didn't have security cameras, I calmly pressed the button for the next floor and exited when the doors opened.

The numbers on the next elevator were still climbing. I dialled new coordinates, trying to gauge velocity and distance and hoped for the best.

The dizzying sensation of spinning through space made my stomach lurch. The impact jarred my knees as I hit the floor, then I was in motion again as the elevator continued to climb.

Husky laughter made me turn my head, and I found myself face to knees with Naamah. Okay, I'd survived the elevator's ascent. I hadn't materialised in the middle of the doors. Now there was the head she-devil to contend with in tight quarters.

Luckily, we were the elevator's only occupants. I scrambled to my feet and fervently wished for a discourager. Probably a good thing I didn't have one. I would have blasted a hole in her grinning face. And probably one in the elevator wall as well.

"Porsche Winter," she said, closing the scant distance between us. I held my ground. It didn't hurt that my back was already up against the wall. I realised she hadn't hidden her tail at all. Beaded black and silver, it circled her waist like a belt. Must be killing her to hold it in that position, I thought. And sincerely hoped it was. "Why am I not surprised?"

I didn't deign to answer the question. "Spill it Naamah. What are you up to?"

"Hades and Heaven have equal access to the Earthly plane," she said with disdain. "I don't have to tell you anything."

"Technically that's true," I bluffed. "Like I'll accept that for an answer."

She gave a haughty shake of her head, sending a cloud of curls cascading over her shoulders. Within that mass of shockingly red hair nestled a pair of very sharp horns, pierced and also decorated with black and silver earrings.

"I don't give a sweet damn what you accept." With that seductive swagger, Naamah sauntered closer still. "And you, fallen angel, are starting to become a real nuisance."

"Someone has to prevent you from doing Lucifer's business on Earth."

I changed tactics, hoping to keep her off balance.

"Lucifer's business?" For an instant Naamah looked truly insulted. She surveyed me, pink-faced from the sun, sweaty from the cloying heat and undeniably human. Visibly, she decided I was no threat. "What are you going to do?" she taunted. "Pull my hair?"

"If that's the best I can do," I told her honestly. "Yes."

Naamah moved faster than my human vision could track. Only the rush of air alerted me. I slid to the side.

Her tail struck the side of the elevator, leaving a dent in the shiny metal. Beads grated against steel. Naamah danced backward. Then, like a charging bull, she lowered her head and pointed those impossibly sharp horns at me.

In the narrow confines of the elevator, I had little room to manoeuvre. I whirled away from her. But not fast enough.

The tip of one horn caught me in the side. I felt the stinging pressure, the shock of sudden pain, and then the hot rush of blood.

Gasping for breath, I raised my knee and slammed it up against her chin. The impact snapped her teeth together. I clasped my hands and brought them down on the back of her neck. I wasn't strong enough to hurt her. That didn't mean I wouldn't try.

Naamah raised her head, Her eyes widened in surprise, then narrowed swiftly in fury.

She lunged at me. I heard the scrape of her spike heels against the floor. I aimed another punch. My fist connected with air.

Belatedly, I felt the tingling of a locator beam on retrieve. And it wasn't mine.

"Oh no," I whispered. "Please . . . not yet."

The world turned over. I flailed in the sudden absence of up or down.

Then my feet hit bleached marble. I caught a flash of white. "No, no, no," I pleaded. But The Big Guy wasn't listening.

I looked up to find myself in the centre of a ring of furious-looking archangels.

"Damnation!" I said.

Gabriel strode toward me, resplendent in his white robes. Towering over me, he glanced down with the displeasure of someone examining a bug.

"Don't use that word here, Miss Winter."
"Sorry," I managed to croak.
"I sincerely hope you are."
I had a feeling I was about to be even more sorry. About a lot of things.

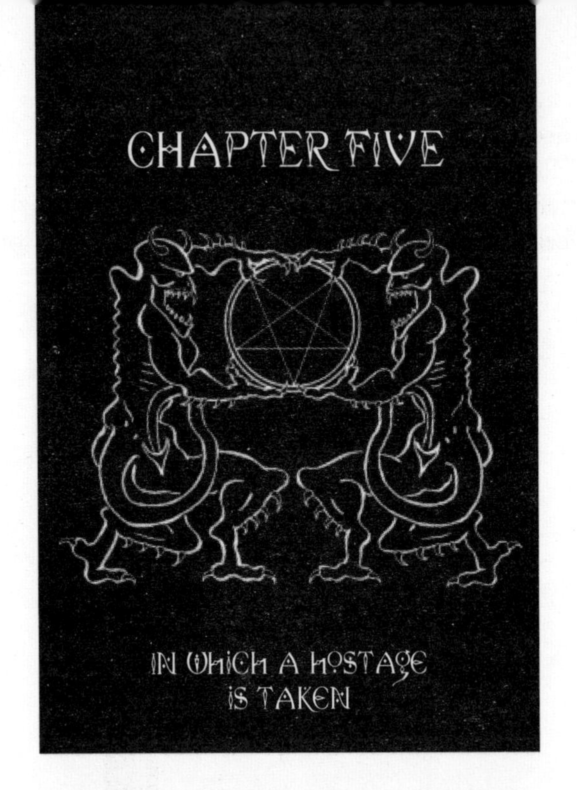

GABRIEL'S GLORIOUS FACE TWISTED IN anger. I risked a glance behind him to find Michael, Uriel and Raphael looking almost as livid.

Raphael shook his head. Golden blond hair tumbled over his shoulders. He still wore it long, despite Gabriel's objections. Today he even wore it loose. That had to irk Gabe just a little. Rafe speared me with emerald eyes, a look full of reproach. I winced. Raphael had been my mentor. He'd recommended me for promotion to Guardian Angel and given me a second chance. If I had Rafe that riled, things were about to turn truly ugly.

By Uriel's furious expression, I guessed he'd rather roast me over one of Lucifer's flame pits than talk. Uriel had been my supervisor that fateful night and Uriel wasn't a forgiving kind of guy.

Michael was the only one wearing a flight suit. Everyone else was in full dress and halos. That didn't bode well. It meant Michael had been somewhere else when they'd called him in. If Michael had joined the quorum, they expected a fight of some sort.

Of all the archangels Michael had the most reason to be angry with me. The clean up and the resulting debacle had fallen to him. Strangely, he didn't look angry.

Grey eyes gazed at me calmly. I stood still while he surveyed my skimpy exercise outfit, my sunburned face and the bloody gash in my side.

He raised an eyebrow at the sight of the drying blood. I shrugged and pretended it didn't hurt. He didn't look convinced.

Contrasted against Earth's multitude of colours, Heaven seemed stark. Strangely, I'd never thought of it that way before. Thrust again into its blinding white, I felt both homesick and foreign.

I glanced at the winged insignia over Michael's right breast and swallowed past the lump in my throat. I'd worn that uniform. I'd owned dress robes and a halo. Gone now, all of it. And being here in Heaven was just a cruel reminder.

"I'll take that locator," Gabriel said. I let him remove it from my hand.

"Care to tell us how you happen to come by it?" Uriel asked.

I couldn't rat on Cupid. Gabriel's temper was legendary. He'd eat him alive. As a department head, Cupid controlled his own territory. But he reported to Gabriel, who reported to The Big Guy himself. I couldn't tell Gabriel that Cupid had given me the thing. So I squared my shoulders and said, "No."

Gabriel frowned at my blatant disobedience, but said nothing. Obviously they already thought the worst of me. I probably couldn't make it worse if I tried.

Gabriel handed the locator to Uriel, who tucked it into the folds of his robes. Robes had deep pockets. Even angels in full dress go armed.

Raphael shook his head again. "What is it with you, Winter?" he asked softly. Uriel just glared.

"Look," I held up my hands in surrender. I didn't have time for this. Naamah could already have seized Alex. "I know this looks bad. But you – "

"Looks bad?" Uriel repeated. His voice rose, echoing around the cavernous white chamber of Gabriel's office.

I tried again. "It's not what you think."

"Trust me, Winter. You don't want to know what I think," Uriel countered.

"Probably not," I admitted. "But you have to listen to me. A man's life is at stake!"

"Oh we're listening," Gabriel said. "In fact we're most interested to hear what you have to say."

I dragged in a breath. And told them. About Naamah, about the falling star and the freak storm. About the locusts that ate a park, my dreams about Lucifer and my meeting with The Four. I told them about Alex losing his job and about Naamah's threats against him.

"That's why I used the locator. I wanted to protect Alex."

"Ah, yes, the human you're . . . living with." Gabriel's gaze told me what he thought of that arrangement.

"I had to live somewhere," I said. A flimsy excuse. If they didn't already know the truth about how things were between Alex and me, I certainly wasn't going to enlighten them.

Gabriel studied me a moment longer. Then he glanced behind him. "Uriel?" he asked.

Uriel drew out the locator I'd surrendered. He dialled knobs, input coordinates, and studied the screen for a moment. "Alex Chalmers is in his study. Alone."

I drew a breath of relief. At least Alex was safe. I wished I were too. "That's because you interrupted us," I pointed out. "She was on her way up to his apartment. I know she was."

"And you know this how?" Michael asked, the first words he'd uttered. And damnation, why did it have to be a rational question? But being Heaven's chief soldier, Michael was a brilliant tactician.

"I – I had a hunch." Stuttering didn't make me sound any more competent. I didn't know it for sure, couldn't prove it. But I'd learned to trust my instincts over the years. Naamah meant Alex harm. I knew it.

Michael raised a blond eyebrow.

"Okay, I know it *sounds* crazy – "

"That it does," Gabriel muttered.

Uriel took another look at the locator. "Chalmers is still in his study. I'm not picking up any other life signs."

I knew I had about two seconds to convince them apocalypse was imminent, before I was shunted back Earth side, defenceless without even a locator to help me in the fight against evil. "Lucifer's behind this. I know it. Naamah's just a decoy."

"Believe me," Gabriel said, "The Dark Angel is amply busy these days. He's been sequestered with his lawyers and spending a great deal of time in court. I doubt apocalypse is on his mind right now."

"Just because he's in court doesn't mean he can't have Naamah rampaging across the Earth doing his bidding. He is the Devil!"

"We're quite aware of that," Uriel interjected into my tirade. "Trust that we know Lucifer a great deal better than you do."

I didn't elaborate that I'd got to know Lucifer a lot better than I wanted. Defeated, I tried another tact. "But you have to admit that an earthquake, falling stars, freak storms, she-devils running rampant, plagues of locusts and the arrival of The Four add up to some serious portents."

The looks on their faces told me they'd admit no such thing.

"Surely you must suspect something if The Four Horsemen were despatched."

"The Four's report was inconclusive," Gabriel conceded.

"But you can't just dismiss the rest of the signs!"

Questioning their judgement was the ultimate impertinence. I waited to be blasted by the wrath of Heaven.

Instead Gabriel studied me for a long time. I had to work not to flinch under that penetrating gaze. "If this is a ploy to regain your place in Heaven," he said at last, "it has failed miserably."

I recoiled, totally amazed at his pronouncement. Their scorn, I expected. After all, I brought the biggest scandal to rock The Great Beyond to light. And it seemed no one thanked me for it. The faster I was out of the way, the faster they could return to the status quo and pretend everything was all right.

Until I'd streaked across their radar again, bringing with me portents and more bad news.

"How can you possibly think that?" By the smug expressions on their faces, they obviously considered me a lunatic. I tried again. "You didn't believe me last time. And I was *right*!"

As soon as I said it, I realised my grave tactical error. The last thing they wanted to be reminded of was that the higher powers of The Great Beyond had misread the situation. *I really should learn to shut my mouth.*

Gabriel's face darkened with anger. "We've endured enough of your insults, Miss Winter. The affairs of The Great Beyond are no longer your concern!"

Now they had the wrong impression all together. I hadn't been looking for trouble. But that hadn't stopped it from finding me. "And I was quite happy to keep it that way!"

They stared at me dumbfounded. This they clearly hadn't expected.

"I was happy on Earth," I insisted. "I had peace, quiet and nothing to do but work on my tan."

Uriel looked at my red face, the significance suddenly occurring to him. He muttered something under his breath, which earned him a dark glance from Gabriel. Raphael ran a hand over his eyes. Michael hid a smirk.

"Until I started dreaming about Hell and weird stuff started happening!"

Gabriel opened his mouth to say something.

I fumbled for a new tactic. I looked at Raphael. "Why am I dreaming about Lucifer, Rafe? That can't be an accident."

Shouldn't have called him Rafe, I realised too late. Apparently, we were no longer friends. His head came up as if I'd struck him, nearly unseating his halo. Gabriel and Uriel glared at him. Michael seemed to be finding the whole exchange amusing.

"Perhaps you'd best search your own soul for that answer," Raphael said coldly.

Ouch. It hurt more than I expected. Rafe and I *had* been friends.

But I refused to be cowed. Damnation, I was *trying* to help. "Oh come on, we've been hacked before," I pointed out. "It is possible."

And I'd said *we*, counting myself among them. The proverbial fallen angel, I couldn't have thought of a better insult if I'd tried. I ground my mouth shut and purposely bit my tongue.

"It *is* possible," Michael said quietly.

Rafe shot him an ugly look.

Michael shrugged. "Perhaps you should look into it."

And now I'd made Raphael a ton of extra work. I doubted Gabriel would fund the overtime.

"Winter – " Raphael uttered my name like a threat. With a deep sigh he pulled out his own locator. I felt the prickling of charged air. Then Raphael winked out.

His anger bristled after him like the tail of a comet.

Leaving me with Gabriel and Uriel, who had never been my buddies. Uriel considered me over promoted and under trained. Gabriel had made no secret of the fact that he didn't consider me proper Heavenly stock.

But my mother was a saint. A saint who was about to get an earful about her errant half-demon, and now human child. A pang of guilt tore through my chest. My poor, long-suffering mother, she certainly didn't deserve any of this.

Maybe Cupid could help put a less apocalyptic spin on it, I thought. But how was I going to get in touch with Cupid without the locator?

I looked hopefully at Michael. Somehow he'd become my champion. An unexpected development, I had to wonder why. But Michael had led the war on Hades. He'd seen first hand what I'd been trying to warn them about. Perhaps it had made a difference. Maybe my predicament simply entertained him. Or, I thought, he might see me as the only one who could get him what he'd wanted for millennia: a piece of Lucifer.

Michael glanced in Gabriel's direction. I gulped. No help there.

Gabriel strode toward me. Robes billowed out from behind him. His face shone like a star. His halo gleamed. The illuminated angel trick.

"Porsche Winter," Gabriel boomed. I wanted to sink into the fluffy white carpet and disappear. "You have caused far more than your fair share of trouble here in Heaven!"

"And yet you were given another chance, The Big Guy knows why," Uriel added.

"Were it up to me, you'd be serving an eternal sentence in our finest jail!" Gabriel thundered. "But we are not here to question The Big Guy's judgement! And so, you will return to Earth, live as a mortal and mind your own business!"

His proclamation echoed through the chamber.

Then I was falling. And this time, I realised, falling was really going to hurt.

I tumbled through the clouds that separated Gabriel's office from the lower administrative floors of Heaven Inc. Arms flailing, I sailed past the master control room where Guardian Angels guarded souls all over the planet. Like a stone, I plummeted past Dream Control and through the last layer of grey clouds. I tensed, waiting to hit the floor of Alex's apartment. Or worse. Gabriel had been in a bad enough mood to dunk me in the middle of Lake Ontario, or maybe even in the centre of the freeway.

Soft cushions gave beneath me. I let my breath go. My head spun enough to make me sick. But there was solid floor beneath my feet. My back rested against what felt like the leather couch in Alex's living room. Cautiously, I opened my eyes relieved to find furniture I recognised. Night had fallen in my absence. The lake's black expanse stretched before the windows, the beacons of passing boats the only lights on the horizon. Alex's apartment. Someone had been merciful, if not Gabriel.

I sagged back against the cushions and felt the wound in my side. Dried blood crumbled beneath my fingertips. At least I was healing. My brief jaunt to Heaven seemed to have speeded up the process. I stretched my legs intending to heave myself off the couch and head down the hall for a shower.

The tiny hairs on the back of my neck stood suddenly at attention. I realised I couldn't hear any movement from Alex's study, not even the radio he usually put on for company. No rummaging in drawers or humming to himself. Maybe he was taking a nap. That's when I noticed the angel standing on the other side of the couch.

I jumped in spite of myself. I took a closer look. Clutching my chest, I glared at him.

"Percy, are you trying to give me heart failure? I'm human you know. My nerves can't take a shock like that!"

Washed out blond hair and watery blue eyes made Percival Thor completely forgettable. His freshly pressed jumpsuit looked too clean. I wondered if he kept a spare one in his locker during his shift should he do something as inconvenient and un-angel-like as sweat.

Human or not, Thorny Percy looked half afraid of me. He muttered,

"Sorry," then glanced down at the floor.

Suddenly it occurred to me to worry about the reason for his visit. But Percy said, "I really shouldn't be here."

"Probably not," I said. "Well, technically we're not supposed to have any contact with our charges." And I'd said *we* again. Like I was still one of them. I doubted the significance had been lost on old Percy. But I continued like my opinion still counted. "But since I used to be an angel and Alex is well aware of our existence, I'm not sure they could hold on that particular breach of etiquette."

I was rambling and embarrassing Percy further. I could tell by the crimson flush of his face, a drawback that went with the fair skin. His eyes flickered to the wound in my side. "So," I said, before he could ask me about it. "What do you want?"

"Want?" Percy asked like the fact that he might want something from me was personally horrifying.

"Why are you here?" I clarified. One had to be specific talking to Thorny. We'd been in the training academy together, along with Wynn Jarrett. On the written tests, Percy had got nearly perfect scores. But he didn't have a lot of depth to him. When it came to spontaneous decisions and emergency procedures, he just couldn't function. I, on the other hand, had no problem with impulsiveness. Which might explain why they'd put Percy in my place.

Percy was still staring at the carpet, as if looking me in the eyes might somehow lead him down the path to damnation. I realised for the first time just how notorious I might have become in Heaven and winced. "You can just talk to me, you know," I said irritably. "It won't rub off."

It was supposed to be a joke, albeit not really a funny one. Percy missed the point, but he brought his head up and managed to gaze somewhere in the region of my left ear.

"I was just coming on-shift," he said. I forced myself to wait patiently and not interrupt. "And I noticed demon activity in your apartment."

"It's not my – " I started to say, then, "What kind of demon activity?"

"It had a she-devil signature."

"Naamah." I said her name like a curse. Uriel had surveyed the apartment. Twice in the space of a couple of minutes, max. Naamah had just waited, biding her time until the powers that be were occupied with hurling me back down through the clouds and engaged in a furious debate over what to do about me.

"Do you really think it's Naamah?" Percy asked, nervously shifting from foot to foot.

You're about to get that uniform dirty, Percy my boy, I thought. Then immediately after, "Oh no, Alex!"

"That's why I'm here," Percy said. "I noticed the demon activity. There was only one human life sign in the apartment. They linked up and went somewhere together. I thought I'd better investigate. I was scanning the living room when you came flying through the ceiling."

"Give me that." I reached out, grabbed the locator from his belt.

Percy jumped back like I'd struck him. But I was too busy dialling in coordinates into the device to argue.

The apartment turned up empty. I couldn't locate Alex's signature on the pier below. I scanned the mall below the condo, and both elevators. I even checked out the rooftop garden. Nothing.

I was just starting to panic when the sound of laughter echoed up from the patio bar. I input new coordinates. The locator screen blurred, trying to separate out the multitude of life signs all packed into a crowded spot. Then it beeped. The screen refocused and spit out its verdict. "She-devil." It fumbled over Alex's signature, having trouble dealing with his refurbished soul, then finally declared: "Alexander Alan Chalmers. Human."

I bolted for the front door, realising only when Percy grabbed my arm, that I was still holding his locator. And travel had suddenly become easier.

"While I was scanning the apartment, I found this."

Percy pointed at something in the centre of the living room floor. Something I hadn't noticed until now. Getting soft, I thought. This human thing might be more damaging than I first suspected.

I looked at the object on the parquet floor. The heads of what had to be two-dozen blood-red roses were arranged in the shape of a heart. Two long stems that still sported dangerous-looking thorns bisected the centre of the heart in a big X.

"What do you think it means?" Percy asked.

The floral motif meant it was a message from Cupid, but I couldn't tell Percy that. The last thing I needed was for him to write it up in his report and implicate Cupid. The heart could refer to Alex or it could be an icon for Cupid. But what about the X? If the heart meant Alex, did that big X mean I couldn't trust him or that Naamah had taken him?

Or had he gone with her willingly?

Percy was still waiting for my answer. Whatever Cupid had been trying to tell me, I'd have to deal with it later. Alex's life might be at stake. Or worse, maybe his soul.

"It's a love note from Alex," I said hastily. I couldn't tell him the truth.

I let Percy chew on that, not caring whether he saw it for the lie it was. I dialled coordinates and grabbed his shoulder. "Come with me."

Percy let out a yelp loud enough to alert the neighbours. But falling, as we were through the dimensions in a short cut to the bar downstairs, I'm sure it was diffused enough that the neighbours would be hard pressed to find the source.

We materialised in the patio bar behind some shrubbery the locusts hadn't yet discovered. Darkness further hid our arrival. Percy clutched at his arms, trying to reassure himself nothing had been damaged in our jaunt downstairs.

"Are you trying to get us killed?" he whispered. He looked around nervously, then held out his hand for me to return his property.

Grudgingly I relinquished the locator. "Oh relax, no one saw us. And no, I'm not trying to kill you, Percy. No matter what they say about me."

He opened his mouth, perhaps to elaborate on just what they had been saying, and then changed his mind.

Percy put the locator in his pocket rather than clipping it to his belt. Harder for me to get my hands on it that way. Fine, let him think that if it made him feel better. I'd frisk him in a second if an emergency arose. I imagined the report that would make and stifled a laugh.

Hot warm nights brought out the crowds. According to Alex the only two months it was guaranteed not to snow in Toronto were July and August. Now it seemed like half the city crammed onto the patio bar. I craned my neck to see over the multitude of heads.

"Percy," I hissed. "We need that locator. Scan for Naamah."

He reached into his pocket and shot me a warning glance. I held up my hands in surrender. He punched in data. A red dot appeared in the centre of the screen. We squeezed through the crowd, following the beacon of Naamah's signature. You'd think the patio stones were made of gold the way people held on to their places. I resisted the urge to snatch Percy's locator and deal with the problem myself. But that would attract attention. Poor Percy was going to have to write that report eventually. And I really didn't want to make trouble for him. I was running out of friends in Heaven.

Percy stopped so suddenly, I ran into him. "There," he said. He nodded toward a wrought-iron table on the periphery of the crowd that still had its umbrella up even though dusk had fallen hours ago.

The umbrella had been angled to block the view from the crowd. And had I been a normal mortal simply strolling by I wouldn't have noticed the she-devil sitting with her back to us. But my well-practiced gaze picked out the shapely form encased in black denim. Unwinding from around her waist, her tail flicked restlessly back and forth like a cat's.

For an instant I wanted to run over there and smack her silly. But then I noticed that one of Naamah's hands rested in her lap below the table. And clutched in her fist, nearly hidden by the darkness was something that to most humans would look like a fat fountain pen. A miniature flamethrower.

And it was aimed point blank at Alex.

Relief dampened my anger. Well, at least he hadn't gone with her willingly. It occurred to me to wonder why that was so important to me, but I filed that thought for future contemplation.

Naamah's tail swished again, then tucked itself back around her waist. I smacked Percy on the shoulder. "She's seen us. Come on."

We strode across the patio, Percy looking a bit out of place in his silver jumpsuit. The faster I got him sitting down the better. Guardian Angels drinking in bars on Earth definitely violated regulations, no matter what the circumstances. Poor Percy was already in above his head, and the night was still young.

"Tell me you have a discourager," I whispered.

Percy nodded. He shot me a wary glance. "Porsche, the last thing we need here is trouble."

"No problem," I said, trying to smile like we were just a couple out for a drink, the guy albeit a little weirdly dressed. "I'm going to get Alex back, no trouble about it." I gave him the boss voice, the one I was used to using, even though I had no one left to boss except Alex, who resented it. "And we will use that discourager."

"Only if we really need it," Percy insisted.

"Oh, we will." That didn't seem to make old Thorny feel any better.

Alex noticed us when we were half way across the pavement. Naamah noted the focus of his gaze and turned toward us.

While still managing to keep the flamethrower trained on Alex she rose and kissed me like we were best friends. I caught the scent of her perfume, intoxicating, like gardenia mixed with honey, but with a tinge of brimstone underneath. She really was playing the seduction game tonight, she'd practically doused herself in pheromones. An unsuspecting mortal might be easily caught up in her sensual aura. I fought the urge to lose myself in her compelling gaze and to let her will overtake my own. "Sit down and make nice or he's a piece of ash," she hissed in my ear, somewhat breaking the effect her close presence was having on me. Her nostrils twitched, letting me know she scented the blood from the wound she'd dealt me. A self-satisfied smile crossed her face.

I smiled back and sat down. *Shoot her Percy*, I wanted to scream. But Alex had that wild *rescue me* look. I cursed myself for letting Percy keep the discourager.

Alex looked down at his untouched glass of beer and swallowed hard. "I'm sorry, Porsche." Sorry about what exactly? I wanted to ask, but there was Naamah to contend with.

"Don't worry," I told him. "I'll deal with it."

Percy nodded his head in agreement, drawing Alex's scrutiny. "Who's he?"

Naamah laughed, that low grating sound I'd come to despise. She studied Percy with interest. "Oh do tell, Porsche. Who is he?"

"One of Heaven's finest. You don't need to know who."

"But I *am* acquainted with our fine representative of Heaven's elite," Naamah said, fixing Percy with her hypnotic multifaceted gaze. The lights of the passing fake riverboat glinted in her eyes like a kaleidoscope. "I just didn't recognise you in your uniform, Thorny Percy."

Percy jumped. He blushed, I could tell even in the darkness.

Now there was a connection I wouldn't have expected. Cupid would pay for not surrendering *that* piece of gossip.

"Ma'am," he managed to croak.

Ma'am? I choked, and quickly covered it with a cough. How on Earth had Percy become acquainted with Naamah? That had the makings of an interesting tale.

But Naamah dismissed Percy like a bug she'd brushed off her sleeve and turned her disquieting attention to me.

"Well, Porsche Winter. Since you wanted to talk to me so badly – let's talk."

AS ONE PERCY AND ALEX TURNED IN my direction. I have to admit, it didn't look good. That I had business with the administrative head of the Underworld and Lucifer's second in command was enough to land me back in one of Heaven's golden cells. Whether they could prove the connection or not.

Thanks for implicating me, Naamah. I hoped I had a chance to return the favour one day soon.

Suddenly Percy's connection to Naamah didn't seem quite so interesting because they were all staring at me incredulously, Alex included. I knew exactly where this choice piece of information was going. Right into Percy's report and straight back to Gabriel via Uriel.

I grabbed Percy's sleeve. Alex I'd deal with later. "This isn't what it looks like."

He shrugged me off. "Isn't it?"

"No!" Briefly I debated diving for the discourager slung on Percy's belt and taking control of the situation. But this could end up involving Gabriel, Uriel and Michael, and the gilded jails that came with satellite TV, but were still undeniably jails.

"As guardian for both *you*," Percy said the word with enough scorn to make me cringe, "and Alex Chalmers, it is my duty to warn you against this conversation."

"Consider me warned." I nodded at the flamethrower I knew was still pointed at Alex under the table. "Alex is obviously here under duress."

Percy's hand moved to rest lightly on the holster of his discourager, making a bigger threat against Naamah than I would have given him credit for.

I shook my head. "That's not necessary. The last thing we need is a fireworks display in public. We're only going to talk." I glared at Naamah across the table. "Aren't we?"

Naamah launched a smile befitting a shark in Alex's direction. "Of course."

"Might I point out that talking to Lucifer sent you to Hell," Percy said.

"That was different."

Percy glanced from Alex back to me. Hiding his feelings wasn't one of his strong points. Clearly he considered me irrevocably warped. Alex, he seemed to be withholding judgement on.

"We're only going to talk." I leaned across the table and looked Naamah in her unblinking faceted eyes. "So put the flamethrower away. You've done enough damage to the Earthly plane for one week."

Naamah feigned shock. "I don't know what you mean."

"The hell," I said. Beside me, I heard Percy gasp. That couldn't have been a surprise. My acid tongue had to be written all over my profile in the database. "Maybe you want to explain about the meteor showers, freak storms and locusts eating up half the greenery in the city." I didn't mention The Four.

Percy stared at Naamah like she was about to gore him on the tips of those prettily decorated horns. Whatever he would have said was interrupted by the shriek of his pager.

"Thor! Where in The Great Beyond are you?" Uriel's voice. It was enough to make me jump even through the scratchy speaker.

"You better go," I mouthed. And really, really hoped Uriel wasn't inclined to go searching for Percy using his locator.

Percy hit the pager's speaker. "Be right there, Boss." We all called Uriel Boss. Unlike Raphael, he didn't encourage informality. He wasn't the kind of guy you got on a first name basis with. Even in the darkness, poor Thorny looked two shades paler than when he arrived. He yanked out his locator, input coordinates and ducked behind the umbrella to conceal himself. Obviously Uriel had greater concerns than tracking down an errant Guardian. If he so much as suspected Percy's whereabouts we'd hear him hollering all the way from Heaven.

"Before you smear my name from here to Hades," I said as he dematerialised, "will you at least try and convince Gabriel something is up?"

He became incorporeal before he could answer. Leaving me without a weapon or even a means of escape.

Naamah laid the flamethrower on the table. From a distance it looked just like a big fountain pen. No one would suspect. A blatant threat, even if I lunged for it, with my human reflexes I'd never reach it in time. Alex glanced at it in dismay, but said nothing.

Naamah's moods changed as quickly as the current in the Styx. Her eyes grew hard, accusing. "You brought a Guardian with you!" she snarled. "Like I'd talk business in front of the competition."

"And you stole my boyfriend!"

"I was merely borrowing him." It sounded so sincere, anyone else might have believed her.

"Right. And if you wanted to talk, why didn't you just talk to me in the elevator, instead of trying to gore me on the tips of your horns?"

My hand strayed to the blood-encrusted wound in my side. Had I not been healed by my time in Heaven, that wound would be hurting like holy Hell. Next time I might not be so lucky. Humans healed horribly slow. I had to keep that in mind. Alex's gaze followed my movement. His expression hardened in anger as he looked at the dried blood. I shot him a look that warned against interference.

Naamah sniffed. "You were the one making accusations."

The last of my patience evaporated. I had been wounded, Naamah had taken Alex hostage, and Percy was probably already ratting me out to Uriel. Which meant I probably had only seconds left before Gabriel discovered the company I was keeping and decided to intervene.

And I really hated jail.

"Just tell me what you want."

Naamah leaned forward. The movement brought her hand closer to the flamethrower. Good sense warned me to lean back, but I refused. Human or not, I couldn't appear to be afraid of her. "We're here to discuss what *you* want."

Now that took me by surprise. "What *I* want?" I managed to ask coolly.

She smiled, showing every one of her small, pointed teeth. It isn't just a she-devil's horns, claws or tail you need to worry about. "To see Lucifer knocked from his onyx throne."

My mouth gaped open. I snapped it shut. And here I'd thought nothing she could say would shock me. Alex's eyes widened. Obviously she'd surprised him as well.

For the record, I never campaigned to dethrone the Devil. Nor did I covet his position. I wanted my job back. I wanted my life back.

In short, I wanted all the things I knew I could never have. That if nothing else, made me a perfect target for Lucifer to warp to his own purposes. Really, I should have known.

But admitting that would end the conversation before it began. So I swallowed my astonishment and said, "Okay, that's . . . interesting. Tell me more." Let Naamah do the talking, let her incriminate herself. Maybe I'd learned a thing or two from Lucifer after all.

"The problem with Heaven is that they judge everyone by their own narrow standards," Naamah said.

True enough, I thought. But I used another of Lucifer's tactics and kept my mouth shut. The Devil knew how to bait a conversation, then to sit back while you spilled your guts. All the while he'd be collecting information to damn you for eternity. Feigning disinterest, I leaned back in my chair and crossed my arms.

"If Heaven thinks the Devil will sit in Hades waiting for the outcome of his court case," Naamah continued, taking the bait, "they are very wrong."

"Likely so," I said. "But why should I care?"

Naamah's eyes narrowed with annoyance. "Because, deprived of his rightful place in Heaven, Lucifer will try to destroy all that The Big Guy has made."

"Heaven is not his rightful place," I snapped. Okay, I knew she was baiting me. But blasphemy was blasphemy. "He has all of Hell to command, what more does he want?"

"Why Earth of course."

Naamah offered us her most dazzling smile, all teeth and glittering eyes. I caught another whiff of her perfume on the air and felt the responding surge of pheromones in my own body.

I heard Alex draw in his breath and glanced at him to see his gaze captivated by Naamah's décolletage as she stretched cat-like in her seat. I gave him a warning look and turned back to Naamah.

"And he plans to do what – conquer his way back into Heaven by annexing The Big Guy's turf one foot at a time?"

"Exactly," Naamah said. "Starting with Earth. Or rather, Hell on Earth."

"The Big Guy will stop him," I pointed out. But Lucifer plotted in cosmic terms. Toppling big opponents netted big rewards to his way of thinking. "And you've forgotten Gabriel, Michael, Uriel and Raphael. Michael's been itching for a bigger piece of Lucifer since the battle."

"And the only thing holding him back is Gabriel."

For the second time in one day Naamah had taken me off guard. I didn't like the feeling.

My eyes narrowed. "Who have you been talking to?" Just because Wynn Jarrett had been dealt with, didn't mean that Hell didn't have another mole in his place.

Naamah batted jewelled eyelashes. "Why no one. We can be very observant in Hell." Her haughty tone grated on my nerves. "When we wish to be."

I said, "Right."

"You can be the one to give Michael what he so badly wants."

Okay, now she had me. Naamah baited the trap. I felt it closing around me.

"Porsche, no –" Alex cut in, realizing where the discussion was heading.

Naamah centred him in her faceted glare. He shook his head and fell silent.

"And what do you suppose Michael wants?" I asked stealing back control of the conversation. I needed to know exactly what was on the bargaining table.

"Lucifer dethroned. Banished."

By leading the conversation in circles, she'd discovered what I deeply desired. Another shot at Lucifer, and a chance to put things right in Heaven. But bargaining with Naamah was a dangerous proposition. It would only help my case if it all worked, something I couldn't guarantee. I teetered on the edge of a treacherous decision.

I looked down at the flamethrower still sitting on the table. "And you think you can do that?"

"With your help."

Mine and who else's? I wondered. Being a powerful figure in her own right, Naamah had allies. But taking down Lucifer would require a ton of manpower. Could Naamah really command such loyalty?

"Porsche, I really think – " Alex started to say.

Naamah snatched up the flamethrower. "Silence, *human*." She sneered the word. If she realised she'd insulted me as well, she made no mention of it. Alex's face darkened, and for a moment I caught a glimpse of the Alex Chalmers he'd been under Lucifer's influence. But then the moment passed. Alex held up his hands in defeat and shut his mouth.

Better sense almost prevailed. I debated telling Naamah to take a hike back to Devil's Mountain where she belonged. But then she said, "Just think of the consequences: meteors gouging giant craters in the Earth, poisoning the waters and the sky, locusts eating up the vegetation, until the ravaged Earth can no longer support itself, Lucifer's minions crawling from the mouth of the abyss until they outnumber every man, woman and child."

Quite a picture she painted. One I'd already seen in my nightmares.

"Okay, I believe you . . . Lucifer might be plotting Armageddon to get back at Heaven for the court case and the corporate raid – "

"He doesn't need a reason," Alex added. "He is the Devil."

Naamah snarled at him. For a moment I thought she might strike him, or use that little flamethrower, but then she seemed to change her mind. "He is the Angel of Darkness," she agreed, as if Alex had given Lucifer a great compliment.

"What doesn't make sense," I said, breaking into the exchange, "is why you want to help me."

The head she-devil laughed, not a pleasant sound. "Of course I don't want to help you, little fallen angel. But you could be useful to me."

"Stop calling me that! I do have a name."

Naamah's look told me what she thought of my unusual given name. She dismissed me with not so much as a blink. "Whatever."

For a moment I almost gave in to an old familiar anger. No one liked my name, including me. My father had named me after his favourite sports car. Why my mom let him get away with it is a mystery to me. Love makes you do stupid things.

"Suffice to say we might have a common goal," Naamah said.

The thought of Naamah and I having anything in common made me nauseous, but I kept it to myself. "And that would be?"

"Neither of us want to see Lucifer lording it over Earth."

A niggly little thought nagged at the back of my mind. Why did Naamah want to see Lucifer ruined? I wanted to ask, but you had to be as careful when talking to Lucifer's minions as when talking to the Devil himself. Every conversation meandered like an eel travelling through muddy water. You never really knew where it was going, or what you might inadvertently be giving away. That kind of verbal sparring wasn't my forte. I decided to try the direct approach. "I certainly don't want Earth falling into Lucifer's clutches. Question is: why don't you?"

Naamah leaned back in her chair. Idly, she spun the flamethrower on the table. Spin the bottle with a surprise ending: the loser got incinerated. I stopped myself from trying to snatch it from her grasp. I didn't want to be the loser.

"Now that," Naamah purred, "is really none of your business."

"If you want my help, you can make it my business."

Alex was shooting me desperate panicked looks with those dark eyes. I read the warning and ignored it.

"Your *boyfriend* doesn't seem to like me much." She said the word like you might say maggot. Alex paled. Enjoying the moment, Naamah sighed and slowly undid the zipper on her denim jumpsuit further revealing more flesh. She gently ran a taloned hand up Alex's leg. "But that could change."

Alex flinched, almost imperceptibly, but Naamah caught that involuntary movement and laughed.

"Leave him alone." I put the sum of my will behind those three words. Gabriel wasn't the only one who knew the angel tricks. As a mortal, it had less impact than it used to, but Naamah felt the impulse behind that command.

Sniggering, she dropped her hand.

Alex sagged back against his chair. I knew what it felt like to be caressed by darkness, terrifying and incredibly erotic at the same time. And totally against your will.

"Fine. Porsche." She said my name like the Devil did, like it was a big joke that everyone but me shared. "If you must know, it suits me to maintain the status quo in Hades."

Damned if she'd get away with that fragment of an answer. "I can't see how it would."

"Of course you can't."

Something was missing in that equation, but damnation, I couldn't figure out what it was. Why wouldn't Naamah want Lucifer to succeed?

Whatever Naamah's motives were, I couldn't allow the Devil to conquer Earth. I had to do something! But besides Alex, I had no allies. I couldn't involve Cupid further. As my best friend he'd be the first person they'd watch.

Naamah offered the only help available. If I was going to prevent Hell on Earth, I thought, examining my dilemma, I was going to have to work with her. I rolled my eyes Heavenward to where I knew The Big Guy had to be watching, if in fact His attention was momentarily on that particular monitor. *Is this in Your plans?* I asked silently. But The Big Guy was obviously otherwise occupied, and no one answered.

"But if Lucifer were to annex Earth, that would leave you in line for a huge promotion." Naamah's head swivelled like a snake from ogling Alex to fixing me in her uncomfortable glare. "He'd definitely need help running both those empires. Managing Hades would probably fall to you."

There, I'd said it. I waited for Naamah to zap me with that miniature flamethrower.

"I already run Hades," Naamah growled. "Lucifer only thinks he does."

How they fit all those egos into Hell was beyond me.

I said, "Really?"

Naamah wasn't entirely out of line. Lucifer loathed the boring, day-to-day drudgery of running a successful empire. He was more a scheming, big picture kind of guy. And once he'd latched on to an idea, it absorbed his full attention. Until it became too much like work, then he delegated it to Naamah.

"Hades suits me just fine the way it is," Naamah said. "The last thing I need is a bigger workload."

So Naamah didn't welcome a bigger chunk of Lucifer's domain. And just when I thought I was beginning to understand the workings of her warped mind, she threw me off balance with a new revelation.

"All right," I said slowly. Deception ran beneath each of her words, I could feel it. But somehow Lucifer had to be stopped, and I had no other allies. "Supposing I agree to this, what's in it for me?"

"Redemption."

The word hung between us in the humid air. Redemption, the one thing I wanted more than anything else. Which made it very dangerous to take.

It couldn't be that simple, came my immediate thought.

But Naamah plucked the flamethrower from the centre of the table and strode off into the darkness.

"I'll be in touch," the head she-devil called over her shoulder.

I realised with a pang of fear that by not strongly objecting, I'd just agreed to it all. The trap sprang shut, trapping me in a deal with Naamah.

Alex watched her leave. A slow shudder worked its way from head to toe, as he realised it too. He turned on me, dark eyes blazing. "How can you even think of working with that . . . that . . . "

"She-devil?" I supplied.

"Whatever. I thought we agreed you were going to stay out of this mess!"

"That was before I saw The Four Horsemen of the Apocalypse in the square in front of City Hall."

"The Four . . . " He let the sentence trail off. "What were they doing?"

"Surveying the territory, I suspect. They said they heard there was work here."

"You talked to them?"

I shrugged. "Sure."

"And is there work for them here?"

"They couldn't seem to agree on that." I stared into the darkness where Naamah had disappeared. His fingers lightly traced the healing wound in my side. "Are you okay? Did she really gore you with her horns?"

I nodded grimly. "Don't worry, I'll live."

He didn't seem convinced. "All this craziness . . . it's never going to go away, is it?"

I wanted to reassure him, to tell him it would all be okay. But the words refused to cross my lips. Truth was: it probably wouldn't be okay.

"No," I whispered. "It kind of goes with the territory." I nodded toward Naamah's empty chair. "She even stuck us with the bill. Probably did it on purpose knowing you just lost your job."

Alex dug into his pocket and grimly tossed a couple of bills on the table. Then he stood and held out his hand to help me up. "Let's get you upstairs and bandaged up."

"I'm okay, really." I insisted.

The encounter with Naamah over for the moment, exhaustion seeped into every muscle. I just wanted to curl up in Alex's king sized bed. Not to sleep, I thought. I'd never sleep after the deal I'd just made. The effects of Naamah's pheromone-laced perfume lingered. I needed distraction and my body craved release. While I'd been sidetracked in Heaven, the she-devil had been busy trying to seduce my boyfriend. The last thing I wanted was Alex going to sleep with Naamah in mind.

Dodging groups of tourists enjoying the warm night, we headed for the condo entrance. No lost tourists or other residents crowded into the elevator with us, so we rode in silence, Alex's hand gently caressing my back.

When we arrived at the apartment, Alex took two steps into the living room and stopped dead in his tracks. "What in G – " God's name, he'd almost said. "What's that?"

I looked beyond him at the heart of flowers on the floor. The scent of roses filled the living room. Deprived of water, the roses had opened their heads. Under other circumstances it would have been a pleasant scent, if you could count dying flowers as beautiful.

"Did someone send you flowers?"

"It's a message." I cocked my head trying to decipher it.

"From whom?" Alex asked in his demanding mover-and-shaker voice. Like that would work on me.

"Cupid, I assume. What do you think it means?"

Alex snorted. "I don't know." He stared at the two stems rife with thorns that crossed the heart of roses. "Love is hell?"

"Ugh!" I said. "You're as bad as he is."

"Do not compare me to that under-tall little tyrant. He calls me names."

I barked a laugh before I could choke it back. It really bothered Alex that my best friend didn't share my enthusiasm for our union.

"He calls our relationship a bad idea, not you," I clarified. Which didn't seem to change Alex's mind at all.

"What do *you* think it means?"

I stepped back, as if greater distance would clarify things. It didn't.

"Well, an X usually means don't or stop or something like that . . ."

"Don't buy flowers?"

I scowled at him, ignoring his comment. "But what the heart means is beyond me."

"He's probably trying to warn you against continuing this relationship." Anger coloured his face. I tried to diffuse the situation.

"Cupid well knows you're off limits. Surely by now, he's given up on that."

Alex paced a slow circle around the flowers like they were somehow dangerous.

"Besides," I added, "he promised to see if he could find out anything about what's going down Heaven-side and send me a sign."

"I'd say he did that." He poked a toe at the rose at the tip of the heart.

"It'd be more helpful if I knew what it meant."

Alex snorted.

I shot him another annoyed glance. "A little help would be nice."

He shrugged.

"Maybe it means that I'm a danger to you." I looked around at the walls of his apartment picturing she-devils with flamethrowers leaping from every corner.

Whatever it meant, the roses were wilting with every passing minute.

I needed to save the image for further contemplation. "Is your camera handy?"

"On my desk," Alex said. "I'll get it."

He disappeared down the hall while I crouched beside Cupid's floral tribute. Only Cupid would know that I liked flowers, especially red roses, the redder the better. It was a well-kept secret. So well kept, no one ever sent me any.

Alex returned with his digital camera. He snapped a few shots from different angles, then previewed the shots on the camera's tiny monitor for my approval. I nodded. He disappeared back into his office to download them into his computer.

I wandered into the kitchen, looking for something large enough to hold two-dozen rose heads. No one sent Alex flowers, either. He didn't own a vase. The best I could come up with was a large aluminium salad bowl. I had a passable avant-garde arrangement made by the time he returned.

Alex glanced at the bowl of roses on the dining room table in horror. "What are you doing?"

I shrugged. "No sense in wasting two dozen roses."

He gave me that 'humouring a lunatic' look again and fell silent.

"So," he said after a moment. The word hung in the air, heavy with meaning for one little word.

I turned, expecting the worst, certain he'd fill me in on the details of how he'd come to be in Naamah's custody. But instead, he said, "You aren't the only one who had a bad day."

A bad day? Alex had a talent for understating the obvious. If only it were just a bad day. I waited for him to continue.

"My lawyer says things aren't exactly looking good for me. And my father found out I was fired."

I said, "Oh no, Alex, that's awful!"

"Dad heard it from a friend of his who works for my former company."

He sounded way more worried about his father's opinion of him than anything else. I certainly knew what disappointing a parent felt like. After all, who could live up to a saint's expectations? "I take it he didn't call to offer his condolences."

Alex offered me the ghost of a smile. "No, he called to yell at me. To remind me of how I've been letting him down since I was born. Now his friends know I've been fired. That's got to bother him even more than me actually getting fired."

"So tell him you were set up."

"That's not going to help at this point."

"Why not, it's the truth, sort of."

"Dad's buddy also told him he heard a rumour I was living with a woman. He thinks I was distracted, and that's why I messed up. He's blaming you."

Great. Now even Alex's dad had it in for me. I hadn't even met the man. Something told me we weren't going to get along.

"So blame me. Everyone else does." I stared out the massive window at the humid sky that was quickly becoming another thunderstorm. I hoped tonight it wasn't blocks of falling ice. "It is my fault, really."

Alex pulled me against him. He glanced at the gathering storm with trepidation, and then ran a hand through my blonde curls. "I'm not going to blame you to make my dad happy. Besides, it wouldn't. Nothing I do pleases him!"

I didn't tell him I'd read his file or that I knew about the other women in his life. "I can't be the first woman you've taken home to meet the folks."

He caught the direction the conversation had veered in and laughed. "Well, no. Dad actually liked my last . . . girlfriend. Of course, she was a stockbroker."

"So why'd you break up with her then?"

"She dumped me, actually."

I said, "Ouch."

Alex pulled me tighter. He'd been spending more time working out lately. I could tell. "Ah, it's okay. It wasn't going well before that. Turned out dad liked her more than I did."

"Meaning he won't like me much," I supplied.

Alex laughed harder. He tipped my chin and studied the side of my face that had caught most of the sun. "Probably not, but I'm looking forward to that introduction."

He kissed me on the end of my nose and I grinned. "Come on then." I turned and headed for the bedroom.

He followed me, still chuckling. "My dad's not as elderly as you imagine. And he's in very good shape for an old guy. But he's influential and he enjoys intimidating people." He laughed again at some private joke. "I think he'll find you a challenge."

Was there no one in the entire universe I could be myself with? Except for Cupid, Alex and my own father who I resembled far too much for my own good, probably not.

Annoyed and not sure why, I headed into the bathroom. Alex's shout of surprise sent me racing back to the bedroom.

Alex stood in the centre of his bedroom, staring at his bed in horror.

Please no, I prayed, *nothing more!* But The Big Guy must have been having a busy night with the locusts, the hail and she-devils overrunning the city because he didn't answer.

Under Lucifer's influence, Alex had changed his taste in bedding. For a while his bedroom had more closely resembled a bordello. He'd put the red satin sheets away since I'd moved in, but someone had obviously found them.

In the centre of Alex's bed lay said red satin sheet, now manipulated to form a striking image.

Alex backed up for a better look, colliding with me. "What the Hell!"

From further away, it made more sense. The sheet had been scrunched and folded to form a devil's head. Beneath the head, a series of pleats formed a skirt.

"She-devil," I said. "No mistaking those horns." I clasped a hand protectively over the healing gash in my side.

"Okay," Alex said, "But what's it mean?"

"Not sure. Perhaps that Naamah might come after you tonight."

"Can't any of your friends just leave a voice-mail?"

"Red satin is more Cupid's style."

"Why did he have to use my sheets?" Alex asked, his tone saying volumes about what he thought of Cupid's taste in bed coverings, among other things. "Why did it have to be my bed?"

"I guess he wanted to put it somewhere we'd notice it." The implications of that weren't lost on either of us.

Alex reached out to pull the crumpled sheet off the bed.

"Wait," I said. "We should probably take a picture, just in case."

"Tell him to stay the heck out of my apartment," he grumbled as he went back to his office for the camera. He took a couple more shots, then looked back at the bed in disgust.

Balling up the sheet, he tossed it into the hamper.

I looked at him across the bed. Thunder rumbled menacingly. I heard the first thump of hail on the roof. As one we stared at the ceiling.

"Let's go to bed." I gave Alex a kiss that left him no doubt as to what I had in mind.

"Hold that thought." I stalked across the room to the bathroom. Behind me he was shedding his clothes as fast as he could.

In the bathroom, I checked my reflection in the mirror. A little bedraggled, but good to go. I ran a brush through my blonde hair and wiped the dried blood from my waist. I opened one of the bathroom drawers and rummaged until I found a tiny pair of red velvet thong briefs, with a matching red lace camisole that I knew brought out the blue in my eyes. I quickly changed out of my sports wear and into the briefs and camisole, reflecting that I probably wouldn't be wearing them for too long anyway.

I reached for the robe hanging on the back of the door. Black silk, it slid seductively against my skin. The robe belonged to Alex, another wardrobe piece leftover from his days under the Devil's influence. Another glance in the mirror assured me I looked at least as hot as Naamah. But as I moved towards the door and to Alex, the air around me shimmered, and the bathroom dissolved into nothingness.

Typical. Percy had filed his report.

I MATERIALISED IN THE WITNESS BOX of Heaven's boardroom. The last time I'd had the pleasure, I was facing a tribunal of Heavenly hosts. Lot of good it had done me. I'd been demoted from Guardian Angel to dream controller. As a mortal I'd been demoted about as far as you could go, except to eternal damnation.

This time no Heavenly hosts lined the long boardroom table. No archangels sat on their golden thrones. Only Gabriel stood on the dais at the front of the massive chamber. And behind him, nearly colourless against the murals of the ages, slouched Percival Thor.

Yanking the belt of the silk robe tighter over my patented seduction gear, I looked down at the golden railing that ringed the witness box. It reminded me of the golden bars of Heaven's jail.

Black certainly made an impression in Heaven. I stood out against the blinding whiteness like a dark smudge. Gabriel glared down at me from his perch on the dais still in his robes and halo. Gabriel nearly always wore formal dress. No working jumpsuit like Uriel and Raphael for The Big Guy's second in command. It had the desired effect. I felt even more underdressed than before.

I looked up into eyes that already judged me guilty and decided the best defence was a good offence. "You could have given me some warning! I was about to go to bed!"

"So I see." Gabriel didn't sound amused. But then Gabe usually came up short in the humour department. Rafe was really the only archangel you could share a laugh with. But these days even Raphael didn't find me funny.

"This isn't mine," I blurted, and then winced when I realised just how much I'd revealed. By his expression, Gabriel had already deduced whom the bathrobe belonged to.

From behind the archangel came a nervous cough. I glanced past Gabriel where Percival Thor was in the process of blushing crimson.

I shot Percy a scathing look. I tried not to imagine the content of his report. Uriel, who was surprisingly absent, had obviously been worried enough to call Gabriel back in. Or maybe I now rated urgent status, which meant I'd garnered Gabriel's personal attention. His fury over having to deal with me again so soon was palpable.

For his part, Thorny Percy appeared completely terrified of the Head Archangel. As Guardian Angels our department reported to Uriel. We rarely had contact with Uriel's boss. Yet rumours abounded, most of them scary.

Having incurred the wrath of Gabriel more than once, I felt sorry for Percy.

"Can't say I approve of the company you've been keeping, Miss Winter," Gabriel said in the booming voice with which he usually addressed the Heavenly hosts. A voice meant to impress and intimidate.

And Gabriel possessed a face perfect for intimidation. Strikingly handsome, he embodied the sleek beauty of a panther poised to strike. If I'd had a passable excuse, I would have used it. But who knew what evidence Gabriel had stored in his high-tech office. Holographic tape surveillance, locator flight plans, all of it sitting in some fat file with my name on.

"If you're referring to Naamah – " I might as well admit it, I figured. "I wasn't keeping company with her. I was trying to rescue Alex Chalmers from her clutches."

"Clutches?" Gabriel had a way of turning a single word into a threat.

"She was holding him hostage at the business end of a flame thrower."

Gabriel turned his penetrating gaze on Percy who promptly turned from crimson to grey. He swallowed hard and nodded. "That's how Miss Winter was injured – trying to protect Mr. Chalmers."

"Trust me. Naamah and I have nothing polite to say to each other."

"I don't trust you," Gabriel said. "That's the point, former-guardian. Which makes me question your motives even more."

"My motives!" Gabriel obviously had his mind made up. What could I say to convince him I wasn't trying to buy my way back into Heaven? And still, even the bitter thought was appealing. "Shouldn't you be questioning Naamah's motives?"

I wanted to box Percy's red ears. Couldn't he have thought up something to get us both out of this mess? Apparently not.

But if Percy had caught wind of the deal I'd inadvertently made with Naamah, he didn't mention it. I had to wonder why.

"Naamah, along with the rest of the Underworld's wildlife, is under our surveillance."

How much surveillance? Where were Michael, Uriel and Raphael? Were they screening holo surveillance while Gabriel grilled me and Percy took notes?

Turned out a chorus of disapproving archangels wasn't needed. Gabriel did just fine all by himself.

"Your conduct as a human is no better than your conduct as a Guardian Angel," Gabriel growled. He shot Percy a scathing look. "And now we have another Guardian following in your muddy footsteps!"

Poor Percy looked like he just might faint, but unlike Wynn Jarrett who would have happily joined in with a list of my sins, Percy kept quiet. So, I took pity on him. "Don't blame Percival, he's just trying to do his job. He was trying to protect Alex and me from Naamah when

Uriel called him back." The archangel's gaze shot to Percy. Apparently, our stories matched. "If there's anyone to blame here, it's Lucifer, Naamah and the minions of Hell!"

Gabriel sucked in an outraged breath. He did that when he intended to yell. "As I said before, Porsche Winter, it is – " Another breath, greater volume. "NOT. YOUR. BUSINESS!"

Ominous silence filled the chamber while Percy held his breath and Gabriel quivered with anger. "Okay," I said quickly. "Not my business."

"And speaking of Lucifer . . . you are this close," he held up a thumb and forefinger, "to spending eternity with him. Only divine intervention is keeping you on the Earthly plane. Do you understand?"

So they couldn't know that Naamah had coerced my help. Or I'd already be stoking Lucifer's boiler. Nor did it seem like the time to fess up.

I said, "Right. Got it."

Then I was spinning.

Down through the clouds, past Master Control and Dream Central, streaking like a comet and messing up everyone's equipment.

I tensed, waiting to hit solid ground, or the prickliest bush Gabriel could find or perhaps the most desolate plateau in Tibet. Instead I fell into the softness of scattered covers and pillows. I almost breathed a sigh of relief, until Alex yelped.

You'd think he'd be used to me appearing out of nowhere by now.

He gawked at me sprawled on his bed, sexy undies barely hidden by his bathrobe. "You were in the bathroom . . . Don't tell me – "

"There is no mercy," I managed to croak.

"Not Gabriel *again*?"

"Himself."

"Dressed like that?" The question painted quite an image. I didn't need to elaborate.

I sat up gingerly. "Yeah well, Percy ratted me out."

"Son-of-a – "

I held up my hand. "Don't. He is your Guardian Angel. And he had no choice, not after Uriel caught him with us and Naamah."

"I gather it didn't go well with Gabriel."

"No, it didn't." I succeeded in standing up without falling down.

"Whatever we're going to do, we're going to have to be quick about it."
"Then we better – "
Someone hammered on the front door, loud enough to shake the pictures on the walls. Alex jumped. As one we turned to look at the clock on the bedside table and winced at the late hour.
"Naamah?" he mouthed.
I shrugged. "She did say she'd be in touch."
He shrugged on another robe and started down the hall toward the door that was still shaking under the impact of someone's fist. I ran after him.
"Let me." I hauled the door open, nearly getting a fist in the face. Instinctively, I ducked.
"Who the hell are you?" demanded a voice above me.
Straightening, I remembered that I was still wearing Alex's black bathrobe and my hair likely looked like a demon nested in it.
And the person standing on Alex's doorstep certainly wasn't Naamah. I looked into dark eyes, so like Alex's I nearly gasped.
Judging by his grey hair and the eerily similar set to his mouth, he had to be Alex's father. And he couldn't be less pleased to meet me.
Behind me Alex said, "Dad, it's late – "
"And you haven't answered any of my calls. Your mother is crazy with worry." Brushing past me, he demanded, "Is it true?"
"Is what true?"
I nearly laughed. I'd used the same tactic trying to evade my mother. Never admit to anything, let them draw it out of you agonising piece by agonising piece. Maybe that way you wouldn't have to tell them it all. And you wouldn't need to lie.
My dad was far more tolerant of my mistakes. I could tell my dad anything. Probably because he'd done worse.
"Did you embezzle money from the firm?"
Alex shut the door. "Come in to the living room, Dad. There's no sense telling the whole building about it."
Colour leeched from the elder Chalmers's face. "Good God in Heaven, it is true."
I said, "Shh!" before I could stop myself, and earned a threatening glare from both of them.

"How could you do this to me!" the elder Chalmers bellowed.

"Relax Dad," Alex said. Obviously this wasn't the first time he'd been on the receiving end of one of his father's tirades. "It's not what you think! I put the money back."

"And you think that makes it okay? What the hell were you thinking? My reputation is ruined!"

Alex's mouth tightened and his eyes darkened with anger. I tried to shake off the uncanny feeling of déjà vu. Under Lucifer's influence, he'd always looked that way. That couldn't be. I'd put his soul back, but hardly in pristine condition. I pondered that thought. Had more happened between Alex and Naamah than I suspected?

"It's always about you, isn't it?" Alex said. "You're not worried about me, you're just worried about what your friends will think!"

For an instant, I thought his dad might actually hit him, but then he shuddered and seemed to crumple in on himself. "This is killing your mother," he said in a broken whisper. For a moment no one said anything.

"And who is she?" his father asked suddenly, like I wasn't standing right there. "Is that why you did it? To impress some little piece of eye-candy?"

Eye-candy? I'd been called weird things before, but never that. I choked back a laugh.

"Dad, this is Porsche, my – my girlfriend. Porsche, this is my dad, Alan Chalmers."

I tightened the belt on the bathrobe and offered my hand. He didn't take it. Alex noted the slight and frowned.

"Por-shee-ah?" His dad drawled my name, pronouncing it Portia. I didn't correct him.

I said, "Hi."

Alan barrelled ahead with his interrogation. "And what do you do, Por-shee-ah?"

Do? Good question. I could tell 'nothing' would hardly suffice. So I said, "I'm kind of in the business of saving souls."

"Good God! Don't tell me you're a missionary!"

"Stop taking His name in vain!" The last thing I needed was The Big Guy listening in on this conversation.

"And no Dad," Alex interjected. "Porsche isn't a missionary, and I didn't do it to impress her. She's been helping me put my life back together."

"There was nothing wrong with your life!" Alex's father bellowed. "Your mother and I sacrificed everything to give you every opportunity. And this is how you repay us!"

"You wanted to make me your clone," Alex retorted. "You don't even know me."

"Apparently not."

Insults piled up between them like a brick wall. A few more words and they wouldn't be talking for years.

Trying to diffuse the situation, I attempted to derail their argument. "Why don't I go make some coffee – " I started to say.

As I passed through the living room into the kitchen, I looked through the window and nearly gasped.

Lightning sizzled across the horizon. Clouds scudded across the lake, moving rapidly inland.

But it wasn't the storm that had me worried. It was the image forming in the grey-green clouds that stood out from the flash of light like a bruise. I held my breath as the dark pits of eyes formed in the vapour. Above those formidable eyes a pair of dark eyebrows took shape. Wisps grew out of the top of what was rapidly forming a face. Wisps that became horns.

Blinding flares of lightning overlapped each other. The clouds drifted closer until the image filled the window. The bottom of the face lengthened. Teeth grew out of the mist, and beneath them, a neat pointy little beard. The mirage drifted closer until it seemed that imposing mouth might swallow the building.

Lucifer.

No doubt about whom that picture was supposed to represent. But whom was it a message from? Cupid? Naamah? Or was Lucifer himself trying to tell me something?

A dark bar formed within the clouds. It cut through Lucifer's face like an arrow. Slicing past one eye, it exited through that mouthful of threatening teeth. I squinted trying to bring it back into focus.

But the clouds passed over the building. I ran for Alex's den, which offered a panoramic view of the other side of the horizon. By the time I reached the window, what had been written in the clouds was gone.

Another bolt of lightning illuminated the den, drawing my attention to Alex's current sculpting project. Turning on the desk light, I bent for a closer look.

"Condemnation!" The word tore from my throat. On the desk sat a partially assembled, yet strikingly anatomically correct sculpture of a she-devil.

Naamah wore her clothes tight and her skirts scandalously short, leaving little to the imagination. And since I'd moved in with Alex, nothing about me had been left to his imagination. Could he be getting sick of me so soon? The thought burned in my mind. I'd believed Alex liked me for well, me. But he'd had a taste of all Hades could offer, including several blatant offers from Naamah. I stared at the sexy little sculpture on his desk. Despite his protests, apparently, he was thinking it over.

What would Alex say if I confronted him about it? I wasn't entirely sure I wanted his answer. All my life I'd been dealing with people's disappointment in me. With one foot in the Underworld and one in Heaven, I never seemed to live up to anyone's expectations. If I'd disappointed Alex as well, I really didn't want to hear it.

And for the moment, I had more pressing concerns than Alex's choice of sculpting subjects.

In the living room I could still hear Alex and his dad arguing, slinging insults at each other with as much vengeance as the storm. I don't think either of them noticed that I'd left the room. Insults could injure as badly as fists, I knew. I had to stop them from doing either.

By the time I returned, the elder Chalmers was standing close enough to crawl down Alex's throat. Rage burned in Alex's eyes. I watched his hold on his temper loosen.

"It was a lapse in judgement." He uttered the words through clenched teeth. "Sorry it inconvenienced you."

"Inconvenienced? You've ruined me."

"You're retired. It's too late to ruin your reputation. You spend half the year on your yacht!" His dad opened his mouth to say something, but Alex cut in, "That's what you're worried about, isn't it? That you'll be the laughing stock at the next yacht club party."

Sure, his dad came on pretty strong, and I knew first hand how difficult living up to parental expectations could be. But this wasn't the Alex Chalmers I thought I knew.

I said, "Alex!"

Which only earned me a vicious glare from both of them.

Time to put those conflict resolution skills I'd been forced to learn at the academy to use. Not that I'd got the best marks. I'd passed. Strangely enough Wynn Jarrett had scored highest.

"I'm sure your dad is worried about more than his professional reputation. He – he just doesn't know how to say it."

The elder Chalmers sputtered for a moment, then fell silent. Finally, he nodded.

"And Alex made a grave error in judgement," I added.

"No kidding," Alex's dad agreed. "Don't tell me it was drugs, son – " I held up my hand for silence, but he slipped in another barb. "Because if it's cocaine, or something else – "

Just when it looked like I'd diffused the situation, his father added more fuel to the fire. "It wasn't drugs, he just gave in to temptation. Which he shouldn't have," I finished quickly.

"I thought better of you son."

Alex shook his head and looked away.

"Look, he made a mistake, for which he's made reparation. And he is *repenting*." I walked into Alex's line of vision. "Aren't you, Alex?"

That question stopped the tirade. We both waited for Alex's answer.

Running his hands through dark curls, he signed. "Yes, of course I am." He faced his father. "Look, Dad. Tell Mom not to worry. I made a mistake, and I'm doing my best to fix it."

Too proud to let Alex have the last word, his father said, "I certainly hope you are."

But this time Alex didn't take the bait. "Tell Mom, I'll – I'll call her later."

Anger crackled the air between them. The conversation came to an impasse. It was either let the argument sputter out or fan the flames again.

"Fine," his father snapped. He stro de toward the door. Alex followed him whether to continue the fight or to simply stop him from slamming the door, I couldn't tell. I followed them to prevent both.

After hauling the door open, his father paused on the threshold. For a moment he stared at Alex and me. Then he sighed and stalked off down the hall. The door swung shut behind him.

"Well, that went well," I said for lack of anything more helpful.

Alex stared at the door. He rubbed a hand across his face. "He's impossible."

"Yeah, well you haven't met my mother. She could teach your dad a thing or two about using guilt as a motivator."

"I thought she was a saint."

"Saints believe a little guilt is good for the soul."

"I shouldn't have got so mad at him." He gave me a sheepish ghost of a smile. "He just got under my skin."

"I noticed. He sure didn't like me much."

Alex laughed. "He has no taste."

"The man has good instincts," I corrected. "He knows I was involved somehow. And he's right."

Alex put his arm around me and pulled me close. "Porsche, we were both deceived."

"How touching," said a snide voice from the living room.

I felt Alex tense and clutch me protectively closer, but I wiggled out of his embrace. I took two steps toward the sunken living room and froze.

Naamah sat on Alex's leather couch flipping through his satellite TV channels.

An image of the Devil's face in the clouds filled the screen of his large screen television.

"VISITORS TO THE WATERFRONT THIS evening experienced an unusual phenomenon," proclaimed the pretty blonde news announcer. I turned my attention from Naamah to the newscast in progress. The shot zoomed in to highlight Lucifer's face in the clouds.

I hoped I'd been mistaken, that what I'd seen was just an unusual cloud formation. But even with crude Earthly broadcasting technology, I couldn't deny that those clouds bore a distinct likeness to Lucifer in his Devil face.

Dark eyes bored out of the clouds, staring back at me through the television set. Within the shifting mists, teeth formed in his widening mouth. Horns formed by wisps of cloud finished off the picture. Even through the video playback that massive mouth engulfed the screen as it drifted toward the camera. Then came that black arrow that shot through the image.

The scene switched back to the news desk. "You're watching video taken by German tourists visiting Harbourfront," the announcer said. "Local meteorologists called it a trick of lightning playing on the clouds. However, we are in for a devil of a storm tonight." She smiled like this was good news.

Alex nudged me. I couldn't tell if it was to alert me to the she-devil in his apartment or to the Devil's picture on the newscast. I gave him a quick nod to let him know I'd deal with Naamah and that I'd seen the image, even if the message was yet to be deciphered.

Naamah had made some wardrobe changes since our last meeting. Tonight she wore a black satin skirt. A train of frothy petticoat material billowed behind it, spilling out over the couch onto the carpet. A black corset squeezed her waist to an impossibly small diameter. Leather straps crisscrossed her collarbone like a bondage halter. A black choker with a huge clear diamond, black lipstick and long satin gloves completed the outfit. Her flaming red hair was piled high atop her head, hiding her horns. She looked like a true Queen of Darkness, Empress of the Underworld, which of course she was.

Alex dragged his gaze from Naamah. I nudged him back, far harder than he'd elbowed me.

Our uninvited guest stared raptly at the television image taking it all in like a big joke. Her smile showed every one of her tiny, sharp teeth.

On the television, the picture changed to footage of decimated crops.

"The Ministry of the Environment has called in experts from Australia to deal with a sudden plague of locusts that started in downtown Toronto and has since spread to the suburbs. Farmers and wine growers in Niagara are taking steps to combat this unusual infestation." The news anchor continued, proclaiming that tomorrow was again going to be unseasonably hot and the beaches were closed due to high pollution levels. No one seemed to have put any of the elements together. No one, except me and The Four Horsemen of the Apocalypse who'd come to the city looking for work and seemed to be finding it.

I tore my attention from the television screen to the she-devil on the couch. "Well, Naamah, what a surprise."

"I said I'd be in touch." She made it sound like we ought to have been waiting with baited breath for her return.

As if. No one waits expectantly for bad news.

"So you did," I deadpanned back. Alex had the decency to look somewhere other than at Naamah's cleavage. But I noticed his gaze kept straying back there, as if lured against his better sense. I thought of the sculpture of the she-devil on his desk and wondered if Naamah knew about it. Probably, I deduced by the self-satisfied smile on her face. Mind you, Naamah always looked like that.

Naamah uncoiled from the couch in a swish of satin, drawing Alex's gaze back to her. I wanted to slap him. Damnation, I wanted to slap her.

Instead I said, "Well, you heard the newscast. What are we going to do about Lucifer?"

"Stop him of course." Naamah walked toward us. Her hips swayed gracefully with each step, oozing sex appeal, none of which Alex missed.

"Sure we want to stop him. Apocalypse is not what anyone needs right now. But the process is already underway, and I'm – " I nearly choked on the words. "Human." I really hated having to admit that to Naamah.

We were desperately short of allies, I reminded myself. Percy ratted me out to Gabriel. And who knew what Gabriel would do to Cupid if he'd traced that locator back to him. Unfortunately, that left only Naamah, who for her own reasons was willing to team up with a fallen angel.

Naamah swatted my concerns away. We faced each other eye to eye, or rather eye to cleavage. In her six-inch spikes she stood substantially taller than me. The scent of her perfume tickled the back of my throat, and I struggled not to fall under her spell. She toyed with the diamond on her choker. "I have a plan."

Great, I thought sarcastically. Naamah had a plan. But then what had I been expecting?

"But it's going to involve some travel." I caught the swish of her tail beneath those voluminous skirts.

"No!" Suddenly I realised where this conversation was heading. "I am not going to Hell."

Annoyance crossed the she-devil's face. And for a moment she looked like a spoiled two year old, who'd just been deprived of her candy. A very malevolent two year-old. "If we want to defeat Lucifer, we must go to the source." She waved at the television screen, but the announcer was now depicting doom on the stock market instead. I noticed that this news item had Alex's complete attention.

"There must be a way to deal with Lucifer from the Earthly plane," I insisted. And to think I'd once worried about being caught in a bar in Purgatory! I could just imagine how Gabriel would take the news of my sudden holiday in Hell. He'd make it a permanent holiday. I swallowed the feeling of a trap closing around me. Naamah's deal got worse with every passing second.

"Trust me," the she-devil said, sounding oh so sincere. I didn't think she even had it in her. "You don't want Lucifer on the Earthly plane, now do you?"

True enough. I sighed, trying to think of a way to deal with the impending apocalypse without sending my body, soul and spirit to Hell.

But before I could object again, Alex said, "You know, she might have a point."

"Oh she has a point, all right. One that might get us killed. We're human, Alex. Hell is no place for a human body. Believe me."

"I do believe you, Porsche. But there has to be a way. Humans have gone to the moon!"

"Yeah," I admitted. "And what for? There's nothing there. We could have told you that."

"For the adventure. To see if they could. To test themselves."

"I've had enough adventures to last me a lifetime," I countered. "And the last time you were in Hell, you were in an incorporeal state. In your human body, the temperature alone would be mighty uncomfortable."

"So we'll wear HAZMAT suits. Or something."

It was the or-something part that had me worried.

Naamah's pointed shoe tapped against the floor. Her tail whooshed beneath her skirts. "We had a deal," she spat.

Technically, she'd trapped me into that deal, taking my lack of objection as agreement. I swallowed hard, debating my next course of action. Every ounce of sense I possessed screamed at me to tell Naamah to slink back to the Hell she'd crawled out of. The she-devil watched my indecision with interest. "Do you really wish to concede the Earthly plane to Lucifer?"

"No!" I admitted, far too readily. Naamah would make a terrible collaborator. But one ally was better than none.

"Then let's go." Before I could protest, Naamah was holding Hell's version of the locator. Like most of Hell's technology, it was a cruder, yet still effective device. Technology differed between the companies of Heaven Inc. and Hell Ltd. Neither trusted the other enough to collaborate on an invention.

I tried not to scream when my human body was wrenched from the Earthly plane and sent straight to Hell.

This was a much rougher ride, but we arrived in Naamah's office in one piece. Immediately I knew I was in Hades, the capital city of Hell. Overwhelming heat gave it away.

Imagine the Sahara desert in the middle of summer, no shade, no water as far as the eye can see, and you'll have some inkling of what the climate of Hell is like. Only there is no sky above you, only miles of smoke, ash and brimstone. The odour of sulphur floods your senses. The oppressive heat saps your strength as the moisture in your body slowly evaporates. Mountains hewn from black rock and swampy rivers round out the scenery. Not much of a vacation destination. Even my dad spent his holidays elsewhere. Usually skiing, or racing his cars.

My feet met rock hard enough to rattle my teeth. Naamah coasted in beside us like she'd been parasailing rather than travelling through planes of existence. With a snap of her fingers, her satin dress disappeared, to be replaced with a form-fitting catsuit: shiny black vinyl with a red pitchfork insignia over the right breast. In her case the red pitchfork was stretched almost beyond recognition. Something Alex picked up on immediately. I wanted to slap him. No, I decided, I would slap him, the next time we had some privacy.

Standing next to Naamah's flaming sexuality fully revealed in the spray-on outfit, I looked like a complete idiot in Alex's silk bathrobe. The stifling heat moulded it uncomfortably to every contour of my body.

Alex dragged his attention from Naamah to look at his surroundings and shuddered. Already sweating profusely, his body tried vainly to cool itself and failed. His denim jeans clung to his body. His faded black t-shirt was already soaked with sweat. He ran a hand through damp curls and raised his chin in challenge. "Well, at least there's no hail."

As a joke, it failed pitifully. "Don't say that! You have no idea what the Devil is capable of. If he thinks your idea of Hell involves hail, he'd make it possible just to torment you."

My personal idea of Hell involved anything on or near Devil's Mountain, the administrative hub of Lucifer's domain. Naamah's private office sat halfway up the hill. Only Lucifer himself rated a perch higher up the peak. But then it was *his* mountain. Hewn from the black rock, Naamah rated some spacious digs. If you consider cavern chic to be a kind of décor.

Lucifer had an office much like it. And though it had been hacked from the same onyx, Naamah's definitely showed a female touch.

In the centre of the office sat a huge slab of obsidian, raised on four oval legs. Behind it stood a chair big enough to be a throne. A carving of a vine of thorns ran across the peaked back and down the sides. The seat was polished smooth to reflect the red light that reflected off the sulphur clouds. I coughed, hard enough to hurt my ribs. But my gasping breaths only drew more brimstone into my lungs.

Alex had pulled the neck of his t-shirt up over his mouth. It made an inefficient filter. I noticed he took shallow breaths in a vain attempt to keep his lungs from rebelling. I tried not to think about what would happen when we actually had to expend some energy.

In front of the desk lurked another couple of high backed chairs carved out of the same stone. I couldn't imagine anyone who'd willingly sit in either one of them. Getting called into Naamah's office rated its own mythology, most of it the stuff of horror stories. The front of the cavern lay open to the air, if you could call it that, offering an impressive view of the scenery. I shot a glance at the gorge that dropped away from Devil's Mountain and took a hasty step backward. Trust me, getting thrown out of Naamah's office wasn't something you wanted to experience.

Tunnelled out of the rock, a corridor led away from the main room of her suite. Rumour had it that it led to Naamah's private torture chamber. Lucifer kept his chains in the open office. This I knew for sure, I'd had the misfortune of being his guest. But, unlike Lucifer, Naamah preferred to take her pleasure in private.

Sweat ran in a hot trickle down my spine, as my human body desperately tried to cool itself.

"Nice office." My voice sounded hoarse.

Naamah nodded like it really was a compliment. Circling the desk, Naamah leaned one shapely hip against it and studied us.

Hotter than Hell, no pun intended, I managed to stare coolly back at her despite the alarm bells ringing in my mind. "So, what now?"

Naamah smiled, showing rows of neat, razor-sharp teeth. "Now, we plot."

That didn't sound like averting Armageddon to me.

Panic threatened to overwhelm me. Alone in Hell without weapons or allies we could trust, Alex and I were in a precarious position. I didn't even have a locator to get us out of there if the situation tilted from bad toward worst. I had the feeling I'd just made the most awful mistake.

But my dad lived in Hell, I reminded the screeching little voice inside. My dad would help us.

Like they'd let him, it snickered back.

I should have found a way to get a message through to him, I realised. Before I left. But the last thing I wanted to do was to involve my family in any more of my dark dealings. They'd suffered enough.

And if my mom found out Dad knew what I was up to, she'd consider it her saintly duty to rid the world of evil by roasting him alive over one of Lucifer's flame pits.

No, the last thing I wanted to do was to land in the middle of another parental argument. I'd take Hell any day.

A small pyre lay to the side of Naamah's desk. Hell's answer to email and teleconferencing. No Internet here. No banks of monitors to keep an eye on the minions of Hades. If you had the misfortune of being a resident, you were considered guilty. Lucifer never needed a reason to torture you.

Naamah waved her hand over the pyre. It roared to life in brilliant red flame. Within the flame darker images began to form. I peered into its depths. Behind me I heard the rustle of cloth as Alex joined us.

I recognised Lucifer's form, artfully rendered in flame. But things had obviously changed a great deal since I'd been here last.

No GQ-Man persona for Lucifer this time. He sat hunched over his great desk, his head in his hands. Dark hair hung in greasy tendrils. His black silk shirt sagged in creases. Stone tablets piled up higher than his desk. More stacks of tablets stood like pillars in his vast chamber. While we watched a puff of smoke appeared in the air beside him. Two weasel-like lawyers shouted at him from out of the mist. And though we couldn't hear the entire conversation, it couldn't have been good because the Devil just shook his head slowly back and forth.

A figure stood in the centre of his chamber. Some lower level demon demanded his attention with another problem. Lucifer raised his fist and squeezed. The demon choked and collapsed on the stone floor.

A flaming arrow clove the air above his head, imbedding itself in the wall of his chamber. The arrow hung there vibrating. A white scroll unfurled from the arrow's shaft, revealing a message from one of Heaven's lawyers.

Lucifer hurled a ball of flame at it. It disappeared in a puff of smoke.

However, peace for Lucifer was fleeting. The flaming arrow had no sooner vanished, when six more broke through the air above the Devil's head. His own pyre roared to life. I caught a glimpse of Frank the former-bogeyman within the blaze. Puffs of smoke burst from thin air all over Lucifer's office. Underworld lawyers, lackeys, minions all demanded his attention.

Lucifer leapt from his carved throne, scattering stone tablets in his wake. Standing in the centre of his cavern, he roared at the ceiling. Creased silk fell from his shoulders as his body expanded beyond the confines of his clothes. Black leather trousers tore from his legs. His jaw lengthened and snapped. Skin stretched over his changing features. He uttered another roar. The whole of Devil's Mountain rumbled.

For an instant nothing changed. Frank stared back at the Devil from out of the flames, dumbfounded. Then Lucifer's pyre winked into ash and was silent. The chattering lawyers froze mid sentence and were silent. The Devil roared again. Puffs of smoke containing the lawyers' messages were blown away like milkweed on the wind.

Lucifer raged about his cavern looking for someone on whom to vent his frustration. Bolts of lightning flew from his fingertips, charring Heaven's flaming arrows beyond recognition. His red eyes glowed in the gloom as he stormed about his office. Saliva dripped from his fangs, sizzling on the hot floor.

The Devil roared again in warning. But the pyre and the puffs of smoke lay silent. Finding no suitable scapegoat, he folded his demon bulk behind the too-small desk and went back to work.

Naamah waved her hand over her pyre. Flames flickered and then snuffed out. "Do you see the problem?"

I nodded. Lucifer definitely had a problem. I'd never seen the Devil so much under siege. But something about it just didn't ring true. That feeling of panic rose to a shuddering crescendo. I choked it back.

Naamah was a powerful enough demon to conjure her own imagery. The scenes in the Devil's chamber could have been live, or they could be carefully edited snippets.

Could you edit the images from a pyre? I wondered. I decided I just didn't know.

Alex was obviously thinking the same thing, because he said, "Wow, things really aren't going very well for Lucifer."

Thinking we'd played right into her hand, Naamah almost purred with contentment. "Exactly why he needs Earth to expand his empire."

That sentiment simply didn't make sense. Lucifer had a tenuous hold on the empire he already controlled, not to mention a pending court case. Not that I'd put it past Lucifer to try solving his problem with another problem. It might make total sense to the Devil that if one empire fell to dust, why not just conquer another? After all, he'd been trying to take over Heaven for all eternity.

"So, what do we do?" I asked Naamah.

"We stop his diabolical plan," Naamah said. She might be in uniform today, but she hadn't forsaken the six-inch spike heels. Leaving her post by the pyre, she sashayed toward us, the metal tips of her heels clicking against the stone. Neatly beaded with regulation black beads, her tail swished behind her.

In those heels, she was taller than me by quite a bit. Still wearing Alex's now sweat-soaked bathrobe, I felt hot and utterly ridiculous. "Okay," I said in the most conciliatory tone I could muster. "But I've got to ask again. What's in it for you?"

She shifted balance, thrusting one hip towards us. Her body moved sinuously beneath the vinyl and the material creaked slightly. Alex's eyes followed the movement with interest. I tightened my hold on my temper. Later, I promised myself. Later, Alex and I would have a heart to heart talk about she-devil sculptures and Naamah.

"What's in it for me?" Naamah repeated. She sauntered back to her pyre, and even I had to admit her backside looked pretty good in that tight material. She waved a leather-gloved hand. Flames roared to life.

"Behold," she said in an imperious tone reminiscent of Lucifer. I noted that inflection for future study.

An image formed within the flames. Naamah sat at the very desk behind us. A line of minions snaked across her office and out into the tunnels beyond. It had to be a scene from the past because the real Naamah stood before the pyre staring with unbridled anger into its depths.

So, I thought with interest. A pyre *could* be used to play back a scene, and no doubt edited to make a more compelling story. That fact had never made it into any of Heaven's training manuals. Maybe they didn't think it was important. Maybe they simply didn't know. None of Heaven's flock had spent as much time in Hades as I had.

I filed that bit of intrigue with the rest and turned my attention back to the scene unfolding within Naamah's pyre. A stack of stone tablets similar to the ones littering Lucifer's office sat piled next to her desk.

More petitioners joined the queue winding down the corridor. The next in line stepped up to Naamah's desk. One of the bean counters from down the hill. I could tell by his slug-like pallor. Bean counters didn't get out of their caves much. He dumped a pile of beans on Naamah's desk and threw up his hands in disgust.

In the replay Naamah stared back at him. Taking this for acquiescence, he continued. Her eyes glowed like coals. Belatedly, he realised his mistake.

Naamah's mouth stretched, showing those rows of nasty-looking little teeth. Her shriek sent him flying backward, arms windmilling helplessly. His bony body hit the cavern wall with an audible snap. The next in line took one look and bolted from her office.

Beans spilled across her desk and ran onto the floor. Naamah shrieked again. Another bean counter was summoned from the depths of Devil's mountain to pick them up.

"You see?" the head she-devil demanded.

I nodded mutely.

"Do you see what I must contend with?" she continued as if I hadn't just agreed with her. I wondered if a requirement for working in Hades involved the ability to whine.

"Dealing with other people's problems is just part of being a manager." A fact I knew well. I'd been one.

Alex nodded in agreement. He'd been a manager, too.

"And Lucifer contrives to add more to my workload!" Naamah complained as vehemently as if Lucifer plotted her murder.

"I'm sure you'd cope," I snapped, then thought better of it. "You're very resourceful."

Naamah preened at the compliment. "I refuse to cope," she snarled. "I prefer things the way they are."

She passed a hand over the pyre to turn it off and straightened, forcing Alex to tear his gaze away from her PVC-encased bottom.

"And that's what this is all about?" I asked, more to draw Alex's attention back to the problem at hand than anything else. I didn't trust Naamah further than I could kick her shapely butt.

"Yessss," Naamah drawled, sounding way more like Lucifer than was comfortable. I forced my feet to stay rooted to the spot and not to take a step backward.

"Okay then," I said, far too quickly. Naamah's multifaceted eyes narrowed. I'd have to be way more careful, I realised. If I aroused Naamah's suspicions, I was quite literally, toast.

"But –" Alex started to say. And then Naamah's pyre roared to life.

She put her back to us, effectively blocking off our view of whatever was happening within the depths of those flames. Over the fire's crackle and the cries of agony emanating from the pit, I couldn't hear what was being said.

But I did hear Naamah snap, "Enough!" Flame sputtered and died. She turned back to us, her mouth set in a hard line. Whatever message her pyre delivered, it couldn't be good. "Wait for me!" she commanded like we were her loyal minions.

And with that the head she-devil vanished down the corridor.

"What do you think that was about?" Alex asked, staring after her.

I turned in the direction of Naamah's departing form. The sound of her clicking heels faded down the hall. "I suspect things aren't as rosy in Naamah's empire as she'd like us to believe."

What had been just a nagging worry became a downright suspicion.

We were being misled. And I had no idea about what.

"But – " Alex said again.

I grabbed him by the forearms. "Listen to me, Alex. I don't believe for a minute that Naamah wants to defeat Lucifer to maintain the status quo here in Hades."

His brows creased in concern, but he didn't look all that surprised. "What do you think she wants then?"

I paced a few feet away from him, careful to stay away from the edge of the cavern. "That's the problem. I don't know really. I've just got a feeling things are about to go very badly for us."

"That's not much to go on, Porsche."

"Yeah, I know." I turned back. "But I really need your help here, Alex. You're good at reading people, you have a talent for strategy."

"Okay . . . " He stared out over the panorama of Lucifer's domain. With his back to me, I couldn't tell what he was thinking, but something must have occurred to him because he spun back in my direction. "What are you thinking? That she brought us here to keep us out of the way? So we won't interfere with what the Devil is really planning?"

"Something like that. I think by coming here, we just made a huge tactical error."

"So what do we do?"

A quick glance around the cavern didn't reveal any weapons. I'm sure she had them, but Naamah knew better than to leave anything in plain view. This was Hell after all.

"We need reinforcements."

Alex laughed harshly. "Here? We *are* in Hell, Porsche."

"Not funny," I said, crossing the rough floor as quickly as I could. "And we don't have much time. Naamah will be back any second."

Squatting awkwardly in front of the pyre, I studied it carefully. Hades used a totally different kind of technology than Heaven. Could a mortal make it work? Only one way to find out, I figured.

I passed my hand over the charred bowl. To my astonishment, it flamed to life. I yanked my hand back. "Okay, so far so good." I felt Alex's bigger body crowding in behind me.

"What are you – "

"Shh!" I said. "I'm trying to think here." But what would make it work?

I decided to try the simplest solution. Staring into the flames, I said, "Charon!"

Flames soared higher, I backed up a step. My father's face appeared from within the fire.

"Isn't that your – "

I turned my head to tell Alex to shut up already, but Dad's image started to talk.

"Hi! You've reached Charon the Ferryman. I'll be on holiday for the next two weeks. Ferry prices are currently set at one gold coin. If you need immediate assistance, you can contact The Grim Reaper at 666-0666. Otherwise leave a message at the beep." The image faded, leaving only the blaze. From out of the flames came a loud beep.

"Dad, it's me, Porsche," I said quickly. "I'm in Hades, staying with Naamah. If you're checking your messages, I could really use a hand with something."

From down the hall came the rapid-fire beat of Naamah's heels. I pulled my hand away from the flame. The pyre sizzled and went out.

As one Alex and I took a step away from the pyre. When Naamah entered the cavern, we were admiring the view.

Hopefully Dad would read the innuendo in that message. He certainly knew I had no love for Naamah, nor she for me. But when it came to insinuation, Dad wasn't the sharpest tool in the shed. And if he got worried and called Mom, I was one dead mortal.

Looking out at Hell's vista, I sucked in a breath of searing air. Either I'd just made a plea for help, or doomed us both.

"I DIDN'T BRING YOU HERE TO SIGHT-see." Naamah's voice cut through the brimstone-laden air.

Shocked by the sheer annoyance in her tone, we turned in her direction. But I barely recognised the she-devil. Tendrils of hair hung from her intricate plait. Her catsuit bore smudges of ash. And the braided tail that undulated like the head of a snake was missing several of its beads. The head she-devil, Queen of Seductresses, looked like she'd been in a bar brawl.

So I let the barb pass and managed to stare back as passively as I could.

Naamah snapped her fingers. "We're wasting time."

And with that she spun on the tip of one of

those spike heels and strode off back down the corridor. Feeling like chastised lapdogs, Alex and I followed her.

The head she-devil did indeed have a cache of weapons hidden in one of the labyrinthine corridors of her private domain. Shackles, nasty-looking knives and flamethrowers lined the walls of one of Naamah's hidden cupboards. Nasty images of what could be done with such weapons sprang to mind.

None of them, or even all of them employed together seemed powerful enough to take down the Devil himself. That nagging little voice inside, the one that had been bugging me incessantly for days, screamed for attention. Everything about Naamah's plan just felt wrong. I had the sneaking suspicion I was being set up for the biggest fall of my life. And I'd be taking Alex with me. But we were in Hell with no way back.

I pondered that thought, growing more nervous by the second.

Naamah yanked an assortment of dangerous looking knives from the shelves and tossed them into a pile. Several flame throwers and a few shackles went onto the heap as well. I scanned the weapons on the wall.

"None of this will hold Lucifer for long."

The she-devil whirled, braids flying in all directions. The beaded tip of her tail snapped. I darted out of the way. Undeterred, I thrust my fists against my hips. Ignoring the sweat dripping into my eyes, I tried to look dangerous.

Reflected in Naamah's eyes I appeared sweaty, dishevelled and utterly ridiculous wearing Alex's bathrobe. But, as my dad had told me years ago, a lot of what went into a good offence was attitude.

"Well, it won't," I insisted.

Naamah hissed in annoyance. "We don't need to hold him for very long," she enunciated as if she was talking to a two year old. "We just need to create a diversion."

"A diversion for what?" Alex had the audacity to ask. Naamah's head whipped around in his direction.

"Enough of a diversion for me to squelch his plans."

Okay, that made sense, sort of. She'd divert Lucifer's attention and then . . . what?

"But how – " I started to say.

"We can spend an entire eon splitting hairs, while the Lord of the

Flies unleashes Hell on Earth," she snarled. Saliva dripped from the tops of her pointed little teeth. Naamah licked her lips. "Or we can stop him," she said in a more civil voice. Civil for a she-devil that is.

Yanking the belt of Alex's silk robe tighter, I snatched a flame-thrower from the pile and slung it over my shoulder. It hung there, a reassuring weight. So reassuring that I added another. Alex reached for one a little more gingerly. Sighting down the barrel, he pressed the trigger and visibly jumped when fire erupted from the nozzle. I grasped one of the knives and slid it from its sheath. The barbed end looked particularly deadly. Probably dipped in poison, I guessed. Not that poison would slow Lucifer down much.

With a groan of disgust, I shoved it back in the leather and strapped it to my wrist. Then, as an afterthought, I tied another to my thigh. With two flamethrowers and two nasty-looking knives, I felt marginally safer. Rummaging around in the pile for a knife that had only one point, I handed it to Alex.

"Don't touch the blade," I warned. His eyes widened. But he took the blade and gingerly threaded the sheath through his belt.

Naamah tested the strength of a pair of iron shackles. That feeling of uneasiness in my gut blossomed into terror. Shackles would work fine on Alex or me. I doubted they'd hold Naamah and they certainly wouldn't contain Lucifer. Not for more than a split second.

According to Naamah we only needed to divert the Devil's attention for a few moments. That I could do. I thought back to the last time I'd had Lucifer's undivided attention and shuddered.

But the images in my mind wouldn't stop. They dragged me back to Lucifer's lair, where I'd been held captive. I could still conjure the hiss of the Devil's scales on stone like it was yesterday. I remembered the smell of his fetid breath as his jaw cracked and his mouth opened wide enough to swallow my head. One second more and he would have sucked my soul from my body . . .

Naamah hefted the shackles, slung the flamethrower in its leather belt around her hips and strapped on a couple of those poison-tipped knives. I had to admit the entire effect was kind of sexy. Alex's eyes followed her every movement. For once I was grateful I couldn't read his mind.

"Ready?" Naamah asked as if waiting for children to tie their shoes. Alex and I nodded.

Naamah led us in a forced march down those obsidian caverns. Within the corridors the temperature rose to intolerable levels. The air lay thick with humidity and heavy with brimstone. I laboured to breathe in the oppressive heat and caustic air. Alex seemed to be doing only marginally better.

The head she-devil marched with neat steps on her heels. Neither the humidity, the heat nor the steep incline slowed her progress. Alex and I wheezed and struggled to keep up.

We took the back corridor, the one that led up the centre of Devil's Mountain. Most of the upper echelon used the more scenic outer stairways that snaked down the mountain. Of course most of the elite never strayed into the bowels of the mountain anyway. That's what minions were for.

So we climbed, nearly running now to keep up. Naamah strode ahead, oblivious to the oppressive air. Erratic torches lit the way in the gloom. It seemed torches were in short supply in Hades. Cutbacks plagued us all.

And I'd bet the cuts to the budget of Hell Ltd. bit even deeper after the last battle with Heaven Inc.

No one passed us in the corridors. Not even a hunched minion balancing one of those stone communiqués on its twisted back. That alone should have worried me.

Worry nagged a persistent monologue in the back of my mind. Nothing about this little trip to Hell felt right. But I didn't know what else to do. I'd asked for help from On High. And been refused.

Where was Naamah's army? I couldn't help wondering. How did she intend to subdue Lucifer with two wilted humans for back up? None of Naamah's so-called plan made any kind of sense. I just couldn't shake the feeling that something was terribly, terribly wrong.

And that I was about to land Alex right in the middle of it.

We rounded a corner. Naamah slung her flamethrower into position. She motioned for Alex and me to precede her.

I hesitated, that nagging voice rising in pitch.

Alex looked back at me, waiting for my okay. Then he shrugged. "This *is* what we came to do."

True enough. Someone had to stop Lucifer. If it all went bad here, at least we would have tried.

I leapt across the threshold into the cavern beyond.

Red light flared, nearly blinding us after the darkness of the tunnel. It didn't matter if I could see, I decided. I lurched forward, got the flamethrower into position and fired. The shot went wide, hitting the ceiling and raining gravel down on us. Beside me I heard Alex discharging his own flamethrower.

Silence greeted us, punctuated only by flamethrower blasts. Then someone laughed, long and low.

Lucifer.

Even through I couldn't see through the haze of debris, I recognised that voice. It haunted the worst of my nightmares.

In that second, I knew I'd just made the worst mistake of my life.

Which meant we'd just been cruelly betrayed. Naamah didn't want to maintain the status quo in Hades. She'd just earned herself a promotion at our expense.

Alex aimed his flamethrower in Lucifer's direction and got off a few shots. Even in the heat of the mountain, I felt the blast. The blaze momentarily whited out everything in my line of sight. I couldn't wait for my eyes to adjust again, so I recharged my own flamethrower and fired blindly.

Cursing under his breath, Alex did the same.

But instead of frying Lucifer to a crisp, the flame met the resistance of a wall of fire. That's when I realised the folly of using fire to fight the Devil. The blast from our flamethrowers merely joined the blaze, effectively blocking our offensive.

"Now that's enough of that," the Devil said. "As amusing as I find all this, I can't have you making a mess."

My eyes struggled to adjust to the brightness. I heard the drumming of Lucifer's talons against stone.

"Well, isn't this a surprise," the Devil continued.

I peered through the flame. Torches burned in bright rows on the far wall. The other side of the cavern lay open to the vista of Devil's Mountain, the Styx and the Pit. But, as Naamah had pointed out, I wasn't there to admire the scenery.

Lucifer sat on the carved throne in the centre of his vast domain. He wasn't wearing the demon face that lurked in my nightmares. Today he wore his cover model persona.

And the Devil had impeccable taste in clothes. His black leather trousers were cut obscenely tight, and his silk shirt stretched over his muscular chest. His silver tipped cowboy boots looked outrageously expensive. I was sure he had a hat to match somewhere close by. Not that his wardrobe mattered much when you knew what was really underneath.

Unfortunately, we commanded the Devil's undivided attention. Naamah was, of course, nowhere to be found.

Lucifer smiled, showing even white teeth. Part of the persona, I guessed. I'd seen his real ones. I didn't need a second look. Then the Devil tipped back his head and laughed heartily.

"And here I thought it was going to take a lengthy court battle to reclaim my property."

He slithered down the dais and sauntered toward us. I heard Alex utter a low gasp as Lucifer stepped neatly through the wall of flame. Then as an afterthought The Devil waved his hand and the blaze disappeared, leaving only a thin line of ash on the onyx floor.

He circled us slowly, giving special attention to me. Finally, he came to a stop in front of me. "I must say you've saved me a great deal of trouble Porsche Winter."

I looked into black eyes tinged with red. "Damned if I have."

The Devil chuckled low in his throat. "Damned, now that's an interesting choice of words."

I snapped my jaw shut. The sound reverberated in my head.

Lucifer gave me another slow once over. My skin crawled with revulsion. The Devil's leering gaze lingered on the sash that was coming undone in spite of my numerous attempts to yank it tighter. "Can't say much for your choice of attire."

"Yeah, well I didn't dress to please you." The comment leaped out before I could call it back. One of these days I had to learn to shut my mouth. I noticed Alex had no such trouble keeping his tongue in rein.

To that Lucifer tipped his head back and laughed again. At least he was laughing. He'd be less likely to turn me into a lump of ash if I amused him. "Oh, don't worry Miss Winter. I'm quite capable of pleasing myself."

No sense dignifying that with an answer.

"But first, your . . . friend." Lucifer smiled at me and turned to Alex who was standing, panting, in the heat. His black t-shirt was soaked through with perspiration and sticking to his body.

"You lay one hand on him – " I started to say, but Lucifer silenced me with a look.

He turned back to Alex, and furrowed his brow. "Yes . . . black I think . . . "

Waving his hand, Alex gasped as his clothing was replaced by a new outfit.

I gasped too, but in appreciation rather than horror.

Lucifer had kitted Alex out in a pair of superbly-cut trousers. Around his waist was a black silk cummerbund. His torso was uncovered, and his muscular chest glistened with sweat. Around his forehead was a black bandanna, effectively keeping the sweat out of his eyes. Alex blinked at the change and looked down at his body.

"Wow," I said.

Wow indeed. If Naamah hadn't wanted him before this, she would certainly think twice now.

Lucifer backed up a step and cocked his head, turning his attention to me. "Red, I think."

"Not the – " *Red leather bustier*, I started to say. The last thing I wanted was to parade myself through Hell again wearing red leather. But Lucifer had something altogether different in mind. Before the words left my mouth, I felt a gust of brimstone laden air rush past my face. The sweat-soaked robe, panties and camisole vanished. I gasped for breath and choked. Lucifer shot me a glance of pure annoyance, and then waved a hand tipped with long black nails.

Suddenly I could breathe again, well almost. I looked down. The tightly laced bodice of a scandalously red dress made a prominent display of my breasts. Taffeta rustled as I moved. And it was a good thing I looked before I moved, because I would have tripped over the voluminous skirt that trailed behind me. From the corner of my eye I caught Alex gawking. I was afraid to look at Lucifer.

My head ached from a headpiece that pulled my hair back into a severe bun. I reached up to undo it, and pricked my finger on something spiny. Swaying on ridiculously-high heels, I fought to keep my balance.

"Much better," Lucifer said. He walked a few steps away, then turned back. "Come, Porsche, walk with me."

When I hesitated, he squeezed his fist and I lurched toward him on those high heels.

"Leave her alone!" Alex roared, throwing himself bodily between the Devil and me. He aimed his flamethrower squarely at Lucifer's chest.

The Devil studied Alex with obvious distaste and his eyes flashed crimson. I expected Lucifer to reduce him to a pile of charcoal. Instead, his laughter shook the mountain. "She has you well trained, doesn't she?" he said, turning Alex's bravery into a joke. Alex set his jaw and kept his weapon trained on Lucifer.

The Devil snickered some more, and then abruptly sobered. His gaze focussed on the flamethrower. "Well, I can't have you annoying me with this."

With a twist of his wrist, the muzzle of the device twisted. The flamethrower glowed red. Alex dropped it with a yelp. It blazed bright enough to bring tears to my eyes, then vanished with an explosion that made my ears pop.

"Alex – " I moved toward him, trying to divert Lucifer's attention by wedging myself between him and my boyfriend. But one of my heels caught in the rock floor. I teetered, perilously close to Lucifer. Alex reached for me. The Devil caught me first.

Heat from his hands singed my bare arms. Shoving off Lucifer's chest, I righted myself. My palms tingled from the contact, but surprisingly, he let me go.

I stared into his fathomless black eyes. In my spike heels, I was nearly as tall as Lucifer. That detail didn't go unnoticed. As I watched, the Devil grew another foot. Let him play his little mind games, I refused to show him a morsel of fear. He'd only use it against me.

"Let Alex go," I demanded, and hoped it sounded assertive and not like the whimper my ears insisted it was.

Lucifer uttered a melodramatic sigh. "Well . . . no."

Belatedly, I realised my mistake. I'd made a request of the Devil. And he had refused it.

"Enough!" Lucifer snapped. "Come Miss Winter. And don't think I'll be letting either of you go this time. Oh no," he added for emphasis. "Not this time."

He allowed me to walk toward him under my own power. Indicating a lump of onyx carved from the very floor, he said, "Sit."

I sat. Lucifer left Alex to stand like some statue of a gleaming Adonis.

The Devil reclaimed his throne. "So tell me Porsche, what brings you crashing into the middle of my work day?"

None of my options looked good at this point. Naamah had delivered us to Lucifer as prisoners. The Devil could keep us as long as he wanted.

And I'd managed to alienate any allies I might have had in Heaven.

Figuring it was all going to Hell anyway, I said, "Maybe you're the one who wants to do some explaining!" And before the Devil could open his mouth in indignation, I continued with, "Perhaps you want to tell us why you unleashed a plague of locusts and you're trying to lay waste to the Earth with freak storms and meteor blasts!"

I waited to be blasted myself, straight into the pit in that fancy dress. But instead, the Devil leaned back against his carved throne and placed one very long nailed hand over his heart, as if he had one. "*Me?*"

Okay, now I know the Devil is the master of deception probably better than anyone, but he said it with such shocked sincerity it rendered me momentarily speechless.

"Don't believe him," Alex said from beside me. "Of course he did it." The comment earned him a sharp look from Lucifer.

"Who else would it be?" I asked. The Devil's head swivelled in my direction. He fixed me in his mesmerising stare. At least I'd drawn his attention away from Alex.

But instead of blasting me into eternal damnation, the Devil stared at me with genuine curiosity in his eyes. "That is a very good question, Miss Winter. Any ideas?"

This time I wasn't going to take the bait. "How should I know? It's your company." Lucifer raised his brows and fixed me with his most beguiling look. And he was very good at it, too. Handsome, sexy, polished and smooth, everything a hot-blooded woman desired, except for the eternal damnation – losing your immortal soul forever – part. I shook myself out of his hypnotic gaze and said, "Because I really do believe you did it." Breath constricted in my throat. For a moment I imagined suffocating here in Hades where my mother would never know what happened to me. Whether the image came from Lucifer or I could just attribute it to healthy mortal fear, I couldn't tell. I forced a brimstone-laden breath past my constricting throat and continued. "It only makes sense that with most of your assets tied up in a court case that will likely go on for eons, you might turn your attentions to Earth. Acquire a new revenue-rich property, as it were."

To that, the Devil really laughed, so hard that fat crocodile tears rolled down his cheeks. The mountain shook with every chortle. Alex gripped my shoulder in alarm, ready for whatever Lucifer might do next.

Finally the Devil stopped laughing. He wiped the tears from his cheeks with the backs of his taloned hands. I didn't even know the Devil could cry! He opened his mouth to utter some pithy comment, then snickered some more.

He pointed a black nailed finger at me. "Ah, now I remember why I wanted you so badly in my corner." Another snicker. "I'll admit, it's not a half bad idea, one I'll have to give some further thought to." He leaned forward on his imposing throne, close enough that his hot breath ruffled the crimson cloud of my skirt. "But you couldn't be more wrong, Porsche." That obsequious use of my name so annoyed me I almost missed what he said next. "I really *didn't* do it."

I said, "What!"

The Devil sat back against his throne, letting the implications of his innocence sink in.

And as I was looking into his self-satisfied face wondering how I was going to get us out of this total disaster, the stone floor beneath me suddenly dropped away.

From what seemed like a great distance, I heard Lucifer cursing loudly.

I felt the impact of cold, hard ground, followed by a blast of frigid air. I blinked, trying to bring the vista into focus.

Somehow I'd landed half way up a mountain, high enough in altitude to have snow. Ski paths stretched an indeterminable distance to a picturesque chalet. A multitude of ski tracks crisscrossed the hill, evidence of the place's popularity. Without a locator, I couldn't tell where I was. Apparently, somewhere they had snow in July.

Snowy peaks towered above me. Drifts marked the boundaries of the ski slopes. Suddenly, I had the most awful feeling just who had yanked me out of Lucifer's clutches.

Alex landed less delicately, face first in one of the drifts.

Then everyone started talking at once.

"Porsche! What in Hades was that message about?"

My dad's voice. I turned, very slowly, trying to hike the bodice of Lucifer's fashion creation higher. Something buzzed across my line of sight, showering me with snow. Cupid, and in a spiteful mood. "Hey!" I brushed ice from my hair.

"What is it with you!" the cherub demanded.

"Do you have any idea how much trouble you've caused?" inquired yet another voice. It took me a moment to recognise that whiny voice. Thorny Percy. Oh no. Which meant it was likely only seconds before we were granted a visitation by either Uriel or Gabriel.

But before I could answer to any of it, my dad took notice of Alex. "Who is *he*?"

I raised both hands toward the sky that threatened more snow. Bad idea, it only made the bodice slip lower, exposing more of my goose-pimpling flesh to possible frostbite. "Everyone just hold on a minute!"

Reaching out a hand to Alex, I helped him to his feet. Half naked as he was, he was starting to shiver uncontrollably.

He took one look at Dad, backed up, slipped and fell back into the snow. I yanked him to his feet again, nearly losing my own footing in those damnable spike heels.

I had to admit, Dad made an imposing figure, even clad in a black ski suit. Snow bleached his skin to greater pallor. The black didn't help, but then I'd never seen my dad in any other colour. To me, he just looked normal. But his skeletal face was instantly recognisable, along with the bony frame beneath the ski suit. Even his ski poles had tiny scythes on the handles.

Dad looked from my outfit back to Alex, visibly drawing all the wrong conclusions.

They were all staring at me now, waiting for me to say something, except for my Dad who was busy sizing up Alex. Obviously, he was not impressed.

"Dad – this is Alex . Alex, this is Charon, my dad."

Alex still stared at my dad like he might eat him alive. Eventually, he remembered his manners and held out his hand.

But Dad marched past me and stuck a bony finger into Alex's chest. "Are you sleeping with my daughter?"

I said, "Dad!"

Alex dropped his hand.

Desperate for his own chance to berate me, Cupid buzzed into the fray. For the first time, I noted he wore a tiny, red ski suit of his own. I didn't even know he owned such a thing. "Are you trying to ruin us all?"

"What?" It was all too absurd. I couldn't make my brain work.

"I sent you three messages. And you ignored them all!"

Mentally, I flipped back through Cupid's cryptic messages. The beheaded roses, the bed sheet sculpture of a she-devil, and Lucifer's face in the clouds. "I didn't ignore them." Anger flared to the surface. I was five-foot one, standing in a seven-foot snowdrift half-naked and being accused by the people closest to me. "I couldn't figure out what they meant!"

Cupid flapped his wings in irritation churning up more of the snow spray. "I was quite explicit!"

I wrapped my arms around myself, too angry at the moment to shiver. "Explicit and obtuse!"

He hovered at eye level, wings creating an uncomfortable breeze. Just moments ago I'd been sweating in Hell. Tiny icicles formed wherever moisture met my skin. Cupid opened his mouth to berate me, but my temper got the better of the situation.

"You made a heart of roses on the living room floor. How am I supposed to know what that means?"

"Love is Hell," Alex piped up. My dad shot him a sharp look, then shrugged. Maybe they had more in common than they realised.

Cupid glanced at Alex in annoyance. "Figures."

"Well?" I asked, "What did it mean?"

The cherub sniffed. "The roses were supposed to represent me. It meant I hadn't found out anything yet and to sit tight."

I said, "Huh?"

"I saw it," Percy piped in. "It really wasn't that clear." I nodded my thanks.

"Well, it hardly matters," Cupid continued in a huff. "Because I sent you another message to beware of Naamah."

"The bed sheet?" I asked incredulously. "That's what it meant?"

Cupid said, "Duh!"

"Wouldn't have figured that," Alex muttered under his breath between shivers. Cupid glared in his direction.

"Fine then." Cherubs might be small, but they have big tempers and Cupid was truly angry now. I couldn't tell if it was because I'd got him in a fix, or that his grand attempt at intrigue had been a dismal failure. "But you'd have to be totally dense to miss the portrait of Lucifer in the clouds!"

"I saw it."

"So did the television news and all the tabloids," Percy chimed in. He held up a selection of tabloids as evidence.

"APOCALYPSE LOOMS!" one of the headlines read, accompanied of course by a lurid photo of the devil's face in the clouds.

Alex took one look at the paper in Percy's hand and groaned. "Oh no."

A competing paper had gone for the more poetic headline: "DOOM MEETS GLOOM!" A closer shot showed the Lucifer's image in vivid colour, then elaborated with a story about the looming apocalypse.

"Okay, I saw it, but . . . " I dragged my gaze from the tabloids back to Cupid who waited for my pronouncement. Seconds dragged on.

Suddenly his eyes widened as understanding dawned that I really hadn't got the message at all. "It's not Lucifer!"

I stared back at him. "Well I know that now! He told me himself!"

Wind whistled through the peaks, the only sound for several seconds. And then everyone started talking at once again.

"Which raises the question – " Percy began.

"Your mother's going to kill me," my dad muttered.

"Don't even go there!" I told both of them.

But Cupid was undeterred. "How could you be so stupid? How could you even talk to that snake?"

"I covered for you with Gabriel once," Percy said. "But covering up a trip to Hades is too much to ask!" Anger twisted his face. I'd never seen him express a strong emotion before.

Resigned to catching hell from my mother, Dad vented his frustration on Alex. "You still haven't answered my question. What are your intentions toward my daughter?"

"Dad!" I stamped my foot against the snow. The spike heel penetrated the ice covering, sinking my foot up to my ankle. I yanked my foot out of the snow and realised I could no longer feel my toes. "Stop it!" I demanded. "Stop it all of you!"

They were all staring at me now, Alex included. "Fine for you to criticise my actions," I said through the deep shivers that worked their way down my spine. "But I asked for Heaven's help and you turned me down!"

"I helped you!" Cupid snapped. "And look at what good it did me! I gave you that locator in case of an emergency and you ran all over the Earthly and Heavenly planes with it." Perturbed, he slowed the flapping of his wings, dipped a little, then resumed fluttering at a more leisurely pace. He had to be getting just a little tired by now. "Wait until Gabriel figures out where it came from," he finished.

"I'm sure Gabriel has it pinpointed with deadly accuracy," Percy said. "He just can't prove it."

Cupid hissed in annoyance.

"Will you be in a lot of trouble?" I asked Cupid.

Another little snarl in my direction. "What do you think?"

"I'm so sorry." I looked up at the sky, which had started to snow on me. Alex was turning blue from the cold, and our breath was creating plumes in the freezing air. "I really was trying to fix things. But now things are more messed up than ever."

"No good deed goes unpunished," Alex growled. Dad glowered at him for a moment, then smiled. Sounded like his philosophy. No wonder my parents didn't get along.

"Forget it," Cupid said. He didn't sound overly sincere. "You're the one in danger of permanent residence in Hell." He shot a glance at Percy, who was digging in the snow with the toe of his boot. The Guardian Angel looked up.

"I've got to admit, Porsche, it doesn't look good." Percy lifted his chin in Alex's direction. "For you or Alexander Chalmers."

"Great." I paced away from them, tottering and slipping in my high heels. Finally, I gave up and simply concentrated on keeping my balance. "How can they pin this one on me? I asked for Gabriel's help!"

"Actually," Percy interjected, "Gabriel specifically told you to mind your own business."

"But locusts were eating up the city!" I protested. "And Naamah was prancing all over the Earthly plane doing the Devil's work!" As one they opened their mouths to object. "Or so I thought," I said quickly.

"But now we know it isn't Lucifer," Percy pointed out. "And you willingly joined forces with the she-devil."

Alex came to my rescue. "That's not true! Naamah tricked her!"

Dad shot him a look that said they'd be settling this later. The look he gave me was slightly friendlier. "You must have known something was wrong because you left me that message."

I sighed. "By then we were already in Naamah's custody."

"So you hinted."

I tottered over to my Dad and hugged his bony frame. "But you rescued us from Lucifer's clutches. Thanks Dad."

Suddenly another thought occurred to me. One more scary than what Gabriel or even Lucifer might do to me. "What were you doing with Cupid?"

Cupid said, "Hey! I was worried about you!" But the look they shared did nothing to calm my fears.

"He's not trying to fix you up is he? Because that's just . . . weird."

"What's wrong with me?" Dad demanded. "I'm not so bad. I have needs"

And neither of them bothered to deny it.

I groaned. "Just send me back to Hell!"

Watch what you wish for.

Because the words had barely left my mouth when I felt my body disintegrating.

"Damnation!" I said into the void. And hoped my next destination would be warmer.

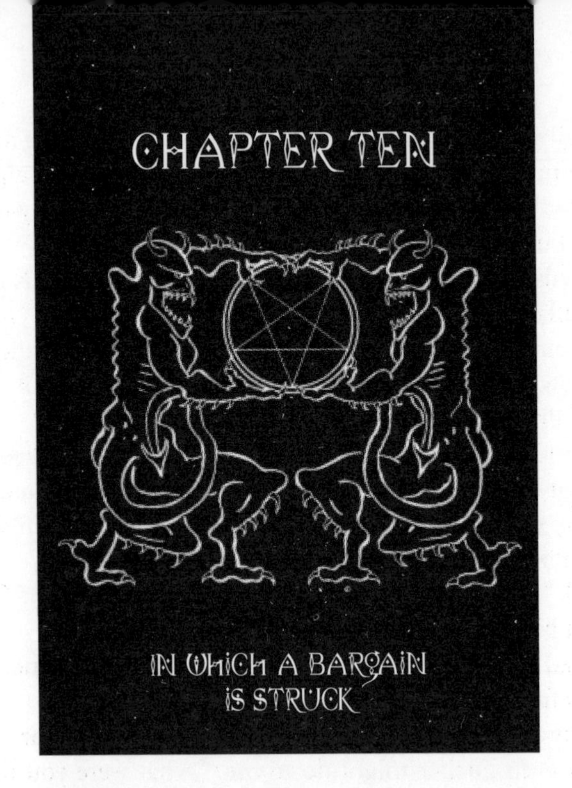

IT WAS.

I landed with a thud hard enough to snap my teeth together. But at least I was sitting upright, even if it was on a chair carved from rock. I gagged on brimstone and choked.

"How dramatic," came a voice from the other side of the room.

A snap of his fingers and suddenly, I could breathe. I raised my head to find the Devil staring back at me.

Anger stole my good sense. I leapt out of the stone chair, scattering my skirts around me. "Do none of you know how to knock?" I demanded.

I faced the Devil and exhaustion caught up with me. Since I'd last been to bed, I'd been hijacked through Heaven and Hell and dumped halfway up a mountain. But it hadn't taken the Devil long to locate me.

"I know everything about you, Porsche. Every petty jealousy, every vain hope." His eyes took another leisurely roam over my body, which was mostly exposed from the waist up. "Everything."

"The details of my life make a boring tale," I bluffed.

Lucifer's smile broadened, showing the white tips of his teeth. "Not at all. I especially enjoyed the pictures."

"Stay out of my personal affairs, Lucifer." I managed to sound suitably insulted. A sudden thought occurred to me. If Lucifer had raided my personal file, hacking into my nightmares wouldn't have posed much more of an obstacle. "And I'll thank you to stay out of my dreams as well!"

His eyes widened slightly, betraying his surprise. He recovered swiftly. "Been dreaming of me, have you? How sweet."

The Devil stood up. Ignoring me, he wandered around his office, coming to stand looking out over his domain.

"I have a proposition for you," Lucifer said at last.

He turned, skewering me with those red-tinged eyes.

"Not interested," I said. "Your last proposition didn't work out so well for me."

"It could have." Was it my imagination, or did the Devil actually sound petulant? "I would have treated you well, Porsche."

Ugh, I hated it when he used my name. It implied an intimacy we didn't share. An intimacy I certainly didn't want. "Define 'well.'"

The smile faded and I knew I'd finally succeeded in angering him. Definitely not a good thing, but at least he'd stopped leering at me. "Do not seek to annoy me, Miss Winter. That wouldn't be at all wise." His eyes blazed crimson. I forced myself to stand my ground.

"Gabriel already tried the glowing eye thing," I snapped. "It didn't work for him, either. And, for the record, I don't work for you, Lucifer. I never did. And unless the Highest Court decides otherwise, my soul is still mine. And you can't have it!"

Lucifer clapped his long-nailed hands. "Quite the speech, Miss Winter, however unnecessary. I do give you points for chutzpah, though."

I desperately wanted out of the dress. Hard to engage in warfare with your breasts on display.

"Just get it over with then. Tell me what you want, so I can refuse."

He sauntered up to me and stared right down my top. "Oh, you won't be refusing me."

I said, "No?"

"No," he repeated almost in a whisper. "Because I have something you want."

"And what would that be?"

"To defeat Naamah and save your precious Earthly plane."

Okay, he had me interested there. But if I gave in that easily, he'd just use it against me. So I said, "Naamah is your responsibility."

The Devil absorbed the verbal blow with another of those leering grins. "Quite true. But on this one, I could use your, shall we say, unique talents."

I was almost afraid to ask, but I had to know. "What unique talents would those be?"

"The ability to blend in on the Earthly plane, for one."

"Yeah, well don't get excited. I probably only have minutes before Gabriel discovers us together and locks me up in his jail again." Or worse. I refrained from sharing Gabriel's threat of eternal damnation with the Devil.

"Gabriel's jail is no barrier to me," Lucifer sniffed.

And I remembered how easily he'd sprung me last time when I'd been willing to pay him with my soul.

That was the problem with the Devil. He could waltz into your life oozing sex appeal and sincerity, while you bargained away your immortal soul. And spent eternity in the bowels of Devil's Mountain.

And the worst thing about Lucifer and his questionable tactics was that he used a smidgen of the truth against you. A tiny jolt of your own fears and a healthy dose of your most desperate need. I did want to defeat Naamah. Most definitely, even if it was just to get even with her for trying to steal my boyfriend.

A terrible feeling of uneasiness crept down my spine. I still didn't know how Alex had come to be in Naamah's custody. Or why he'd suddenly taken to sculpting she-devils. I filed my confused feelings for Alex under 'Deal With Later'.

Much as I hated to admit it, Lucifer had a point. I'd risked everything to ask for Heaven's help, and they'd refused me. But I simply couldn't allow Naamah to unleash Hell on Earth, not if I could prevent it.

I chewed my lip and considered the Devil standing before me. For the first time in my life, I didn't know what to do. Right and wrong blurred until I couldn't tell them apart. To join forces with Lucifer meant risking more than jail. I wanted back in Heaven. I wanted my life back.

I wanted *me* back.

If I helped Lucifer I could lose it all. Forever. And yet, the Devil was asking, almost politely, for my help.

That in itself deserved careful consideration.

Lucifer yawned. His forked tongue flicked over his lips, testing the air. Testing me. "Hurry Miss Winter, I don't have all day."

Don't do it, that squealing voice inside counselled.

A flaming hourglass appeared above my head. Lucifer glanced at it quizzically.

"What's in it for me?" I doubted I could believe the answer. I knew I couldn't count on the Devil to keep his word. But I asked anyway.

To my complete amazement, Lucifer said simply, "Nothing."

The Big Guy be praised, an almost honest answer from the Devil. "Nothing?"

"You help me get what I want. I help you get what you want. We'd be even."

"And what I want is?"

"To stop Naamah from stealing your current squeeze and unleashing Armageddon." The Devil paused. "And to prove to your mother you aren't your father's daughter after all."

I stifled a groan. Trust the Devil to push my most volatile buttons. But the sad truth was that I was most definitely my father's daughter. Lucifer was mistaken if he thought he could use that against me. I'd accepted the truth long ago. Not that I'd ever share that with the Devil. "And you want to help me do this why?"

Lucifer glanced at the hourglass. The trickle of flaming sand was almost gone. "At the moment, it suits my purposes to rein in an over-ambitious employee."

So the Devil had uncovered Naamah's attempt at corporate espionage.

But the head she-devil still fell under Lucifer's influence. Who knew how he'd taken the news. Or what he meant to do with that knowledge. "At the moment," I repeated. Which implied that could change with every passing second.

"It suits my current plans," Lucifer qualified. "Which means this is a red light offer, Miss Winter. Decide. Now."

Panic set my heart racing. I'd managed to trap myself in the worst of dilemmas. Above all, I wanted to protect life on the Earthly plane. If the Devil thwarted Naamah's plans, Earth would be granted some peace. At least temporarily. The last grain of flaming sand trickled through the hourglass.

"Okay. I'll help you," I said quickly. And felt iron bands clench around my heart.

"Good." The Devil smiled.

My stomach clenched. "Now explain to me how we're going to defeat Naamah, and next time I want some warning before you scatter my atoms over half the Nether Regions!" I stamped my foot against the rough floor and winced as my spike heel caught and wrenched my ankle. "And we're not even going to discuss the specifics until I get better clothes!"

To demand anything of the Devil was lunacy beyond belief. It left you beholden to him. But I simply had to get into something better suited to the climate. Something I felt I could cope better in.

Lucifer regarded me without emotion. Only a slight flaring of those red eyes betrayed his anger. "Such a shame," he said. "I suppose you want something less . . . revealing."

"I want a proper uniform."

"Done," the Devil hissed.

By the suffocating feel of tight PVC encasing me from neck to ankles, I knew I'd made a grave error in judgement. I glanced down, finding myself in the same form-fitting black catsuit Naamah wore, with the red pitchfork insignia over the right breast. "Not *your* uniform," I said, enunciating each word. One had to be specific when dealing with the Devil. "*My* uniform."

"You have no authority to be wearing such a thing," Lucifer reminded me.

"Then leave off the insignia," I growled back.

The Devil yawned. "Whatever."

Soft silver fabric enveloped me, material that allowed me to move and breathe. I flexed a flat-soled boot against the stone and sighed in relief. As I'd requested, well demanded actually, the right shoulder lay devoid of any rank or designation. *Quit now*, the little voice inside advised. I ignored it. "And I want weapons."

One of Naamah's miniature flamethrowers appeared in my hand. I shrugged. "That'll do."

Lucifer raised one black eyebrow. Dressed casually this time, he wore black jeans and a black t-shirt that clung to every muscle. I forced myself to remember that his form was as changeable as the weather. "Will it?" He nodded to the flamethrower in my hand. "With that tiny lighter you would march into battle against Naamah and my former minions?"

So the Devil *had* discovered the extent of Naamah's betrayal. I wondered how many minions he'd tortured to gain the truth, or if he realised what he'd just revealed.

I hefted the flamethrower and shrugged, trying to look nonchalant. "Well, yeah."

"Not much of a plan."

"Got a better one?"

"Of course." Lucifer looked so stunned that I might have doubted him I almost snickered. Almost.

But before he had a chance to expound on his grand scheme, my body became incorporeal once more.

"No!" I screamed as I found myself sailing back through the dimensions.

Diffuse light made my eyes water after the gloom of the Devil's lair. The scent of flowers should have lifted my spirits. Would have, if I hadn't materialised practically under Gabriel's nose.

"Well, Winter, you do get around." Gabriel glared down at me.

I let my temper loose. "Will you stop tossing me around like a ping-pong ball! What is it about me that everyone wants a piece?"

My outburst took Gabriel off guard. "Why don't you tell me?" he asked in a dangerously quiet voice.

I sighed. "I wish I knew."

The Head Archangel shot a disgusted look at my uniform. Devoid of insignia, technically he couldn't say anything about it. Thank The Big

Guy he hadn't seen the red dress.

I took stock of my surroundings. Gabriel had the biggest office, but with Michael, Uriel, Raphael and Percy crammed into it, a few more square feet would have suited me fine. Especially with Michael standing there in battle armour as if he expected serious trouble to arrive momentarily. Gabriel wore formal robes like he'd been summoned from somewhere more important. One glance at Percy's guilty expression told me exactly how I'd come to be in Heaven just now.

"Percy – " I wondered if smacking him could possibly land me in more trouble with Gabriel.

He glanced down, abashed. "Sorry, Porsche. I didn't know what else to do."

I gave him a glower to rival Gabriel's. Percy blanched and fell silent.

"Since relieving you of your locator didn't stop you from invading every plane in The Great Beyond, obviously we need a more effective method of restraining you." Anger rolled off him in waves. "And believe me, Porsche Winter, there are worse things than jail and eternal damnation."

Worse than eternal damnation? My heart thumped in panic. "Surely that's not necessary – "

But Gabriel wasn't listening. "Don't think I don't know where you got that locator, either."

Percy cleared his throat. "She may have purchased it on the black market. Lots of hardware went missing during the war."

I beamed my thanks at Thorny. I didn't want Cupid catching the wrath of Gabriel on my account.

"It could have," the Head Archangel conceded. "But I much doubt it."

"The war's not over," I said, pointedly and earned myself a challenging glance from Michael. A long silence followed.

The other archangels remained uncharacteristically mute, and that frightened me even more. I couldn't imagine Uriel giving up a chance to blast me again. I looked in their direction and discovered what held them in such thrall.

During our raid on Hell, Gabriel had converted his office into a war room. A huge bank of monitors still covered one wall. He hadn't re-arranged the furniture yet. I glanced past Gabriel who had opened his mouth to give me another tirade. And then the view on those monitors changed.

"That's why we thought we should withhold judgement," Michael said.

Raphael cast an unreadable glance in my direction. I couldn't see Uriel's face from that angle, but Gabriel just looked grim.

I gawked at the scene unfolding on the monitor. Considering me out of the way for the moment, Naamah had obviously stepped up her plans.

Armageddon reigned in high-end holographic Technicolor. The downtown core with its glass buildings had taken the brunt of the brutal hailstorm. Smashed windows gasped like toothless mouths. Store awnings had been shredded. Deserted streets had emptied of cars and people. The abandoned automobiles that remained had broken windshields and roofs nearly as dented as the surface of the moon. Locusts had stripped the city and surrounding farmland of vegetation. Wind and rain had ripped down tree trunks and toppled light standards. Without power, the city lay in darkness.

A wasteland. One about to get worse.

No stranger to inclement weather, demons crawled from under manhole covers and emerged from drains and sewers. Bogeymen leapt from under beds and out of closets.

Everything in Hell that crawled, slithered or lumbered was now emerging on the Earthly plane.

"NOW WILL YOU DO SOMETHING about this?" Anger battled my good sense. My voice rose in spite of my fear of Gabriel's wrath and the promised fate worse than eternal damnation.

"Porsche," Percy's voice trembled. "As your Guardian Angel, I really have to advise you to – "

Gabriel turned on both of us, a flurry of white robes and blazing azure eyes. The movement nearly unseated his halo. I winced, sincerely wishing I'd kept quiet. Percy shut his mouth quickly.

"*We* have to do something?" Gabriel's whisper rose to a near shout. "For the second time you've meddled in things that were none of your concern." He waved to the monitors still broadcasting the carnage on Earth. "This is all your fault!"

"*My* fault!" Somehow we'd become caught in a circle of finger pointing and name-calling, behaviour more typical of Lucifer's minions than angels. No longer a member of the Heavenly host, I was still ashamed. But that didn't stop me from flinging the blame back at Gabriel. "I warned you this was coming! I asked for your help. Twice," I added self-righteously, holding up two fingers.

"The time for debate has passed," Michael said, the only voice of reason in the room. He nodded toward the monitors. "We must act swiftly and decisively."

Uriel glanced from the lurid holos back to Gabriel. "I agree with Michael. We can deal with Miss Winter later."

I said, "Hey!" By dealing with me, Uriel likely meant locking me in one of Gabriel's golden jails while I awaited my doom.

Michael cocked his head, studying me with grey eyes. "I disagree."

"What?" asked the three remaining archangels in perfect chorus. Even Percy looked surprised.

"Our Miss Winter has some . . . hybrid talents that might be useful."

"Porsche Winter has dealt with the Dark Angel on two occasions – that we know of," Gabriel said in a shuddering breath. "She has proven only that she cannot be trusted." He virtually panted with indignation. "And she is no longer Ours!"

"Thank The Big Guy," Raphael muttered. Uriel nodded his agreement.

Ah, thanks Rafe. It hurt that I'd never been able to convince Raphael I hadn't been in league with Lucifer. Not willingly in any case.

Gabriel was still intent on doing battle with Michael while Uriel, Raphael and Percy hovered nearby ready to intervene. Gabriel ramped up the wattage on those eyes and glared at Michael. But then Michael was not only an archangel, but also Head of Special Projects a.k.a. the Commander of Heaven's army.

"Be that as it may." Michael made a valiant attempt to stare Gabriel down. "She still falls under our jurisdiction. She's an asset we should put to our use."

"Hello? I'm standing right here!" It was too much to bear.

Punish me, but don't discuss me like I had neither ears nor feelings!

Uriel strode up to me. "And you'll stand there silently," he snapped.

Looking up into his face, I couldn't see a shred of mercy. I said, "Yes, sir."

"Lucifer trusts her, even if we don't," Michael argued.

Oh, thanks, Michael, you're a huge help!

But Gabriel turned his attention back to the monitors and the steadily worsening news. "Perhaps," he said thoughtfully, conceding Michael that one point.

"Gabriel – " Raphael stood between Michael and the Head Archangel. "You can't be considering this! I gave Winter a second chance. She used it to contact Lucifer."

"I used it to impress upon Alex the dire consequences of consorting with Lucifer," I corrected, coming to my own defence. "And I'm the first to agree that I used questionable tactics, but I did uncover the biggest scandal ever to rock the Beyond."

"Silence!" Uriel ordered. "We're all well aware of how you handled the matter."

I ground my jaw shut.

Gabriel studied Michael for a long moment while we all fidgeted with nervous energy. "When it comes to Lucifer, you and I will never agree," he admitted finally.

Michael accepted that pronouncement with a nod.

"But, much as I hate to admit it, when it comes to Miss Winter you might have a point," he said with distaste. "Being half-demon, she has an affinity with the netherworld none of us share. We should take advantage of that."

Suddenly jail wasn't looking so bad after all.

"Gabriel, you can't be thinking of – " Uriel began.

"It won't work out the way you hope," Raphael warned.

He ignored their protests with a wave of his hand. "As you say, Michael," Gabriel nodded to the monitors, "this matter requires our immediate attention. And, the former guardian Porsche Winter might be useful in infiltrating the Dark Angel's stronghold."

Uriel, Raphael and Percy waited for his pronouncement.

"So," Gabriel said, as if the words burned his tongue, "I'm putting you in charge of this project."

Michael hefted his helmet, ready to depart.

"But if you fail," Gabriel's voice drew him back. "We will be doing things my way."

"Allow me to assess the situation first hand." He shot an unreadable look in my direction and blatantly discarded Raphael's warning. "I'll take Miss Winter with me."

Relief washed over me. At least Michael didn't intend to leave me for Gabriel, Uriel and Raphael to vent their anger on. But then he grasped my arm. I looked up into fathomless grey eyes that studied me and sized up my worth all in one fraction of a second. Trouble was: I couldn't decipher the answer.

Before I could protest, or as much as look back at the other archangels, my feet left the ground. I flailed slightly, still not used to be being hauled all over the beyond in this human body. But Michael steadied me.

I looked behind me into the clouds and saw a multitude of glowing lights following us. Michael's army assembling. But instead of following us in a flaming wave, they halted there in the haze, waiting.

"Let's start with a little reconnaissance."

Reconnaissance! I wanted to scream. *We're out of time!* I opened my mouth to protest. But one look at Michael's severe countenance silenced me. He was the most intense of the archangels. Gabriel might be famous for his temper, but he had far more bluster than impact. With Michael, a great deal went on behind those grey eyes. A great deal I should have worried about. It was suddenly obvious that I'd been on Michael's radar for some time. And right now he hoped I'd deliver him Lucifer's head on a plate.

When he realised it wasn't Lucifer's head we wanted, things were bound to turn ugly.

Tossed again into the ether against my will, I fell Earthward.

We coasted in for a perfect landing in downtown Toronto. Or at least it looked like downtown. Hard to tell with the glass in nearly every building smashed and the streets devoid of even a passing car. Hail beat upon us. Michael donned his helmet. I put my hands over my head.

Grey eyes slid sideways. I said nothing about my discomfort. Trust me, Michael wasn't the kind of guy you wanted to whine to.

He waved his hand. A rush of warm air surrounded me. I stood under an invisible, protective umbrella. Rain and hail cascaded around me. I looked at Michael and grinned.

The archangel stared past me. His face changed, focussed. A demon crawled out of a dark storefront. Glass crunched around and beneath its bulk as it exited through one of the plate glass windows as though it wasn't there.

Michael raised his discourager and fired. One neat shot, so smooth I barely noticed him draw. The reek of charred flesh revealed that he'd hit his target. But it didn't matter because more demons crawled from every dark crevice, quickly surrounding us. I unclipped the flamethrower from my belt. Michael glanced at me and smiled. A grim smile, the kind you'd give an adversary.

I dealt a few demons some third degree burns. But their hides were a great deal thicker than mine. And they kept coming.

Rats poured from beneath a sewer grate. Their claws clicked against the pavement as they raced toward us. In the darkness of the abandoned storefront, I saw a horde of minions assembling.

Around us every kind of creepy thing that inhabited Hell skulked and shifted in the shadows.

"Enough reconnaissance for you?" I asked Michael as I fired off another blast of flame. The flamethrower would soon be out of juice. "I don't suppose you brought a spare discourager?"

He shook his head. "You're no longer one of Heaven's flock, Miss Winter. You're not licensed."

"So change the rules," I grunted, ready to use hands and fists if need be.

But just as I was about to toss the spent flamethrower on the ground in disgust, a low chuckle cut through the sounds of battle.

"Well now, isn't this a sight." Naamah sauntered into view. My jaw dropped. She was still wearing a uniform, but a somewhat abbreviated version of it. A blue leather halter top impressively displayed her breasts, and the effect was heightened by a faux bullet belt casually slung over one shoulder, diagonally crossing her body. Her flat stomach was bare, revealing a golden pitchfork charm dangling from her pierced belly button. She wore a pair of blue leather micro-shorts, and her legs were encased in matching thigh-high stiletto boots.

She stopped and regarded us, one hip thrust outward as her tongue licked her lips suggestively.

"Slumming are you, Michael?"

Rats lined up behind her in furry rows. Minions assembled in the shadows. The demons shifted nervously from foot to foot awaiting her orders.

I glanced at Michael, who was raptly staring at her. Good grief. Was that all it took to throw Heaven's finest . . . a pair of legs that went on forever and a bust you could drown in!

Naamah's eyes bored into mine as she sauntered closer. "Wouldn't have thought Heaven would take you back so easily," she said.

She walked a slow circle around us. "Or that Lucifer would have let you go."

That Lucifer had let me go came as a huge surprise to the head she-devil, but she covered it swiftly. Obviously, Naamah hadn't expected me to survive that encounter. In order to have escaped his clutches unscathed, she knew I had to have made some kind of deal. And that meant Lucifer now knew of her deception.

I watched as understanding dawned in her disconcerting eyes. Understanding, and something infinitely more evil. That Lucifer had let me go instantly convicted me. One glance at Naamah and I could tell she had the death penalty in mind.

I elbowed Michael in the ribs to try and snap him out of it, and heard his discourager start to charge up.

Her face lit up. "How dramatic. Oh, do shoot me, Michael. It won't change anything. My minions will conquer the Earthly plane. There's nothing you can do about it." A good bluff. Anyone else would have been fooled. But I read fear in her faceted eyes.

Undeterred, Michael merely laughed. "Now there's where you're wrong, little she-devil."

"Very, very wrong," said a honey-smooth voice from behind us. Lucifer's voice. My hackles raised at the sound.

Michael tensed. The grip on his discourager tightened. His gaze slid sideways, trying to decide whether Naamah or the Devil posed the greater threat. For a split second, he wavered.

Foolishly, he settled on Lucifer.

"No!" I screamed as Michael whirled, discourager blazing.

Laughing, the Devil dematerialised. The beam gouged a smoking hole in the pavement where he'd been standing. Demons shrieked. In a wave of scaly hides, they retreated. Only for a second though, on Naamah's orders they surged forward again. The rats followed after them. Minions overflowed the abandoned storefront.

Still chuckling, Lucifer reappeared. "Surely, you didn't expect to hurt me with that *toy*," he taunted Michael.

Tossing his discourager aside, the archangel went after Lucifer with his fists.

Everything happened at once. A wave of demons gushed toward us. I emptied my flamethrower into their front line. The smell of burning flesh seared the air. I didn't have enough juice left to deal with the rats, and minions rushed to close ranks with the demons. Michael dived at Lucifer. Wrapping his hands around the Devil's throat, he knocked Lucifer off his feet. They fell to the pavement. Lucifer got in a lucky punch. Michael grunted, and for a moment I thought the Devil had the upper hand. But then Michael rolled on top and proceeded to try and grind Lucifer's face into the pavement.

I hesitated, not sure whom to try and grab for. I knew from experience you really didn't want to get between those two. Not even Gabriel would try that. Hail began to fall on my head as Michael's attention to my protective bubble wavered. Somehow, I had to divert his attention from the Devil and back to the battle, I realised.

Throwing caution to the wind, I lunged at Michael.

I shouldn't have let my attention lapse.

A sudden blow from the side knocked me sprawling. The flamethrower hit the ground with a metallic ping. I saw a flash of blue, then one of Naamah's sharp heels gouged my leg. So much for Michael's protection. In his haste to get at Lucifer, the archangel had let his concentration lapse. His bubble had collapsed, leaving me vulnerable. And Naamah, if nothing else, was never one to miss an opportunity.

I slammed my knee into her stomach. She absorbed the blow with barely a grunt. In retaliation she bashed my head against the concrete. Stunned, I tried to keep my wits about me. I wasn't going to win this fight, I realised. Trapped in a human body, I couldn't match the she-devil's superior strength. And my only weapon was a spent flamethrower.

The overpowering lure of her perfume urged me to surrender, but panic kept me fighting.

Still struggling against Naamah's weight, I groped on the ground for a rock, but there were only pebbles within reach. My fingers closed around the barrel of the flamethrower. I forced my body to relax, feigning surrender. The she-devil grinned in triumph. I slammed the flamethrower against her head.

My unexpected offence caught her by surprise. Heaving her off me, I ran.

Naamah shrieked in outrage. She scrambled to her feet and gave chase. Even in those stiletto heels, I couldn't outrun her. Rats covered the ground like a furry carpet. They raced between my feet, trying to aid their mistress by tripping me.

"Michael!" I yelled. But the archangel was too busy trying to pummel Lucifer to notice my distress.

I ducked behind the rubble of an abandoned storefront, barely escaping a bolt from the she-devil's flamethrower. Nearly falling over chunks of brick and plaster, I dashed in the direction of what I hoped was a back door. Flames licked at my heels as Naamah incinerated everything flammable in her path.

A minion snatched at me as I barrelled through the back door, now hanging by a single hinge, and raced down the garbage-strewn alley. The passage opened back onto the street where Michael was still doing battle with Lucifer.

I gauged the distance between the archangel and me. Surely, if I wedged myself bodily between the Devil and Michael, he'd protect me, wouldn't he?

Not much of a plan, but it was the only one I had. I raced toward Michael.

Searing pain and burning flesh seized my attention. Agony hit with such shock it stole my breath. I gasped and spun dizzily. The smell of my own charred skin made vomiting a definite possibility.

Naamah hauled back on her flamethrower. A satisfied grin spread across her face. I was afraid to look down and assess the damage.

Even in my angel body, that blast would have done considerable damage, as a human it became deadly. I didn't need to look down to know it was bad. Very, very bad. Ironic, I thought, that after all the battles I'd fought, after all the demons I'd faced, after I'd braved the depths of Hell, I might die as a mortal on Earth.

Darkness encroached from all sides. I couldn't think past the pain. I fought to stay conscious. I floundered, trying desperately to remain standing.

Awareness swam away from me. I thought of Alex, Cupid and my dad, all wondering what happened to me. I thought of my mom.

I barely felt the impact as I hit the pavement.

For an instant, everything seemed to slow down. I saw Michael raise his head and let go of Lucifer. The Devil craned his neck for a better look.

Shouting, all around me. And none of it made sense. I dragged in a gasping breath around the pain that seemed to constrict my throat. Then my body became incorporeal.

Michael, I thought distantly. It had to have been Michael.

Why? I thought as my atoms spun through space. Why, when Heaven could have so easily been rid of me, had Michael saved me?

What happened after that is still unclear.

I remember sailing through space in pieces. At least they were pieces that didn't hurt. I couldn't seem to make my brain work. And for a while everything seemed to swirl in a bright fog. At some point they must have put me back together in one piece. I recalled Gabriel looking down at me with disapproval, while Percy begged for Heaven's intervention.

Uriel and Raphael also passed through that dream state, or perhaps it was just a nightmare. I think even my mother put in an appearance in one of my hallucinations.

Lucifer came and went in my delirium, asking banal things like how I was feeling.

Like hell, I think I told him. His laughter echoed through the chamber.

This can't be Heaven, my scattered brain reasoned. They never would have let Lucifer in while the question of his ownership was still contested in court, not even dragging my smoking corpse.

I wanted them to contact Alex and Cupid, tell them I was all right. But I wasn't all right. And I couldn't make my mouth work.

I realised the haze had cleared. I sat up. Gingerly.

I wasn't in Heaven. I was lying in the middle of Alex's king sized bed. I felt my right side, where Naamah's flamethrower had barbecued half my body. The skin was tender, but whole.

More scars. Just what I needed.

I took stock of the room. Michael and Gabriel conferred quietly in the corner. Alex sat in the big chair by the bed. Cupid stretched out on the bureau, toying with the arrows in his quiver. Percy leaned against the wall.

And standing at the foot of the bed, like a dark shadow, was Lucifer.

I groaned. "What are you doing here?"

"Tsk tsk, Miss Winter, is that nice?" the Devil asked. "And after I was so concerned for your welfare."

"Your concern is not a good thing." I barely recognised that hoarse croak as my own voice.

Seeing I'd gained control of my faculties, the room stirred to life.

"I agree, the Dark Angel's notice is not a good thing," Gabriel repeated with a scathing glance at Lucifer. "But we are powerless to remove him. He holds joint custody on the Earthly plane."

I knew that. He didn't need to explain metaphysics to me.

Time was missing from my memory. It seemed like hours had passed. But that couldn't be. Unless they had managed to defeat Naamah and her legions of minions, they'd still be out there fighting.

I opened my mouth to ask, but just then something crashed outside. Loud and close by. Percy glanced out the window and winced.

"How long – " I began, then cleared my dry throat and started again. "How long has it been?"

"Not long." Alex got up from his chair and went to the bathroom for a glass of water. My fingers curled around its comforting coolness. I held it to my cheek. "We were all wondering where you went." He shot a furtive glance at Lucifer. "Well, we had a pretty good idea."

"Until you came crashing in here with Michael," Cupid added. "And Lucifer." He brandished one of his arrows at the Devil, reminding him of how much damage those little arrows could do. Lucifer merely snorted in return.

"My dad?" I asked.

"He went to talk to you mom," Cupid supplied with a sideways look at Alex. And again I had to wonder what had been said in my absence.

"That can't be good," I muttered.

"Probably not," the cherub admitted.

Hail pelted the roof. It had been going on for so long, I was almost used to the insistent drumming. But then the sound of breaking glass from somewhere outside shattered the uncomfortable silence.

"We have to get back out there!" I levered myself off the bed and held onto the wall for support. "We can't let the forces of darkness win!"

Everyone glared at Lucifer.

"No offence," I said hastily.

"The minions of Hell *are* Lucifer's concern," Gabriel proclaimed.

"And this is no time for a turf war!"

Gabriel's face coloured with anger at my outburst.

But just then Michael said quietly, "I agree." He moved toward Lucifer, every step screaming menace. The Devil held his ground. The air practically crackled with the tension between them. "As much as I'd like to take this opportunity to settle things with the Dark Angel once and for all – " he continued, then sighed heavily in disappointment. And he looked really, really disappointed. "We cannot allow Lucifer's usurper to conquer the Earthly plane."

"It's plain that the Dark Angel is not in control of his domain," Gabriel added.

"Liar!" Lucifer snarled. "You're the one that allowed them to overrun the Earthly plane." The Devil appeared ready to take a shot at Gabriel, but with Michael standing between them, there wasn't much he could do without despatching Michael first.

"With Naamah on the rampage, it's obvious that Lucifer is not *completely* in control of his domain," Gabriel amended with much restraint.

"Many legions are still loyal to me." The Devil sounded like he was trying to convince himself as much as the archangels.

"And many aren't." Another comment from Michael full of quiet malice.

Lucifer tensed, ready to launch himself at Michael. But then he swallowed uncomfortably and admitted, "So it would seem."

"Leaving Hell Ltd. ripe for a takeover," Gabriel said. He let the significance sink in.

"Seems that while Lucifer was gunning for a piece of Heaven, he neglected his home front," Michael observed dryly.

I waited for Lucifer to hit him for that. Shockingly, he didn't.

"While Gabriel has a point," I cut in, "if we allow Naamah to gouge herself a place on Devil's Mountain, it will completely destroy the revenue stream from the Earthly plane."

Just standing made my world spin. Percy reached out to steady me. "All the more reason for us to work together to avert this – this disaster," I added weakly.

A heavy silence followed.

"Surely," Gabriel began, "You aren't suggesting we work with Lucifer – "

By the expression of distaste on the Devil's face, I could tell he found it equally repugnant.

"I will not," Lucifer's voice rumbled through the room, "work with the likes of . . . them!" There was a momentary puff of sulphur as the Devil spat the final word.

Seeing that I was still swaying on my feet despite Percy's steadying grip, Alex eased me back down onto the bed. But even sitting on the side of the bed made my head spin and I leaned against him for support. He was still wearing the well cut jeans that Lucifer had outfitted him in, but he'd pulled a t-shirt on to cover up his chest. "It's not a half-bad idea, Porsche. But I can't see it panning out."

Hell raged outside. The minions of Hades crawled across the city, destroying it in their wake. And this bunch of so called experts picked this moment to debate corporate culture. I just couldn't let the discussion die. Somehow I had to keep them talking.

"Perhaps what we need is an impartial judge," I suggested. "A mediator."

Cupid caught my train of thought. His eyes brightened and he hovered at eye level. "Who did you have in mind?"

"I was thinking Nemesis."

Lucifer hissed at the mention of the Angel of Retribution's name.

Michael shrugged. "Might work."

"I hardly consider your lawyer an impartial source," the Devil snarled. He drawled the word lawyer.

Thunder rumbled. Lightning sizzled across the sky, momentarily blasting the bedroom into searing light. Something crashed below on the Pier. Waves smashed against the shore.

Gabriel looked up as if he could see through the ceiling of Alex's apartment. He still wore his formal robes. His halo was still balanced precariously above his head, and not a hair was out of place. Don't know how he did it. Except for Michael, the rest of us looked exhausted. Even Lucifer looked the worse for wear. His designer clothes were ripped and stained with ash. But then, none of us knew what was happening in Hades. The Devil was already doing battle in his own realm.

The head archangel looked from Michael back to Lucifer. Me, he studied for a long moment. I tried not to fidget. "All right then. Send for Nemesis."

No sooner had he spoken the words, when I felt the static of a locator beam. Down the hall came the rapid-fire tap of high heels on parquet flooring.

"Well, I can see my help is definitely needed here," said an efficient female voice from the bedroom doorway.

Nemesis.

She wore an expensive-looking navy blue suit. It clung to every curve, while still managing to maintain an air of authority. Her blonde hair was still cut in a bob and every hair was sprayed into place. And her brown eyes blazed with challenge.

She nodded to Alex and me. She shook hands with Michael and Gabriel and waved to Cupid. Her eyes slid past Percy, noting him with interest. Stopping in front of the Devil, she merely said, "Beelzebub."

Lucifer curled his lip in distaste.

"So, what brings me here?"

"We need you to negotiate an . . . agreement," I said.

At the sound of the word agreement, her eyes widened in surprise. I had to admit, just thinking of an agreement that involved Lucifer, Gabriel and Michael was incredulous enough in itself. But other than that, nothing betrayed her emotions. "Interesting, tell me more."

"We find ourselves in a situation." Every word seemed to burn the Devil's tongue.

"Actually, *you* find yourself in a situation," Michael corrected.

Lucifer clenched his hands and his nails lengthened into claws in preparation to take a swipe at the archangel.

"A situation that concerns us all," I said, jumping into the fray before the whole thing degenerated into name-calling and hair pulling. Perhaps that kind of in-fighting had been part of Naamah's plan all along, I thought.

Quickly, I filled Nemesis in on everything that had happened in the past few days, including a few details I'd neglected to tell Gabriel and Michael. "So, I promised to help," I finished. And hoped it didn't sound as lame as I thought.

"Inadvisable," Nemesis snapped.

"As the Guardian Angel on duty, I agree," Percy said.

The two of them sounded remarkably like my mother. The effect was spooky. I regarded the square of carpet between my feet. "I know."

In my torn silver flight suit with a foot-long burn across my midriff, I made quite a picture. The kind you see in war movies. Nemesis inventoried my many scrapes and gashes silently. "But you do have *unique* talents to offer this cause. And they deserve . . . compensation."

"Now wait a minute!" The Devil's eyes blazed crimson. Skin stretched across his face as his jaw lengthened. I thought for a moment he'd degenerate into Demon Face right in Alex's bedroom, but then he controlled himself and the transformation reversed. "I will not be held hostage here. This joint . . . undertaking benefits us both."

"I'd say you're already being held hostage," Nemesis replied coolly. Lucifer's outburst hadn't ruffled a hair on her sprayed bob. Nemesis considered Lucifer to be some bizarre kind of extreme sport.

The Devil's eyes brightened. His face tinged crimson. A streamer of steam billowed from the neck of his shirt and curled in a lazy spiral from his head.

Michael glanced at him and shook his head in disgust. "Oh cool it, Lucifer. You did ask for our help."

"I asked for Miss Winter's help," the Devil said in an amused whisper.

"And she asked for ours," Gabriel pointed out.

I didn't add that they'd refused.

Cupid flitted to the window and looked out. "Forgive the interruption, but we have no time to waste here." The gathering whirled in his direction. Lucifer's annoyed glance alone looked ferocious enough to blast him into ash. But Cupid had also done battle with the Devil. "And if things are this bad on the Earthly plane, I shudder to think about what's going down in Hades," he said quietly.

Lucifer let his breath out in a slow hiss. Some more sulphurous steam escaped. "Fine," he snapped. "Let's discuss the terms."

Everyone turned to Nemesis. Laying her briefcase on the bed, she snapped it open and took out her notepad. She jotted a few notes in red ink with an engraved fountain pen, and then considered her handiwork.

Rumour had it that Nemesis' red ink was blood. I didn't want to think about it. From within her sleek briefcase Nemesis produced a handheld computer and called up a boilerplate contract.

She tapped the tip of her stylus against the screen in her hand. "Here's what I propose – "

"Do enlighten us." By the Devil's tone, you'd think he was bored. But he clenched his taloned hands into fists.

Nemesis looked from Gabriel to me and back to Lucifer. "A settlement – "

"No!" said Gabriel and the Devil at once.

The Angel of Retribution held up her hand.

"You haven't even heard the terms," Alex said. Everyone glared at him. He shut his mouth quickly.

Michael said, "I doubt I want to."

Nemesis tapped the toe of one tasteful shoe against the floor. "Listen up, time *is* of the essence."

"Agreed." Gabriel said reluctantly. "Tell us the terms."

"Heaven Inc. will loan Hell Ltd. the, ah, resources, to defeat Naamah and return the company to its former power structure with Beelzebub at the helm."

There had to be more to it than that.

"And in return, Hell Ltd. will relinquish its claim on its shares of Heaven Inc."

"No!" the Devil roared. "I will not settle!" Losing his precarious control, his face contorted. Fangs lengthened. His jaw snapped, bones rearranging. With difficulty, he brought his temper and his face back under control. "I bought those shares in Heaven Inc. on the open market, with legitimate funds."

"*Legitimate*?" Michael scoffed. Nemesis shot him a warning glance. With surprising acquiescence, the archangel fell silent.

Nemesis turned to Lucifer. "It is unlikely the courts will decide in your favour."

"That remains to be seen." He said the words with conviction, but the Devil didn't look quite so sure.

Lucifer's bluster didn't faze Nemesis at all. "Time is running out for you, Beelzebub. The more likely outcome is that you will lose your claim to both Heaven Inc. and Hell Ltd."

Something crashed against the side of the building. Debris kicked up by the storm, or a rock thrown by one of Naamah's catapults.

Nemesis fixed Lucifer with her penetrating gaze. They faced each other, worthy adversaries. "Do you really want to take the chance of losing Hades as well?"

ANOTHER SECOND TICKED BY PUNCtuated by the thump of more hail against the roof. I imagined the Earth as Naamah wanted to make it with desolation stretching in all directions. The destruction wouldn't last long. With that kind of power, it wouldn't take Naamah long to rebuild. I pictured she-devils and demons driving in refurbished cars, riding on escalators in shopping malls and commanding the Earth's financial centres . . .

"Hurry up, Satan!" Michael's voice cut into my thoughts. "You can fight with us or against us. But if you fight us, remember you'll be fighting on two fronts. And you'll probably go home empty handed."

It was too much for the Devil to take. "Shut up!" he roared. "Let me think!"

"The time for thinking is long past," Nemesis pointed out. "We have an offer on the table. A worthwhile offer. Take it or leave it."

With an audible snap, the bones in Lucifer's face shifted again. His mouth grew into a wolfish snout. His shoulder blades popped out of alignment, drawing back into his spine. Clothing peeled back from his body like the skin of a rotten banana. Liquid skin flowed over his arms as they lengthened and became wings. But the black talons at the tips of each finger remained. His legs shortened until two hawk-like feet stretched out from his torso. A spiked tail cracked the air.

The Devil rose above us, cracking the top of his bony skull on the low ceiling of Alex's apartment. Sinking his claws into the wall, he hung upside down from the ceiling and regarded us with glowing red eyes.

"Hey, that's my ceiling – " Alex started to say. One blink of those red eyes and he quickly shut up.

Cupid looked at Nemesis. "Was that a yes or a no?"

I glanced at the Devil hanging from the ceiling. Fond of offering dilemmas, Lucifer now choked on a gulp of his own medicine. "Looks like he's thinking it over."

The words had no sooner left my mouth, than the Devil launched himself from the ceiling and swooped down over us, sending Cupid sailing across the room. Alex ducked. I made a grab for Cupid. Michael, Gabriel, Nemesis and Percy held their ground. Until today, I wouldn't have given Thorny credit for having that much backbone.

Hovering in mid air, the Devil's body reformed. His spine lengthened, arms and legs grew out of wings and talons. I sincerely hoped his new persona included clothes.

Fortunately Lucifer materialised in battle armour. Encased head to foot in padded leather, black of course, he strode up to Nemesis. "I accept your terms."

A breath that I'd been holding seemingly forever escaped. Under the terms of Naamah's settlement, Lucifer would have to surrender his disputed shares in Heaven Inc., thereby undoing the events set in motion the night Gnurr escaped with Alex's soul. Everything would be put back the way it was. Finally, I had a true chance at redemption.

And all I had to do was live through the next few hours.

"Fine." Nemesis tapped furiously on her computer. She offered Lucifer the stylus. "Sign here."

The Devil shot a dubious glance at the tiny screen.

"We'll carve it in stone for you later." Nemesis offered.

Lucifer took the stylus between his talons. Flame leaped from the tip of the stylus searing itself permanently across the screen of Nemesis' computer.

"No need." The Devil handed it back to her.

Nemesis swallowed her annoyance. She looked to Gabriel and Michael. "So witnessed?"

"So witnessed."

Nemesis tucked the ruined palmtop back into her briefcase and snapped it shut. "Then gentlemen, it would appear we have a deal."

With that she strode from the room. The sound of her high heels echoed down the hallway, then abruptly stopped as she returned to business elsewhere.

Michael took control. "Very well Satan – assemble your troops. You have five minutes."

Lucifer's lip curled at the order. The floor of Alex's apartment disintegrated. The Devil disappeared in a plume of brimstone. The hole closed over with a thud. Carpet repaired itself, except for a dull smudge where Lucifer had been standing.

Michael looked at Cupid. "Arm the cherubim."

"Aye sir." With a warning glance in my direction, Cupid winked out.

"Wait a minute," I said into the silence that followed. "We can't just wage war in downtown Toronto. We'll be seen!"

Gabriel peered out the window. "We'll use the storm as coverage." He raised his locator. "I'll be in the war room." He nodded to Percy, "Mr. Thor?"

Percy raised his own locator and followed Gabriel. Every angel who knew how to wield a discourager would be pressed into service in this battle, I thought. Instead of fighting the minions of Hell on one front, we now had two.

"What about me?" I asked Michael as Gabriel disappeared. "You have to let me fight."

Michael gave me an appraising glance. "I don't have to let you do anything."

I strode up to him. "It's a matter of honour."

"You should have thought about your honour before you allied yourself with Lucifer."

"Ouch," I said. "That's not fair. I had no other choice!"

"Perhaps," he relented, and looked hard at me again. "But you're human."

"You could restore me to angel form," I ventured. A risky proposition. But I so wanted to fix everything, to put things back the way they'd been and forget the past few weeks had ever happened. Like anyone else would let me forget. "Temporarily," I added.

Tilting his head, he pondered that thought. "That would require special authorisation."

"I imagine it would." I nodded to the smudge where Lucifer had been standing. "But you know I can handle a discourager."

That almost got a smile from the archangel. "I'll see if I can secure that authorisation."

Alex stood up. "I want to fight too."

"Out of the question," Michael snapped.

"I go where Porsche goes." Alex said it with such authority he almost made me believe it was actually up to him. Perhaps I'd been wrong in suspecting something between Alex and Naamah other than a captive–captor relationship.

I started to agree with Michael that Alex had no place on the battlefield, but just then Alex said, "I have as much of a quarrel with Hades as anyone."

Michael input coordinates into his locator. "I'll see what I can do."

The archangel winked out of existence on our plane, leaving Alex and me alone in the bedroom. My uniform still bore a foot long gash across the middle. I looked like I'd already been to war and it hadn't even started yet.

"Think they'll let us fight?" Alex asked.

"Don't know. It's up to The Big Guy."

Alex looked at the claw marks Lucifer had left in his wall and ceiling and winced. "What do you think He'll decide?"

"I wouldn't hazard a guess. He's The Big Guy. I have no idea how He'll see the matter. But I doubt our dealings with Lucifer will please Him."

"But Lucifer's agreed to a settlement."

"And that's a deal with the Devil. You ought to know how those go."

"Hardly the way you want," he said with a grim smile. He glanced at the healed wound across my middle. "You okay?"

I offered him a wan smile in return. "Yeah. But I'm going to have a shower before all hell – "

A rush of air carried away my words. I reached for Alex as the gale whipped through the bedroom, scattering pillows and blankets and churning up anything not nailed down.

"Or not," I added.

The Big Guy must have decided in our favour because a split second later we stood at the foot of Yonge Street dressed in white battle armour. Silver combat boots and helmets completed our uniforms. One glance at Alex made me laugh.

Encased in padded leather, the winged insignia over his right breast, he looked every bit a dark angel. Not darkly dangerous like Lucifer, rather like an oversized cherub with exotic blood. Black curls and eyes contrasted with the white leather. Strangely though, it seemed like he belonged in those clothes.

"What?" he asked self-consciously.

"You make one weird looking angel," I said and laughed again.

Hail beat down the ground around us. I donned the golden helmet. Alex followed suit. Wearing the helmet, he looked even more like one of Heaven's Hosts.

"Am I an angel?" He looked horrified at the thought.

"I don't know." I studied him. Other than a new outfit, he didn't seem any different. "Try and make wings," I suggested.

His eyes widened. "*Make wings.* How?"

"Imagine wings, you know, on your back. Like this!" I pictured a pair of fluffy white wings, the kind you see in renaissance paintings. My spine prickled. I moved my shoulder muscles, flexing a suddenly huge pair of wings. Okay, that was a little ostentatious. No one needs wings that big. I made them disappear.

Alex stared at me, mouth gaping.

I grinned. "I'm me again! I'm restored!" Reality set in then. "Well, for the moment." Depending on how it all turned out.

My hand strayed to my waist, finding a new locator clipped to my belt. An interceptor was slung across my back. I even had a discourager in a stiff new holster. So did Alex. Apparently, The Big Guy intended us to fight with everything we had.

He scrunched his face in concentration. Then he glanced over his shoulder, looking, I guess, for those wings. But the only thing on his back was an interceptor in its white sling. "If I can't make wings, does that mean I'm not an angel?"

Personally, I'd take a fully charged discourager over a pair of wings any day.

"Unfortunately," I said.

Relief washed over his face followed swiftly by worry. "But I still have weapons, right?"

"Right." I thumbed the catch of that brand new holster and drew the discourager. "This one is the most important."

Alex tentatively pulled his from its holster as well.

"Okay, Combat 101." I showed him how to change the blast setting from stun to maximum destruction. You'll want to leave it there," I said. "As long as we're in battle. No sense stunning something that'll rear up a second later and come after you."

Alex gave me a nervous nod. Sighting down the discourager, he pressed the trigger. A lump of concrete rubble disintegrated, taking with it a swarm of locusts that had landed there simply because it was green. But even a discourager blast at full power didn't do much against a horde of cockroaches crawling out from beneath a sewer grate.

The air shimmered around us, our brothers in arms were arriving. I checked that Alex had his interceptor slung securely behind his back and his locator clipped to his belt.

"I'll have to explain Soul Retrieval and Teleportation later."

Alex nodded, but didn't look convinced. As long as he had discourager basics down, he'd be okay, I told myself. And I hoped that was true. I could always tow him with me with my own locator.

A golden chariot coasted in beside us, landing without so much as stirring up a cloud of dust. Michael had the helm with Cupid riding shotgun. Being the best marksman, Cupid always rode with Michael.

Two more chariots followed. Raphael and Uriel, looking terribly grim.

On the back of each chariot rode a cherub in miniature white armour with a golden helmet. I didn't recognise the cherubim. A couple of Cupid's subordinates wrenched from other duties. They didn't look friendly.

Through the storm, I saw the glimmer of other chariots coasting in. Michael's army. Finally. Percy winked into existence, commanding his own unit. Bright as shooting stars, a multitude of angels and cherubim in battle armour formed columns behind Michael.

Lightning lit up the sky, camouflaging the arrival of the Heavenly hosts. Hail pounded the empty streets around us. Every living thing with a brain had taken cover. Locusts had stripped the entire area bare of vegetation. The stubble of bushes and trees big enough to withstand the hail poked out of gardens and boulevards. Rain drenched everything else.

Oblivious to the weather, we waited for Lucifer and whatever minions he could rally to his cause. Empty streets stretched before us. Minutes crawled by and there was still no sign of the Devil.

Sighting the assembling angels, Naamah's minions crawled out from every sewer and crevice. Demons loyal to Naamah stretched across the boulevard, blocking our access to the rest of the city. Sandwiched by the lake and a line of unfriendly looking underworld wildlife, we waited.

From beneath the raised expressway sauntered a line of she-devils. No surprise there. Naamah wouldn't have risen to her post if she couldn't command her own department. Every one of them wore black, form-fitting armour. Their braided tails bore shiny black spikes. Their platform combat boots also had some nasty hardware on the toes. I sure didn't want to be kicked by any of them. And every she-devil in the column also had a souped up version of Naamah's nasty little flamethrower.

Obviously, the head she-devil had been doing some serious acquiring on the sly.

And at the front of the column of undulating scaly bodies sauntered Naamah. Instead of the form-fitting black catsuits her she-devils wore, Naamah came dressed for a party. A tiny red leather blouse tried to contain her breasts and a matching mini skirt barely covered her crotch. I caught a glimpse of red panties underneath. Her braided hair and tail bore red and black spikes that coordinated with the ones worn by her minions. The hardware on her black shoes gave literal meaning to the term "spike heels". How many outfits could one she-devil have?

We stared at each other from opposite sides of the street, Lucifer conspicuously absent.

Had the Devil found a way to worm out of the deal so soon? Everyone seemed to be thinking that same thought.

A geyser of brimstone split the tarmac. Chunks of pavement tumbled down around it, competing with the hail. Out of the steam, strode Lucifer. Not a hair out of place.

No demon-face for the Devil today. Lucifer seemed intent on maintaining his banished angel image. He wore a nearly identical version of Michael's armour, black of course. Instead of the golden helmet Michael donned, his gleamed chrome. The red pitchfork he carried matched the insignia on his uniform.

Behind Lucifer came a line of bogeymen. Pasty white faces contrasted with their black uniforms. Leather uniforms stretched to the breaking point over fat bodies. I noted an old acquaintance, Frank, at the lead and resisted the urge to wave.

After the bogeymen marched a loose formation of those demons still loyal to Lucifer. Their ranks were shockingly thin. How had Naamah managed to steal so many of the Devil's most trusted in so little time?

One of the demons recognised me. Gnurr. My hand tightened on the butt of my discourager. Gnurr curled his lip in greeting.

When this is all over I'll eat you for dinner, that expression said.

I smiled back. Gnurr and I had a history. When this was all over, if we were both still standing I'd welcome a round with Gnurr. In my angel body, hopefully. As a human I wouldn't last a second.

Lucifer led his rag-tag army to stand beside Michael. Neatly assembled, they appeared ferocious, but if that scared Naamah, she gave no sign.

The sight of all that black set against Heaven's shining white made me hold my breath.

The Big Guy must be having fits! I let the thought go. It might also be part of The Big Guy's plans, His way of putting things back the way He wanted them. That was the problem with trying to second-guess The Big Guy. He didn't share His plans.

Michael shot Lucifer a frigid glance. "About time."

Lucifer surveyed Naamah's army, the neat rows of traitors lined up against him. "Well," he said finally. "Since we're all here, let's have at it."

"Fine with me." Michael drew his discourager. With precise aim, he fired a bolt into the pavement at Naamah's feet.

That was all it took. With a roar, Naamah's army surged forward.

So much for diplomacy. But then, by demolishing a major North American city, Naamah's minions had put up enough of an offensive.

Chariots lifted gracefully from the ground, taking command of the air. The storm intensified. Columns of rain obscured our vision. Gabriel had promised to cover our activity with inclement weather. I wished he'd kept it on the other side of the street.

I let the mental gripe go. With the archangels, seraphs and Percy's guardians in the air, Michael left the ground war to the lower ranks. Meaning me, Alex and Lucifer.

Alex and I stood shoulder to shoulder, even though his shoulder was a good foot taller than mine. A minion tried to dart between us, bumping me off balance. Old reflexes came rushing back. My discourager was in my hand. I didn't even remember drawing it.

The shot hit the minion nearly at point blank range. It hissed in pain, doubling up over its middle. But then it straightened. How much firepower did it take to topple one of the things? Apparently, minions had tough hides. I flung my discourager to my other hand, ready to use my right fist, if I had to. The claws of one gnarled fist whipped out, burrowing a long furrow in the front of my armour. And I'd looked so tidy in my new white clothes. Thankfully a thin layer of leather remained. Who knew what poison tipped the points of those talons.

Alex let off a blast of his own, discouraging a demon encroaching from the side. Seeing my difficulty, he drew back a muscled arm and let the punch fly. The minion went down hard. It didn't get up again.

I nodded my thanks. As one, we turned to deal with the demon.

Chariots soared overhead. Discourager blasts furrowed the pavement. How Gabriel intended to clean up after this was beyond me. But then Gabriel had access to assets no one else did.

Michael had an entire column of she-devils on the run as he ploughed up the ground behind them. Cupid's silver arrows rained down with more intensity than the storm.

A growl brought my attention back to Alex. A demon raced toward him, faster than he could get his discourager into position. Not that he didn't try. Heat sizzled as his weapon discharged. But Alex, for all his hand-eye coordination was still only one human trying to take on the supernatural. The demon sidestepped the beam and reared back to deal Alex a killing blow.

I fired my discourager. Heat arched overhead. The demon's arm disappeared. It roared in fury and pain. I grabbed my locator, dialled coordinates and hauled Alex out of the way.

"Thanks," he said as our feet touched down several feet away.

A horde of rogue demons and bugs of all sorts had Lucifer surrounded. Even with Frank and Gnurr on his side, the Devil was losing ground.

I hated the thought of coming to his rescue, but we'd promised. Gabriel and Lucifer had pledged their joint forces to the cause.

With a sigh, I grabbed Alex's hand and hauled him with me into the fray. We worked out a system: punch, kick, shoot, with me doing most of the shooting. But Naamah had absconded with substantial numbers of the Devil's most trusted, and they soon had us surrounded.

A sudden blow knocked me on my backside. For all my enhanced strength, my head spun. It took an inordinate amount of effort to make my jumbled brain work. But the wide expanse of gleaming teeth and fetid breath sent a clear enough message. I scrambled to my feet. Alex let go a discourager bolt over my head. I heard a roar of pain, smelled burning flesh.

Demon flesh smells bad enough fresh, when cooked it defies description.

The demon swung at Alex. I lunged toward him, but I couldn't make it in time.

The impact knocked him flying. His feet cleared the ground by several inches. That was going to hurt, I thought even as my finger stabbed my locator's retrieve button. The beam snagged Alex mid-tumble. Damnation I was good.

Vanity is a sin, I reminded myself. And pride goeth before a fall that's going to hurt like hell. I forced my thoughts to be more humble.

Alex yelped as I set him down more gently on his feet. Then, his eyes widened as he caught sight of something over my shoulder.

Demon. I could tell by the stench. Alex raised his discourager. A nice gesture, but too slow to help me. I knew it already. I was a goner.

I had a fraction of a second to turn in the direction of his gaze when a discourager blast rippled the air. The demon collapsed in a foul smelling pile of scales. I looked skyward for my saviour.

Raphael's chariot whizzed overhead, close enough to ruffle the hair that escaped my helmet. I saluted. He smiled back, offering me a glimpse of the old Rafe. The cherub behind him hissed. Obviously I couldn't count all the cherubim as friends. Everyone, it seemed, had an opinion of me, most of them bad.

With Rafe's help, Alex and I had managed to clear away the outer knot of demons. But closer to Lucifer the fighting was more intense. Even the mighty Gnurr tired under the strain. Frank had plenty of weight to throw around and he had considerable skill with a flamethrower, but as a strategist he failed terribly. Frank just wasn't that smart.

A demon reared up. Frank swung and missed, leaving the Devil wide open.

I fired. The demon wailed in pain. His barbed paw hung in a charred lump of meat. But taking a demon down isn't that easy. Wounded, they just get mad.

It towered over me. The stink of smoking flesh took my breath away. From the corner of my eye, I saw its other paw coming toward me.

Oh no, here it comes, I had time to think. And then I remembered my Dad's tip.

My leg shot out, catching the demon in its knees. Demons have notoriously bad knees.

The impact jarred my leg up to the hip. The demon's knees collapsed and it fell in a lump of burning flesh.

Freed of his assailant, Lucifer let off a mega-bolt from his pitchfork. I squinted against the blast. Blinking back tears, I saw only a crater where the demon had fallen.

Gnurr straightened, giving me an appreciative look. "Rrrr," he growled, which could have been a compliment or a challenge. With demons who knew? He turned his attention to the lessening ranks of Naamah's army.

Lucifer dusted the demon's ashes off his black leather sleeve. He glanced at the hole the demon had left and bowed. "Why thank you, Miss Winter."

Oh, oh. Having the Devil beholden to you couldn't be good.

"Don't thank me," I snapped. And looked around for something else to shoot.

"Oh, but I do." The scariest thing about Lucifer was that he could be courteous when he wanted to be. He could almost seem nice.

But courtesy from the Devil came at a high price. One I could scarcely afford.

Frank rolled on the broken pavement in hand-to-hand combat (or in Frank's case, fist to flab combat) with a demon. The demon gained the upper hand. He hauled a meaty arm back, ready to take out Frank's windpipe with his barbed claws. If he could find it under the rolls of fat that ringed Frank's neck.

Lucifer raised his pitchfork, but I'd seen it first. I emptied the charge of my discourager into the demon's back. A three-pronged bolt from Lucifer's pitchfork followed. Alex added another discourager bolt for emphasis.

Frank flailed on the ground, blinded by the blast. I reached down, braced my heels and levered Frank to his feet. But the last thing I wanted was for Frank to take that the wrong way. He'd asked me out more times than I could count. And he was likely the only person in any part of the beyond who wasn't bothered by the rumours about me. I didn't want to encourage him.

I dropped my hand and wiped it on my leg.

Frank stared at me. "Hi Porsche," he said as if he'd suddenly remembered my name. His eyes shifted from Lucifer to Alex. I could have sworn his pasty flesh blushed.

Then I remembered Wynn Jarrett had told Frank the Devil wanted me for his own.

Alex glowered protectively in Frank's direction. Frank kept his eyes on the split pavement.

We'd broken through the knot of demons around Lucifer. And Naamah's she-devils were turning out to be more about fashion than hand-to-hand combat.

"Look!" Alex said from behind me. I sighted down the length of his leather-clad arm, noting it wasn't so white anymore.

Michael's chariots flew in formation, blasting down on the ranks of the she-devils from both flanks. No longer sauntering, the she-devils bolted across the expressway toward the city. But Uriel circled above them, trailing his own air force and cutting off their escape.

She-devils broke ranks and ran. Naamah's demons turned scaly tails and followed them.

Climbing up on a pile of rubble, Lucifer stared after the departing she-devils and roared in triumph. In the centre Naamah's red panties gleamed like a bull's-eye as she fled.

"Don't let them get away!" Lucifer ordered. "This isn't over!"

Michael chased after them. A multitude of chariots soared behind him. Uriel and Raphael circled around, closing in for the kill. The archangels and their squadrons attacked in unison. I couldn't help but admire their skill and efficiency. Raphael and Uriel seemed to know instinctively what Michael intended to do, even before he gave the command. Chariots hovered in the air. The archangel's forces issued a circle of discourager bolts, hemming in Naamah and her forces. Cherubim put arrows to their bows, ready to reinforce the archangel's discourager fire with a rain of arrows.

I pictured Gabriel in the war room watching it on his wall of monitors. The archangels had Naamah and her troops surrounded. Victory appeared imminent.

But then the ground in front of Naamah split in a geyser of steam. Rubble tumbled into the void. Locusts raced toward the crevice. Naamah and her she-devils leaped into the steaming mist.

Michael's forces issued another stream of discourager fire. Cherubim loosed their arrows. But with a crack that split the air, the crevice sealed over.

For a second there was utter silence. The relentless pounding of hail ceased. A ray of sunshine escaped the black clouds.

Then, from one of the leafless trees on the waterfront, came the hesitant chirp of a sparrow.

For a moment everyone froze mid-stride. Naamah's demons glanced around nervously. Then, *en masse*, they headed for every sewer grate and dark hole they could find. The archangels took down more than a few of them. But they scattered, like ashes on the wind.

Just because Naamah was in retreat, I realised, didn't mean she was beaten.

Above us came the crackle of Michael's pager. "As much as I hate to admit it – " Gabriel sounded wearier than I'd ever heard him. "Lucifer is right. This isn't over. Follow them!"

"You heard him!" Lucifer roared. "Follow them!"

Chariots winked out of existence. I pictured them soaring above Devil's Mountain, chasing Naamah back to the home front. I raised my locator, ready to follow Naamah's departing signature back into the steaming depths of Hell.

"Wait!" Alex said suddenly.

Gnurr froze in position. Frank shot me a nervous shifting glance. Lucifer looked at Alex with pure boredom.

How could he look bored beyond belief while his whole world fell apart?

"I'm coming with Porsche."

Lucifer yawned. "Mr. Chalmers, are you still here?"

Alex raised his chin and stared the Devil down.

I jumped into the argument before it could get truly ugly. "I want safe passage through Hell for Alex, or I'm not going, either." I'd learned from bitter experience to be very specific when talking to the Devil.

Lucifer planted his fists on his hips. I suppose he thought it gave him an air of superiority, but really he looked more like a spoiled two-year-old. "Mr. Chalmers wasn't part of our deal, Miss Winter."

"You asked for our help – "

"Your *help* came at a high price."

"Porsche – " Alex whispered. "Let me handle this."

But I couldn't. The Devil would just laugh off Alex's demands. Mine held slightly more weight. After all, the Devil had stopped just short of saying he needed me. And no way would I allow Lucifer to separate us. Who knew what Naamah would try while everyone was otherwise occupied. "He's not a half-bad shot," I added.

Lucifer considered him for a long moment, while the rest of our forces winked out of the Earthly plane and headed for the Underworld.

The Devil sighed. I knew that sigh. It sounded like he was doing you a favour. And if you believed that you were truly doomed. "Very well."

Lucifer snapped his fingers. Alex jumped. I had a split second to wonder what he'd done to him before the Devil disappeared in a wall of flame.

I had to hope Lucifer wanted our help more than he wanted revenge. "Come on," I said. And grabbed Alex's hand.

My locator brought us cruising in above the caldera of Devil's Mountain. Lucifer had set up his command post there. Below us, demons loyal to Lucifer prowled the caverns looking for Naamah's traitors. Bogeymen leapt out from behind every rock, chasing down Naamah's she-devils. I pictured the new upper echelon of Lucifer's forces devoid of female workers and without most of the demons who staffed it, and wondered how Lucifer would make it all work once he'd banished Naamah. But then, the Devil was nothing if not resourceful. And he had a myriad of doomed souls at his disposal.

Bogeymen corralled she-devils at the foot of the mountain. Trapped between the Styx and the pit, they had nowhere else to go. A few dived into the murky depths of the river to take their chances swimming. I caught sight of my dad in the fray. He'd barricaded the mouth of the river with his ferry and was using his pole to dunk any she-devils who succeeded in swimming the river back under water. Demons splashed into the water after them.

Alex seemed to have survived the journey with no ill effects. But even in my angel body, the heat sapped my energy. Just because Lucifer pledged safe passage, didn't mean he intended to make it pleasant.

Chariots raced across the sky. Discourager blasts rocked the mountain. Michael had an entire department of she-devils fenced in with a ring of discourager beams from the chariots under his command. Silver arrows enforced the boundaries. Demons still loyal to Lucifer moved in to relieve them of their flamethrowers and knives. They weren't going anywhere this time. Hell left nowhere else to run.

Raphael and Uriel chased down another of Naamah's legions, cornering them by the pit. A few jumped in. The rest threw up their hands in surrender.

I scoured the wildlife scaling the mountain, looking for Naamah, but I spied no red panties in the sea of black leather. Maybe she'd changed her clothes. It couldn't be easy running in that short skirt and spike heels.

"Well?" Lucifer roared behind us. "I brought you here. Make yourselves useful. Find Naamah!"

I whirled, ready to tell him I didn't take orders from the Devil. But

I'd caught him in the midst of yet another transformation. Demon face couldn't begin to describe this new persona.

The Devil's body grew to huge proportions. Hands ten feet across gripped the edge of the volcano. And still Lucifer stretched and expanded until he filled the sky. Clothes peeled from his body, discarded in tiny scraps. Gleaming horns grew out of his forehead. His fifty-foot tail snapped the air, nearly knocking Alex and me from our perch.

"We don't want to see this," I counselled. "Let's go!"

Taking Alex with me, I sailed through air thick with brimstone to give Michael some back up on the ground.

I landed in the middle of the fray. On the ground I met an orgy of flailing limbs as she-devils and bogeymen slugged it out.

It took me a moment to realise that Alex was missing.

"Alex!" I screamed. Devil's mountain bounced my voice back at me, barely audible above the fray. I cast around me. But no white uniforms brightened the knot of Lucifer's forces in black leather. Furiously, I jabbed at the locator's retrieve button. I even tried to link into the signature broadcast by Alex's locator. Static buzzed across my screen.

As far as I could determine, Alex had disappeared from the plane.

CHAPTER THIRTEEN

IN WHICH A RELATIONSHIP IS PUT ON ICE

"ALEX!" I CALLED AGAIN, EVEN THOUGH I knew it was hopeless. The sounds of the skirmish absorbed the sound of my voice.

Immediately I suspected Naamah. She had to be behind Alex's sudden disappearance. But how had Naamah managed to snag him in the middle of a locator jaunt? Technically it shouldn't have been possible. Still, we knew little about the technology Hell Ltd. had. Lucifer kept a tight lid on that kind of information.

Battle roared around me. On Devil's Mountain, Lucifer warred with the remnants of Naamah's forces. On the ground it appeared Michael, Uriel, Raphael and the guardians under Percy's command would soon declare victory. The ranks of Naamah's army thinned by the moment. Our unexpected alliance caught her by surprise. That I'd been able to unite the forces Heaven Inc. and Hell Ltd. against Naamah and her army must have come as a big shock.

So Naamah had done the one thing guaranteed to divide the sides once again: she kidnapped Alex. By diverting my attention, she'd dissolved the glue that held us together. It worked well. Already my thoughts had turned away from the war in progress to locating Alex.

Static hissed through my locator's speaker. With his refurbished soul, perhaps Alex no longer matched the database. Making allowances for that variation, I refined the signal. Devil's Mountain was about as impenetrable as lead. Still, some kind of signal should have leaked through. I tried again. Nothing.

If a she-devil wanted to hide a human being, where would she go? If the head she-devil now found herself on the run, where would she hide?

My stomach clenched at the answer. The Nether Regions of course. A plot of territory so forbidding no one would go there willingly. Souls wander forever lost in its chilling fog.

Thanks to Michael I temporarily had my old body back. If I was going to look for Alex it had to be now, before the battle ended and the final accounting was done.

I really, really did *not* want to travel through the Nether Regions. But I couldn't leave Alex stuck there with Naamah.

I stared up through the sulphurous haze of Hell. Lucifer seemed to have most of Devil's Mountain under his control. Michael and the other archangels were making considerable progress on the ground. I looked again at the grey static fuzzing up my locator screen and pressed send.

Cold mist cloaked me. I dragged in a damp breath and glanced at my locator screen. Nothing. Not even a blip.

Don't think about it, I warned myself. *Don't think about Alex, don't think about errant souls lost forever.*

I looked around. Nothing but banks of billowing mist.

You're a professional. You know how to do this, I told myself in a vain attempt to stop my imagination from running off with my better sense.

Or you thought you did, my conscience nagged. *Maybe you had just a bit too much pride.*

That might well be true. Anger shocked me back to my senses. I'd gladly do penance for that extra super helping of vanity and pride once I had Alex back.

I widened the locator field, scanning all axes. Fog swirled around me, chilling me until I shivered uncontrollably. X turned up only more static. Y showed a mountain range suddenly forming. The geography of the Nether Regions changed continuously, making tracking impossible.

Difficult, I lectured myself, *not impossible.*

I focussed on the Z-axis. The locator tugged me along in the eerie grey light. Topography morphed around me. I nearly collided with a wall of ice.

But there on the tiny screen I could barely see in the gloom came a sudden blip. I stared at the blinking light. *Please*, I prayed to The Big Guy, *just let me find him.* I coasted closer. The blip grew brighter. Not an anomaly, but a real signal. I input the coordinates into my locator.

The signal kicked in, dragging me through mist as fast as I dared go in the changing landscape. Alex's blip beeped steadily, growing brighter. I lined up the dots on the screen until the blip of Alex's refurbished soul matched the coordinates.

And still I found nothing. The red light flickered, and then dropped off my screen.

Naamah was on the move.

I widened the scope as far as the locator's settings would permit and prepared to pursue the she-devil. If I'd been faster by a split second, I might have escaped.

As it was, I didn't see the massive fist descending on me out of the bank of fog. The punch sent me spinning into the mist. My entire skull vibrated under the impact. Ignoring the shock and pain, I forced my body back to combat readiness and tried to get my trajectory under control. I needn't have bothered, because a pair of huge arms snatched me mid-turn and hauled me close.

I looked up and *up*! Into the pits of tiny eyes set into a mass of scaly black flesh. The demon stood easily ten feet tall. Gigantic wings sprouted from his gnarled shoulders. They cracked the air with a leathery snap. *Oh no*, I thought, recognising him instantly. Malacoda. *This is bad, very bad.*

But that's where it all stopped making sense. The kind of scheming and politicking that went on in Hades really wasn't Malacoda's scene. His only purpose was causing pain, and he didn't much care to whom. So what was he doing prowling the Nether Regions instead of tormenting the spoils of Lucifer's war? Unless Naamah *had* persuaded Malacoda to join her cause, which would mean a grievous loss for the Devil.

I didn't have much longer to consider this new development, because the demon prince hauled me up to eye level and examined me much as he might inspect an exotic bug. "Little annngelll," he growled. His breath was pure sulphur. I gagged and attempted to smother the sound.

"Well, see that's where you're wrong," I managed to say, desperately trying to buy myself some time. "I'm technically not an angel anymore, so if you'd just put me down – "

He roared in outrage. Scalding saliva stung the skin of my face. His tail whipped out. I flailed in his iron grip. Angel reflexes saved me. I managed to twist my lower body out of its path.

My locator was still clenched in my hand, but my arm was going numb under the pressure of his grip. I couldn't move my other hand to reach for my discourager. I doubted if the blast would do more than annoy him.

He shook me, rattling my brain even further. I kicked out with all my strength, aiming in the direction of his crotch.

It was like hitting a brick wall. He didn't so much as grunt. Pain reverberated up my leg. I had a second to hope I hadn't broken any bones. Then, with a casual fling of one hand, Malacoda sent me sailing off into the gloom.

I tired to raise my tingling hand to engage my locator. But an ice wall formed as I soared through the fog. I slammed into it back first. For a second I hung there, held up by the crater my body had created. Then I slid helplessly to the ground. Before I could draw a breath, Malacoda snatched me up by the collar. Holding me aloft, he cuffed me with a giant fistful of barbed claws. Instinct made me jerk my head away, but not fast enough. I felt his nails bite into my upper chest, rending cloth and skin. Blood fell in crimson drops, sizzling in the frigid air.

Panic cut through the pain. I couldn't die in the Nether Regions. I had to save Alex. My hand clenched. With numb fingers, I groped for the locator's recall button and prayed it was still in my hand.

My body went weightless. I heard Malacoda's grunt of surprise. His huge wings snapped the frigid air in annoyance. I felt another swipe of those deadly claws, but by then I'd become incorporeal.

The locator shot me back to my previous coordinates. I hung in the gloom for a moment, stunned, in pain and out of breath, but still miraculously in one piece. Precious minutes had been lost. I needed medical attention, but I couldn't spare the time. Cursing, I switched back to the Y-axis, retracing my steps. The bottom of the world fell out. I followed my tumbling stomach to new coordinates.

My feet met ice-covered ground. I inched forward cautiously. The fog parted. I skidded on the slippery ground, nearly colliding with a giant monolith of ice. And there, encased in a wall of ice, was Alex.

Damnation! I shouldn't have let him come with me. I'd thought I'd be able to protect him.

Instead, I'd played right into Naamah's hands.

In his human body, Alex had to be suffering. If he was conscious enough to know how uncomfortable he was. I had to get him out of there. And fast.

"Well, well." Naamah sauntered out from a curtain of fog. "Not so self-assured now, are we?"

"Give it up, Naamah, you've already lost. Michael's got your she-devils on the run. And Lucifer's already resumed control of Devil's Mountain." I purposely didn't mention Malacoda.

Naamah leaned casually against the block of ice that encased Alex. "Ah, but where does that leave you?"

How did she manage not to shiver dressed in that tiny top? My hands were starting to shake from adrenaline and the cold air.

"I'm hardly the issue here. The question is: where does that leave you?"

The head she-devil blinked her eyes. "An admirable trick merging the forces of Heaven and Hades. A trick worthy of me." She stared at me with uncharacteristic openness. "Are you sure you won't join my cause? It's not too late."

What was it about me that everyone wanted to warp me to their own purposes? Lucifer seemed determined to have me in his camp. Heaven disciplined me and cast me out, yet refused to relinquish me completely.

And now the traitor Naamah intended to lay claim to me. It was all too much. I just wanted to be . . . well, me.

I planted my hand on my discourager. "Too late, Naamah. You've already lost."

But the former head she-devil saw through the bluff. "The outcome is still to be determined, little angel. You're the one in trouble. No one will think to look for you here." She tilted her head at the ice block that held Alex. "Or poor Alex. Not until it's too late."

Poor Alex indeed. He ought to be getting at the very least a serious case of frostbite in that slab of ice, I thought, risking a quick glance at his frozen face. His eyes bulged in horror. His hands pressed against the ice. Morbid thoughts raced through my mind. Had he tried to escape? Or had Naamah taken him completely by surprise? Would a concentrated discourager blast melt the ice without reducing Alex to cinder?

If I shot at Alex's ice prison, what would stop Naamah from turning me into a pile of ash?

Clearly, taking Naamah out first was my only option. But could Alex stand a few more minutes in the deep freeze? I decided I couldn't wait any longer.

I strolled up to her until we stood eye to eye, or we would have if she hadn't been wearing those absurd high heels. Time to bring her down to size. I hooked my foot around her right ankle. She went down, backside first, onto the ice. Those miniscule panties couldn't be keeping out much of the cold, I thought with satisfaction. For an instant, I saw a rare expression of shock cross her face before it twisted into anger.

Her nails snagged the leg of my flightsuit. I lost my balance on the slippery ground. I tried to regain my balance and failed. Flailing, I tried to roll out of Naamah's way, but the she-devil dealt me a vicious kick with one of her spiked boots. It hurt – like hell. I turned the pain to fury and snatched at her tail, yanking it hard. With most of it coiled in my hand, at least she couldn't whip me with its barbed tip.

Naamah shrieked. She twisted, throwing herself on top of me. I let go of her tail and slammed the palm of my hand into her nose. Anything to get her off me, anything to prevent her from reaching for my discourager. Hot blood dripped onto my face, stinging the wounds Malacoda had dealt me. The she-devil retaliated by biting my hand.

I snatched my hand away in time to see Naamah licking my blood from her lips. She brought her face down close to mine, forcing me to look into her eyes. Looking would be a grave tactical error, I realised just in time. She was the Queen of Seductresses, after all. I forced my eyelids shut. Blindly I groped for a handful of her crimson hair and yanked with all my might. She grunted in pain, but didn't shift her weight. I slapped her across the face as hard as I could.

Her head jerked backward. She tried to return the favour, but I opened my eyes just in time. I twisted my head out of the way, wrenching the muscles in my neck. Naamah's nails grazed my face. Her hand continued its path across my chest, following the path Malacoda's claws had taken. I yelped in pain. She seized my wrists and held them over my head.

I bucked against her, trying to throw her off, but in doing so, I turned my head and looked into her eyes. With her face only inches from mine, I couldn't look anywhere else. Waves of her pheromone-laced perfume wafted over me. I choked and inadvertently breathed in even more. Reflected in her jewelled eyes, I stared back at my fractured reflection.

"Such passion, Porsche," she cooed. "Think of what we could do together." I caught the innuendo in her words.

"We won't be doing anything together," I snarled back.

"Really?" she asked. The question hung between us. I struggled for a tart reply, but between the effect of her perfume and her mesmerising gaze, I couldn't tell where Naamah's desires ended and mine began.

"Really," I repeated stupidly.

My voice sounded flat and hollow to my own ears. I was having trouble concentrating. Naamah's eyes bored into mine. I saw myself reflected in the prism of her gaze. But not the way I saw myself – the way Naamah saw me – as an object of her desires.

Not me personally, came the dull plodding thought. Naamah only wanted what she found useful to her. The Underworld was full of horror stories about what happened to those who'd outlived their usefulness. But in that moment Naamah desired my compliance, and she intended to get it by any means necessary.

She pressed my shoulders against the ice. Trapped in the net of her gaze I was having trouble remembering that Naamah was a danger to everything I held dear. I felt the heat of her body–a sharp contrast to the stinging cold of the ice. "Are you entirely sure of that?"

Of what I couldn't recall.

My senses were overloaded with the intoxicating scent of her perfume, the warmth of her scaly skin, and the weight of her stare. "I . . ." I hesitated, knowing I should be doing something vitally important, but I just couldn't focus enough to remember what it was.

Seeing my confusion, Naamah smiled. She leaned closer. Her forked tongue flicked out to caress the side of my neck.

Another second and I might have done anything she wanted. But in that same moment, Naamah had broken eye contact with me, and I lurched back to my senses.

The chill of the ice penetrated the back of my uniform, pressing urgently against my consciousness. *Ice*, I thought. Why was that so important? And then I remembered. Alex – who was counting on me to stop him from freezing to death.

I didn't want to join Naamah. The she-devil had betrayed me. And she'd just as soon kill me, and Alex.

Something must have shown on my face because Naamah frowned. I noted that lapse in concentration and turned it to my advantage.

I raised my knee and slammed it into her back. The impact unseated her. I used her momentum to scramble out from under her. She sprang to her feet like a cat.

My discourager snapped into my hand. The bolt hit Naamah squarely in the middle of that sexy little leather top she wore. I had a split second to watch her fall before I hit the send button on my locator with my other hand.

But even wounded and tumbling to the ice, Naamah managed to aim her flamethrower.

A blast of heat hit me in the arm as I winked out. Pain tore from my elbow to my shoulder, wiping out all other thought. Instinct made me keep a vice-like grip on both the locator and the discourager. Naamah was an excellent shot, I thought with grudging admiration. Better than I'd given her credit for.

I flickered out of existence, jumping to the X-Axis, and then circling behind the monolith that held Alex. Naamah's hand covered the wound I'd dealt her. Green blood leaked between her fingers. But she remained on her feet long enough to take another shot at me.

My finger jabbed the locator's send button again. I felt the heat whiz by my ear, singeing my hair as I disappeared from the axis. If I lived through this, I vowed, I'd cut it all off.

Pain brought tears to my eyes as I materialised again. The foggy landscape spun before me as I kept a tenuous hold on consciousness. I forced my eyes to focus and aimed another discourager blast at Naamah.

My shot hit her in the hand. She dropped her flamethrower. I skidded after it and snatched it up.

Keeping the discourager trained on her, I fought dizziness. Practically at point-blank range, I didn't need to be a great shot to do serious damage to Naamah. I changed the controls to maximum stun and fired. Naamah collapsed in a heap on the ice.

But how could I keep her in that state? Even maximum stun likely wouldn't keep the head she-devil down for long. Perhaps a taste of her own medicine . . .

I levelled Naamah's flamethrower at the top of Alex's ice prison. Fire spewed from the muzzle. Ice melted. Water ran down the front, hissing as it turned to steam in the humid air. Under the steady flame, the ice began to melt. I saw Alex blink, heard him drag in a ragged breath. Then he started to struggle, adding his efforts to mine.

Lunging forward, I grasped Alex around the waist. I could barely stand myself, but he managed to free his lower body from the ice and stagger free.

I glanced at what remained of the monolith of ice, measuring it against Naamah's crumpled form. The base seemed big and solid enough to serve. But making a body materialise within a solid substance took skill. I dialled coordinates on the locator and pointed it at Naamah and pressed the button.

Her body disappeared from the ground and reappeared within the ice. "That ought to keep her for a while."

Alex stared at Naamah, now a she-devil version of an ice cube, and shuddered.

Together we were barely standing, holding each other up. I raised the locator to make a quick getaway.

But where could I take Alex? We both needed medical attention.

Heaven and Hell likely still battled the last of Naamah's forces for control of Hades. And the Earthly plane was still recovering from a near miss with Armageddon. I couldn't count on being welcome in Heaven.

And even an ice prison wouldn't hold the indomitable Naamah for long. Out of options, I took the last one open to me. Encompassing Alex, the she-devil in her block of ice and myself in the beam, I punched in coordinates and aimed for Gabriel's war room. For better or worse.

Light blazed around me, impossibly bright after the orange haze of Hell and the dull grey of the Nether Regions.

"Porsche!" Alex cried in alarm.

Shouting came from all directions. Gabriel bore down on us in a flurry of white robes. Grim-faced seraphs followed in his wake.

The head archangel stared in amazement at the ice block that held Naamah like a fly in amber. He muttered something unintelligible, then motioned for a couple of seraphs to see to the matter. Arms seized me, separating me from Alex.

It took only seconds for more seraphs to appear with a large silver metal stretcher. They loaded Naamah onto it, block of ice and all, and trudged off, leaving splashes of water on the marble floor. Prison was too good for her, I thought bitterly as they hauled her away. But matters were now out of my hands.

Gabriel stood over me, demanding an explanation. Light glinted off his halo. Behind him a row of monitors showed the progress of the battle on Devil's Mountain. It looked like we'd won, but I couldn't seem to make my eyes focus. Static buzzed through my head. Whatever reprimand Gabriel had in mind, it would have to wait, I thought with fuzzy satisfaction. Fainting seemed a distinct possibility.

"Where's Alex?" I demanded, but I couldn't raise my voice above a whisper. I swayed on my feet. The floor rushed up to meet me. I tried to raise my arms to stop my fall and failed. Gabriel snagged the collar of my uniform.

White flashed across my vision, then quiet, featureless black.

I came to my senses with the feeling that a great deal of time had passed. Movement demanded my attention, but I couldn't will my eyelids to open. I heard the flutter of wings, felt the breeze on my face.

I lay on something soft and familiar. I cracked one eye open and gazed cautiously upward. It took me a moment to recognise the ceiling of my own apartment in Heaven.

"What?" I started to sit up.

Cupid planted a small foot on my chest and pressed me backward. "I wouldn't be moving just yet, if I were you."

Good advice, because even that small a movement made me dizzy again. I felt the sting of at least a dozen scrapes and the dull ache of even more bruises. The pain in my arm buzzed with a ferocity that made me nauseous. I moved my head slowly to the side and found my arm heavily bandaged. It didn't seem like a good idea to look underneath.

"Alex?" I barely recognised my own voice.

Cupid didn't look so good himself. His blond curls hung in greasy waves. His white armour was smudged and ripped. "He's in the living room." Cupid's tone spoke volumes about what he thought about that. He kept one toe against my chest in case I decided to leap up and go see. "He's okay, just a little frostbite. Don't worry."

If things hurt this much, I had to be back in my human body. Apparently my enhancements had only lasted as long as the battle. Goodbye enhanced strength. Goodbye wings. I'd never cared much for wings. Most of the time I found them a huge annoyance, but I missed them now.

I sat up gingerly and looked around my bedroom. My fluffy white bedspread still covered the bed. The closet door stood open the way I'd left it. Uniforms from Dream Central, formal robes and my silver Guardian Angel flight suits hung haphazardly. The brush on the sparkling white bureau still had blonde hair in it.

"What am I doing in my apartment?" Another more troubling thought occurred. "What is Alex doing in my apartment?"

Cupid sat on the feather pillow beside me. "I guess they didn't know what else to do with him. Because – "

"Because what?"

He assessed me, visibly debating whether I could take the bad news.

My good hand clenched the bedspread. "We didn't lose the battle, did we?"

"Of course not."

"Then what is it?" I couldn't stand it anymore. Cupid's half-answers drove me crazy. "Naamah didn't get away, did she?"

"Oh no. Naamah is still in Heaven's custody. They have her in stasis. They haven't defrosted her yet."

Coming from a warm climate, Naamah had to be hating that.

Cupid toyed with the buckles of his white armour. "You set off alarms all over with your discourager fire and your constant locator jaunts. They had to know you were incoming."

"Heaven having Naamah can't make Lucifer happy." Not that Heaven cared a wit about the Devil's state of mind. And that raised a truly troubling worry. One reflected in my best friend's concerned face.

Cupid fidgeted uncomfortably. "Actually, you're . . . under house arrest and awaiting sentencing."

So that's why I was still in Heaven. And why I had Alex as a houseguest. I guess they were waiting to see what The Big Guy intended to do with me, before they made any decisions about Alex.

Things were not nearly as neatly tied up as I'd hoped. Something had obviously happened while I was unconscious, something that made Heaven terribly unhappy.

"Oh no! What did Lucifer do?"

"Well, nothing we can pin on him, of course." Cupid punched the pillow. "But Nemesis' palmtop is missing." He gave me a moment to absorb the significance of that thought.

Suddenly I felt sick again. I measured the distance to my bathroom sink and doubted I'd make it. "If Naamah's palmtop is missing, then so is the only record of our settlement."

Which meant that we'd come to Lucifer's aid and gained nothing. Unless we could locate that palmtop, the settlement didn't exist. Lucifer still had a claim on his shares of Heaven Inc.

Along with my soul.

"But Michael and Gabriel witnessed the agreement. That has to count for something!"

"And they'll testify, but it'll still be held up in court for eons."

"But at least the Earthly plane is safe, isn't it?" I asked, desperate to find something good in this horrid turn of events.

Cupid nodded toward the holographic set in my living room. "According to the most recent newscasts, things are slowly returning to normal on the Earthly plane. They're blaming the violent weather on the thinning ozone layer."

I didn't ask about the locusts. Hopefully the reporters would find a reasonable explanation for them as well.

Earth was safe. At least Alex had a home to go back to, I thought with relief. If they'd let him.

Cupid busied himself stroking the nap of my velvet bedspread. I grabbed his chubby hand. "Okay Cupid, what else?"

He looked up at me, blue eyes wide in a soot-streaked face. "You have an another audience with The Big Guy. And," he added quietly, "a meeting with Nemesis."

Thankfully, he didn't say, *if you survive the audience.*

I shut my eyes and prayed for the room to stop spinning. "I guess that's to be expected."

My doorbell chimed. Heavy human feet moved toward the door. A familiar voice echoed down the hallway.

I grasped Cupid's shoulder. "Oh no, Cupid. My mother!"

And she was in the living room with Alex.

"You have to do something."

But Cupid only shook his head, ruffling more of his blond curls. "No."

"Tell her I'm too sick for visitors," I pleaded. "Tell her I'm dead. That way she could mourn and get over me."

My pathetic attempt at humour only angered Cupid more. The cherub leapt to his feet. Standing on the pillow he was a couple of inches taller. He planted his fists against his hips and gave me a surprisingly dangerous look. "She's your mother, Porsche. You *deal* with her."

And with that the cherub vanished, leaving me to my own devices.

Alex's head appeared around the doorframe. He looked extremely relieved to find me conscious and sitting up in bed. "Porsche, there's a saint in the living room who says she's your mother."

His eyes pleaded for rescue.

I glanced at the closet, looking for my robe and found it slung over a chair where I'd left it.

I sucked in a deep breath. No sense praying. I'd have to deal with my mother, The Big Guy and my lawyer. In that order. No escaping. "She *is* my mother, Alex. Tell her I'll be right there."

"Okay." He wandered back in the direction of the living room, not looking much relieved.

I imagined my mother sizing Alex up. What she'd think of him, I couldn't guess. But nothing I'd ever done had met with her approval. I doubted she'd approve of Alex Chalmers, former stockbroker and criminal. Fitting company for a fallen angel.

Choking back a laugh, I stood up and tried not sway on my feet. I stripped out of the filthy uniform and put on my white robe. One glance in the mirror told me I was fooling no one.

In the living room, I heard Alex say, "She'll be right with you, ma'am."

I bit my tongue to contain another snicker. Poor Alex. You'd think after all he'd been through, a saint wouldn't faze him at all. But I suspected my mom could make even Lucifer feel guilty. He'd probably call her ma'am too.

By the time I staggered to the living room, my mother was sitting on the couch while Alex milled about nervously.

"Hi, Mom." I sank down into the chair across from her a little too heavily. My mother noted the involuntary movement of my obviously human body, but said nothing.

"Porsche." With a sigh my mother acknowledged the bandage on my arm. Her blue eyes catalogued the other cuts and contusions. Death warmed over described me adequately, while my mother shone with righteousness.

She wore a sackcloth dress with a wooden cross. Her greying blonde hair was scraped back into a bun. Mine looked like a family of birds nested in it.

Alex gave off enough anxiety to electrically charge the air. I raised my head to tell him to stop shifting from foot to foot and sit down. But suddenly he blurted, "I'll wait in the other room."

Before I could stop him, he'd bolted off down the hall. I shut my eyes in embarrassment. The only other room in my apartment was my bedroom. The last thing I wanted my mother to think was that he was a frequent visitor there. By her disapproving frown, I could tell that was exactly what she thought.

My mother turned her accusing glance from Alex to me. "This time you've even got your *father* worried," she said, with emphasis on the word father. Oh poor Dad. I well knew how that parental conversation went.

"Dad had nothing to do with it."

"So he says."

"Really, Mom, he didn't."

Always the same story, arguments so familiar I might as well number them. Then I could just shout:

Yeah, well number one to you. And Mom could yell back: *Well, two and six to you! And so is your father.* Except that being a saint, my mother never hollered.

Wisely, I caught myself before I laughed out loud. Or cried. The urge to do both suddenly possessed me.

"Must we do this?" I asked. "Who knows how long they'll let me stay here for."

"Not long," my mother said.

"Well, thanks a lot."

She gave me a look filled with pain. "There isn't anything I can do to help you this time, Porsche."

I said, "I know that, Mom. It would probably be best if you stayed out of it."

"Probably it would. But you are my daughter – "

Even if you're just like your father. That could be argument number three, I thought in the darkest of humour. Mercifully, she didn't finish the sentence.

What she said next shocked me so much I could only stare back at her.

"And a great deal of your suffering is my fault."

I said, "Mom – "

"Let me finish, Porsche." Her use of my name hit me like a spear to the heart. Only my mother could use my name as such a potent weapon. "I thought if I brought you back to Heaven with me, that I could subvert your demon nature. I hoped that by raising you in a positive environment that you'd turn out to be – "

"More like you?" I supplied.

"Maybe," she admitted with a sigh.

Did it ever occur to you that I'm not what you think I am? The words stung my tongue, but I couldn't say them. Exhausted, I hurt all over, and the last thing I wanted to do was to have this conversation. But Mom showed no signs of granting me a reprieve.

"Your father and I hoped that as you matured, you'd find your own way. But what place can there truly be for someone like you – who doesn't fit in entirely in Heaven or Hell?"

A blunt, but strikingly accurate assessment of the state of my life. I opened my mouth to deny it and found I couldn't. She understood me far better than I'd realised. "I'm all grown up, Mom. It's my problem to deal with."

"Still, I wanted you to know how much your father and I regret placing this burden upon you."

Her pity twisted my gut into knots. "It's not so much of a burden being me," I protested. "The Big Guy must have a plan. Even for me."

"The Big Guy gave you another chance. He may not be so understanding this time," she said in a broken voice.

I pondered that for a moment. "No, I don't suppose he will."

Tears welled up in her eyes. And now I'd made my mother cry. Add that to my list of sins.

"I did save the Earth from Armageddon. Surely that counts for something!"

"Well," my mother said. She smoothed her sackcloth dress and stood to leave. "Let's hope so."

I stood stiffly and walked her to the door.

She hesitated, her hand on the doorknob. "I'll tell your father you're okay, for the moment. I have a feeling you're about to be very busy."

"Thanks Mom."

"Porsche – " She clutched my good arm. "I will pray . . . "

I choked back a sob. Crying would only make me feel worse. "That's probably a good idea."

She nodded, pressed her lips to my cheek. The door closed behind her. I sagged against the wall.

Alex peered out of the bedroom doorway.

"Coast is clear," I said.

He stepped cautiously into the hall. "Your parents are intense."

A polite way of putting it. "They make me crazy."

He looked tired enough to fall asleep right there. But, as my mom hinted, bigger stuff gathered in the ether. The air practically vibrated with it.

"I expected Heaven to be more serene," Alex remarked.

We sat together on the couch. "It is serene, well, most of the time."

"Like when you're not here?"

I leaned against him for support, emotional and otherwise. "Yeah, there are archangels who'd attest to that."

For a moment there really was only the serenity of Heaven to enjoy. Silence and diffuse light cocooned us. Home, I thought. I took a deep breath and relaxed against Alex's comforting warmth.

"Porsche?"

The worry in his tone made me sit up.

"I didn't want to bring it up while your mom was here, but . . . "

"But what?"

"If I'm in Heaven . . . am I dead?"

Laughter burst from my lips before I could smother it. I'd expected him to say something far worse. "No, Alex, you're very much alive."

"How can you tell?"

"Because this is the administrative level. Souls go . . . " I stopped, not sure how much I dared tell him. Poor Alex was still human, though every interaction with the beyond altered him. "Elsewhere," I finished. Still, some things he really needed to know. "Given what you've been up to lately, I can't guarantee you'd actually end up here."

Relief followed swiftly by dismay crossed his face. "Oh."

"But don't worry," I said. "Hopefully, you'll have a long time to fix that before the ultimate judgement."

"So why am I here then?"

"Guess they didn't know what else to do with you."

"But they're going to let me go home, aren't they?"

"I hope so."

Everything in my body cried out for some heavy-duty painkillers. I longed for the angel body that healed faster. Somehow I had to gather my wits before my audience with The Big Guy. Getting up, I wandered over to my music collection and set a disk spinning in midair. Alex jumped as crystal clear notes filled the air. He gaped at the disk. He came over to look at it from above and below. Finally, he stuck out his hand, stopping the disk mid-note. Soothing notes died into silence.

"Hey, don't get your fingerprints on it!"

He let it go. The music resumed.

"How does it work?"

"Superior technology. Trust me, the less you know, the better."

He nodded nervously. "I thought your apartment seemed awfully . . . sparse. I never dreamed that," he pointed to the tiny silver dome on my desk, "thing was a stereo."

From across the room he spotted the TV remote for the holographic set peeking out from under the couch where I'd kicked it weeks ago in a rushed fit of housekeeping. Alex picked it up and pressed the red button.

Holographic images shot upward from the transmitter hidden in the floor.

"Wow!" He walked a slow circle around the Utopia Channel logo. The scene dissolved as the station went to news. I snatched the remote from his hand and turned it off. News was the last thing I needed, especially when I was guaranteed a starring role. A grey smudge marred the white wall behind, evidence of the last time I'd been unhappy with the content of a newscast. I'd heaved a boot at Lucifer's image. "I don't suppose they'd let me take that home?" Alex asked with a hopeful glance at the nearly invisible transmitter in the floor.

I shook my head.

"Too bad," he muttered wistfully.

"Like I said . . ."

"The less I know, the better."

"Right."

"Okay then. I'll just sit here on your couch some more and behave."

"Please." I glanced in the direction of my bedroom. "I'd better clean myself up before . . . well, before whatever's coming."

What came wasn't the summons I'd been expecting.

I was just turning to head for the bathroom when the holo set roared back to life. The logo for Hell Ltd. burned across the image. I glanced at the remote in my hand, but my finger was nowhere near the power button.

"Oh no," Alex said. My thoughts exactly.

Lucifer's face filled the picture. Somehow he'd managed to hack into the transmission signal. But then Lucifer's garrison included demons, bogeymen, lawyers, network specialists and hackers.

He'd hijacked a strong signal, too, because I could see most of the Devil's private office in the background. Naamah's forces had done considerable damage in Hades if the carnage in Lucifer's lair was any indication.

"Porsche, Porsche, Porsche," the Devil said.

Dressed in tailored black pants and a silk shirt he was seated on his imposing throne. It seemed things had returned to normal in Hades.

I resisted the impulse to say *Lucifer, Lucifer, Lucifer,* or worse, *that's my name, don't wear it out.* Instead, I just nodded. "You're hijacking a private signal, Lucifer."

The Devil yawned. "Oh, I know." He looked around my apartment with interest.

His perusal made me feel invaded and violated. Heaven had to be tracking this. It sure didn't help my case. "What do you want?"

"Why, I wanted to thank you, of course."

I said, "Don't bother."

"Oh, but I must. I'm in your debt, you see." He said it like that was a good thing. Gabriel would be eavesdropping on every word, while my estimation in The Big Guy's eyes steadily dropped. If it hadn't hit rock bottom by now.

"Fine, I expunge your debt."

"Oh no, Miss Winter. That just wouldn't be right."

Anger squeezed out my pain and exhaustion. "Since when do you care about what's right? You went back on our deal, Lucifer. You never had any intention of honouring our agreement!"

The Devil leaned into the image, filling it. "Prove it."

"I'll testify against you."

But Lucifer only laughed. "I'm sure you will." Sitting back in his throne, he toyed with the skulls on each armrest. "Say hi to The Big Guy for me," he said.

His image disappeared.

"Oh, that's all I need," I said to the empty air.

"It's never over, is it?" Alex asked quietly.

I shook my head.

A chime echoed through the apartment.

Alex looked around as if something else might appear out of nowhere. “What’s that?”

“A summons,” I said.

And I ran for the bathroom to squeeze in that shower before I faced The Big Guy.

TIME MIGHT FLOW DIFFERENTLY IN Heaven, but I took the shortest shower in recorded history. Wrapping a towel around my hair, I barrelled out of the bathroom, nearly running down Alex who'd followed me into the bedroom.

"Wait for me here," I told him, shrugging out of the bathrobe and snatching up the nearest formal robe in my closet. "That is, if they let me come back."

I stuffed my feet into silver slippers and dumped the towel on the bed. Running the brush through my hair didn't improve things much.

"What if they don't?" Alex looked around my bedroom, barely suppressing panic.

"Don't worry, I'm sure they won't leave you here."

"What if they do?"

"Cupid will help you." I automatically reached for the spare halo still sitting on the shelf. It gleamed fluorescent gold in the subdued light. I wondered if it would make any difference.

"Oh great, that makes me feel much better," Alex said.

I longed to stay and reassure him, but any second that summons would drag me to my audience with The Big Guy. I had to be presentable.

One glance in the mirror made me groan. "Oh, The Big Guy have mercy! I look like a drowned rat."

Alex mumbled a noncommittal reply, still irked at the possibility of having to rely on Cupid.

Holding the halo above my head, I gave it a quick spin. Did I even have the right to wear the thing? I expected it to come crashing down on my nose.

But to my total amazement it spun there, perfectly balanced above my head. My damp hair sprung into place, fluffy and dry. My arm abruptly stopped hurting. I flexed my hand, finding it healed. I gingerly removed the bandage. I was whole.

I gawked at the stranger in the mirror, now nearly as unrecognisable as my human twin.

My face glowed with health. The scrapes and bruises had vanished, leaving perfect, unblemished skin. My eyes were clear, and sparkling. The dark circles that betrayed nights without sleep had faded. My white robe clung to me in all the right places, hinting at the perfect muscle tone I had so missed as a mortal.

For once I actually looked like an angel. I practically shone from inside. Someone wanted me to make a good impression.

From the mirror, Alex stared back at me. I couldn't read the expression on his face. He looked . . . stunned.

I turned to face him. "What?"

He closed the space between us. He raised his hands to grasp my shoulders, and then thought better of it. "You're . . . different. You're gorgeous."

He stared at me the way he had the first time I appeared in his apartment with an equal mixture of awe and terror. Really seeing me for the first time.

I shrugged, accepting the compliment. "Well, this is me. Or at least it was."

His hand traced the shape of the halo spinning over my head, feeling the vibrations in the air. It took more energy than I remembered to keep it there. Abruptly, he pulled his hand away.

A variety of emotions crossed his face. I watched him struggle to accept the reality of what I really was, and the cruel truth that with me in his life, he'd never have a moment's peace. If they let me come back to him. He seemed poised on the edge of making a big decision. I couldn't guess the verdict.

"Alex – " What could I say? What should I do? When it came to Alex, I no longer knew right from wrong.

Fate intervened on whatever I would have said to him. The air snapped with the power of a strong locator signal.

"Wish me luck," I called into the void.

I didn't hear what Alex said back.

Light this time, instead of the darkness I expected. My feet touched down on something solid. But when I looked down my white robes and silver slippers gleamed as brightly as everything else.

I shut my eyes against the brilliance. When I opened them, the illumination had sunk to a more comfortable level.

I stood in the bright silence and waited.

In the distance a desk appeared. White, like the light, like the floor and everything else. I walked toward it.

A chair materialised in front of the desk. An order, not an invitation. I sat down.

Behind the desk tiny pinpoints of light swirled in the brilliance. Light became energy. Energy became head and shoulders, arms and torso. In the next instant The Big Guy sat behind that massive desk.

White suit, white shirt, white tie, white hair. No beard. A very different Big Guy than I'd met last time. Obviously, today He was in a minimalist mood.

Clear eyes stared back at me. Eyes that reflected the universe.

I gasped, blaringly loud in the silence. But then I reasoned it didn't hurt to show a little awe in front of The Big Guy.

Nothing stood between us. Nothing to distract The Big Guy from me or from what I'd done.

Stillness stretched into eternity, The Big Guy merely gazed at me. No expression crossed His face. What went on behind those clear reflective eyes was anyone's guess. Sometimes they seemed still as a pond at dusk, at other times monumental events rippled beneath their surface. So many things overlapped within them, I felt humbled to have troubled Him.

"Porsche Winter," He said finally. No big booming voice fit to shake Heaven and Earth. The Big Guy didn't indulge in Lucifer's false grandeur or pyrotechnics. He didn't need to.

Still, His outward calmness unnerved me.

I swallowed and tried to think of something to say that might ease the reprimand which was certain to come.

But The Big Guy waved His hand. "Behold Wynn Jarrett." Beside Him a nucleus of light began a slow spiral.

I stared into those pinpricks of light, but if Wynn was in there, there wasn't enough left of him to tell. Suddenly I understood. What The Big Guy showed me was Wynn Jarrett practically reduced to his component parts. Wynn Jarrett reduced to atoms, destined to spin like a decorative snow globe beside The Big Guy's desk.

A stab of panic shot through me. Did The Big Guy show me my own fate?

"Does he – " I began and then realised I talked out of turn, before I'd been given permission.

But He merely stared back at me with those eyes like smooth glass, waiting for the rest of my question.

"Does he know?" I whispered. My voice came out ragged and hoarse.

Something churned beneath the surface of those eyes, but his face remained as compassionate as ever. "Oh, yes, he knows. Every minute passes for him, just as it normally would."

I stared at the raw materials of Wynn Jarrett trying to imagine the horror of living out every passing second in the equivalent of cosmic goo, unable to participate in any of it. My mind couldn't quite grasp the terror.

"It seems like an extreme punishment to me," I blurted before I could stop myself. The Big Guy hadn't asked for my opinion.

I looked into His eyes expecting to find condemnation there. But all I saw was kindly pity, so I continued, "I know Wynn sold Heaven's secrets to the Underworld, which allowed Lucifer to plot a hostile takeover, but still . . ."

"And who do you suppose is punishing him?"

A simple, yet deceptive question. I pondered it as Jarrett continued to circle in front of me.

Suddenly I realised I had it all wrong. Jarrett *was* being punished, but by no-one other than himself.

"He *chose* this?"

The Big Guy nodded sadly. "Such is his remorse."

Guilt wasn't an emotion I would have attributed to Wynn. I'd never seen him express regret for anything. That he would opt for such a severe form of atonement made me wonder if I'd ever known Jarrett at all.

"How long does he have to stay like this?"

"As long as he chooses."

"You wouldn't leave him like . . . that would you?"

"Of course not," The Big Guy said with a reassuring smile.

My gaze kept straying back to Wynn. "I . . . I feel sorry for him," I stammered.

"You pity him?" The Big Guy's question drew my attention back to Him.

"I loathe what he did. I can't understand why he did it. But I feel compassion for his suffering," I answered truthfully. The Big Guy would know the blatant truth whether I sugar coated it or not.

"Ah, and therein lies the contradiction within you."

He was leading me on, showing me the circuitous path of my own mistakes. I had no idea what to say.

"I know what it is to be confused," I admitted finally. "I know how easily someone can be misled."

If The Big Guy intended to reveal something to me, I'd better pay attention. Even if it hurt.

"It comes down to wisdom," The Big Guy said. "And free will."

"And knowing the difference." Suddenly I understood.

"There are moments when I almost regret adding free will to the mix," The Big Guy mused.

Now why had he told me that? "I . . . I wouldn't presume, I – "

He leaned across his desk and regarded me with those reflective eyes. "Oh yes you would."

I dropped my eyes and regarded the flawless surface of his desk instead. When I looked up He regarded Wynn's sparkly residue almost wistfully.

"Is that – " Dare I ask? "Is that my fate?"

"You would wish such a thing?"

"No," I said quickly.

The Big Guy tipped back his head and chuckled. "Don't worry, Porsche Winter, I have something else in mind for you."

That didn't sound so good.

"Might I – " I cleared my throat. "Might I speak?"

"Oh do," The Big Guy said. He already knew what I'd say. The Big Guy knew everything. But then, as he'd said, free will added an amount of uncertainty. "I'd be most interested to hear it."

"I want you to know how hard I've tried to fit in here in Heaven. Perhaps I'm just not meant to be here."

It sounded so whiny and false, I held up my hand. "And that's not exactly true." Words tripped over each other, too fast to make sense. "Well, it is, sort of. What I mean is – it's no excuse. I did what I did of my own free will even when Gabriel told me not to."

"So he has said," The Big Guy prompted, ignoring my outburst. "My archangel is quite perturbed with you."

I shot a glance at what was left of Wynn and shuddered. "I'll bet."

"As are Raphael and Uriel." He didn't mention Michael. Had getting at Lucifer, however briefly, satisfied Michael?

I nodded. "I can imagine. I didn't mean to interfere – "

The Big Guy raised white eyebrows. "No?"

I took a deep breath and laid it all on the table. The ugly, unadulterated truth. I'd be judged for it one way or another, I reasoned. I might as well get it over with.

"I interfered even though I knew I shouldn't."

The Big Guy sat back in his chair. Holding out one palm, he motioned for me to continue. So I told him it all.

"I was afraid Naamah would conquer the Earthly plane in spite of

Gabriel's attempts to stop her."

"And you took it upon yourself to stand between Naamah and the Apocalypse." A statement, not a question. The Big Guy well knew what I'd done, what I'd been thinking. He wanted me to admit it, too.

"I look at things differently. I see things other people don't. It's the demon blood," I blundered, and then wished I'd had the sense to shut my mouth.

"Maybe," The Big Guy said.

That seemed to please him. Or maybe my willingness to admit it pleased him.

"And, I wanted to put things back the way they were . . . well, before I interfered."

Ready to defend that argument, I waited. But The Big Guy continued his compassionate stare, compelling me to fill the silence by spilling my guts. "And they are. Sort of." I shut my mouth and ground my teeth into my tongue. Whatever He had in mind for me, self-justification wasn't going to help.

He pursed His lips, conceding me that small point. "Granted, things are somewhat the way they were." He held up one white finger. "But you were betrayed, Porsche Winter."

"A deal with the Devil couldn't have turned out any other way," I said at last.

"Ah," The Big Guy murmured. "Now you *see*."

And I did. With crystal-clear hindsight, I saw how I'd been manipulated. And all the time, I thought I controlled the situation. "No good could have come from it. You can't make something good from evil."

"No, you can't."

"I just wanted to put things back the way they should be. I felt responsible for causing this whole mess."

"That endeavour caused a lot of damage."

It took every once of courage I possessed not to flinch from His gaze. "Forgive me. I am so very sorry."

"Your regret fixes nothing."

I tried to swallow past the rising lump in my throat and couldn't. "I know," I croaked.

His wrath, I expected. But The Big Guy sat still in his chair, waiting for me to continue. Apparently, judgement wasn't coming just yet. I made one last desperate plea.

"But I did just foil a plan to dethrone Lucifer. At least the Devil is back where he belongs. And with Gabriel, Michael and Nemesis to testify against him, it has to shake his claim on Heaven's shares just a little."

"Perhaps," He admitted. He ran one hand over His chin and studied me some more. I stared at a spot on the bright floor and remained silent. "That still leaves the problem of what is to be done about you."

I dragged my eyes upward. "I am at your mercy, Lord."

The Big Guy pushed back his chair and stood up. He walked a slow circle around me.

"I have come to a decision, Porsche Winter." That voice could crumble mountains and raise the sea. I sat stone still and tried desperately not to tremble.

"As you say," He continued, "you do see things differently from anyone else. You see things others overlook."

Lotta good it's done me, I wanted to say. I took that rare moment to practice restraint.

"And you have uncovered corporate espionage in both Heaven Inc. and Hell Ltd. That *talent* might be put to better use."

Dare I breathe? I wondered and decided to hold my breath a moment longer.

"Perhaps that talent needs to be further developed."

He regarded me shrewdly. "The Earthly plane is under control for the moment, yet still volatile. I need someone with your skills to look after our interests in that territory."

Breath rushed into my lungs. I didn't know whether to thank him or curl up and cry with relief.

"But this time you will accept Michael's direction."

The words echoed in my head, refusing to make sense. Had he just given me to Michael?

"Are you listening, Porsche Winter?"

"Yes Lord. Got it. I'll be good."

"Very well then. I reinstate your Guardian Angel status. You are hereby posted to the Earthly plane under Michael's guidance." He raised His hand to make it all so.

I should have accepted his proclamation and remained mute. But instead, some perverse little voice piped up. "What about Alex Chalmers?"

The Big Guy lowered His hand. Lightning flashed beneath the surface of His clear eyes. For an instant I expected to take up residence beside Wynn, but then He said, "Ah yes, Alexander Alan Chalmers."

I imagined Alex diving under my bed screaming, *Why didn't you just shut your mouth, Porsche?*

Good question.

Silence stretched like an elastic band ready to snap. Storm clouds drifted across The Big Guy's eyes. I imagined I heard that far-off thunder as he pondered Alex's fate.

"Mr. Chalmers is best kept in our camp," The Big Guy said after a time. He sounded like an army general giving orders. A convincing act to put things in a context I understood. The Big Guy could sound any way he chose.

The light in his eyes dissolved into serenity. I wasn't sure which unnerved me more.

"We don't want him offering Lucifer any more stock advice," I agreed. "But he's human – "

"A human being with far too much knowledge of The Great Beyond."

"My fault," I readily admitted.

"Not entirely. Lucifer had been watching him for some time."

That The Big Guy had taken my side shocked me so much I could only nod.

"I am removing Alex Chalmers from the roster and assigning him to you. Exposure to The Great Beyond has given Mr. Chalmers some unique talents as well. Gifts better used for good than evil."

His very words made it so.

But what did it all mean? I tried to unravel the conversation, to decipher the strands of subtext. He'd reinstated my angel powers along with the freedom to come and go on both the Heavenly and Earthly planes. With that came the responsibility for Alex's soul. Well, at least poor Percy was off the hook – for both of us.

Still, I had the most awful feeling something swelled beneath the tranquillity of the Heavenly plane. Something known only to The Big Guy, and possibly to Michael and the other archangels.

As ombudsman for Alex's soul, my first act involved getting him off on a technicality if I could.

"Alex Chalmers still has a hearing scheduled," I pointed out. "Even though he returned the money he embezzled under Lucifer's influence." By now Alex would be screaming, if he knew how much of The Big Guy's attention I'd focussed on him.

"Alexander Chalmers will face up to his sins."

No such luck, Alex. But at least I tried. "And you will see to it. Is that clear?"

Plainly, I'd delayed my departure long enough. I said, "Yes, Lord. Obey Michael, behave myself and make sure Alex behaves as well."

The air shimmered around me. I found myself standing in the hallway outside The Big Guy's audience chamber. Alone.

Looking down, I found my body encased in a silver flight suit that felt like a second skin, complete with winged insignia. I felt for the locator clipped to my belt and sighed. A discourager rested in its holster against my right thigh. I twitched my shoulders and tested the weight of the interceptor in its sling.

Armed and dangerous again, I supposed that meant I should report to Michael before I talked to Nemesis. I turned down the marble hall and headed for my new boss' office.

Michael's headquarters contrasted sharply with Gabriel's high-tech domain. Where Gabriel filled his workplace with the latest gadgetry, Michael's office was sparse to the extreme.

Grey marble covered the floors. The walls were the colour of dove's wings. Easily as big as a dancehall, the single piece of furniture made it seem even more spacious.

A marble desk dominated the far end of the room. Devoid of paper or clutter, it was a shade darker than the floor. A single monitor sat on the corner of the table.

It had a view to rival Raphael's tower, though. An entire wall looked out into the slowly drifting clouds. The vista was calm, meditative and very unlike the Michael I thought I knew.

Mounted on the wall behind the desk was a dangerous-looking sword. I had no doubt Michael knew how to use it – well. Special Projects indeed, I thought. But the owner of this impressive domain was nowhere in sight.

Well, Michael certainly knew how to find me – on any plane, I reasoned. I turned to head back to my own apartment. A discreet cough stopped me.

Uriel and Raphael stood in the doorway blocking the only way out.

For a moment we stared at each other. I didn't know quite what to say. Both wore clean flight suits, which meant for the moment the Heavenly plane was secure.

"I suppose you've heard," I began.

"Oh yes," Uriel said, "we've heard."

From Uriel that counted as small talk. I looked to Raphael for rescue.

His green eyes stared calmly back at me. Then his face broke into a slow smile. "Well Winter, never a dull moment, is there?"

"In all honesty, a few dull moments would be most welcome, sir."

"Well, I doubt you'll be getting any," Uriel remarked. He voice held traces of grudging respect mixed with pity. "Seems we're going to be needing you, after all."

What in the Heavens did that mean? I wanted to ask, but the archangel continued. "While I don't agree with your tactics, you do get results. You did manage to secure the revenue stream from the Earthly plane."

High praise from Uriel, or at least as close as he ever came to passing out compliments. I had no clue how to respond.

While I was trying to come up with a worthwhile retort, one that wouldn't get me into further trouble, Raphael brandished his locator. "Go home, Winter. You look beat."

The Heavenly plane swirled in a cosmic blender.

When the universe stopped spinning I found myself staring though a window at shining blue water that stretched out before me. It took a moment to recognise my surroundings.

Alex's apartment. *Oh no.*

I'd promised to take Alex back to Earth with me. I imagined him alone in my apartment in Heaven panicking. But The Big Guy had supposedly given me the ability to travel both planes. Hopefully, that meant I could retrieve him.

Through the windows, the lake gleamed in the sunshine. I peered down at the docks and saw workmen replacing windows in the mall. A crane hoisted a ruined boat from the water. Apocalypse averted, the Earthly plane dug itself out. Repairs were underway.

All was quiet, and I was refurbished and fully armed. Now all I had to do was find Alex and bring him home.

Unclipping the locator from my belt, I dialled coordinates.

"Not so fast," said a voice behind me.

I spun, nearly knocking myself over with momentum.

Michael sat in the middle of Alex's leather couch. Dirt streaked his face. Blond hair tumbled haphazardly over his shoulders. He appeared every part the warrior angel at rest.

He gave me a quick once-over with those grey eyes that missed nothing. "Winter."

I cleared my throat. "So, Boss."

The corner of his mouth quirked in a half smile. "Don't look so relieved, Winter. I doubt I'm going to be the kind of boss you have in mind."

What should I say to that? I settled for a mute nod.

Then suddenly the intricate strands of a puzzle knit together in my mind. The dreams about Lucifer, the numerous portents and Michael's curious interest in me. "You sent me those dreams, didn't you?" I blurted.

Michael raised one blond eyebrow, neither confirming nor denying my accusation. I noted he didn't ask which dream I referred to.

"Does Rafe know?" He couldn't know, I thought, answering my own question. If Raphael found out Michael had hacked his system, he'd have fits. But why? I couldn't help wondering. Why send me dreams about Lucifer. To warn me? To prepare me for that big bad something I had a feeling was coming our way? A something that had Uriel feeling sorry for me, and Michael collecting Uriel's former guardians. I wondered suddenly if I'd been wrong about Percy. Perhaps he hadn't been Gabriel's spy after all. Maybe he was Michael's.

"What's to know?" Michael asked in that enigmatic way of his. And I realised he hadn't been threatening me earlier. He wouldn't be an easy boss to work for.

He held me in his slate eyes a moment longer. A commander inspecting the troops, or in my case, perhaps a new weapon. Nearly as penetrating as The Big Guy's scrutiny, I tried not to flinch. "I suspect you're going to be an asset to me in the struggle to come."

Another enigmatic half answer. One that certainly didn't calm my fears. Again that reference to a big bad something. I said, "Yes, sir."

"Well, I have a report to deliver. He wiped a hand across his grimy face. "We'll have to have that staff meeting later."

"I'll wait for you here."

After I find Alex, I thought. But I didn't tell Michael that.

I expected him to disappear. Instead, he raised his locator. "You forgot something."

I followed the glint of its energy in the sunlight. He aimed the beam in the direction of Alex's bedroom.

When I turned around Michael had disappeared.

Please! I prayed. And bolted for the bedroom.

CHAPTER FIFTEEN

IN WHICH EARTHLY MATTERS MUST BE SETTLED

ALEX LAY MOTIONLESS ON HIS BED, HIS eyes closed, probably trying to determine whether it was safe to move.

I scrambled closer and shook him hard. "Alex!"

His eyes flew open. "You're back." He looked around the bedroom. "I'm home."

"Everything's okay," I said. I guess, at that moment, everything pretty much was. Except for one last detail.

"And you're – you!"

Again that wary look, the same one he'd given me when he'd seen me in my halo. I had looked every bit a supernatural being. That had to make even the bravest of men think twice.

I sat down on the bed beside him. "I'm me."

"What does that mean?"

"That things are back the way they should be. Well mostly."

He reached out and touched the smooth silver material of my flightsuit, and then curled a blonde lock of hair around his finger. "Are they sending you back to Heaven?"

I sighed. "No."

"They're not sending you to jail, arc they?"

"No." It didn't seem fair to keep him guessing. "I've been posted here on Earth. Though, I guess I'm somewhat free to come and go in Heaven." He still had that wide-eyed look, like he expected Lucifer or some other minor demon to come leaping out of the woodwork. "I guess I really should have asked about that."

"What about me?"

Now for the bad news. "Well . . . "

Alex grew still. "Porsche?"

"Damnation, Alex! I tried to get you off without having to go through a hearing for embezzlement. Really, I did. I went to the highest authority."

His eyes widened, but he didn't move. He didn't even breathe. "And?"

"You still have to face the tribunal." There I'd said it.

"The Earthly tribunal?" Alex asked. "Not – "

"Oh!" I said, understanding suddenly what had him so spooked. "No, I meant the securities commission."

He let his breath go. "Compared to the wrath of Heaven or an eternity in Hell, that's not so bad."

I had to agree with him there. "Trust me, you don't want to face the Heavenly one."

"I believe you."

He seemed so relieved, I hated to tell him the rest of it. "Alex, there's more."

Alex groaned. "There always is."

"You've been . . . well, drafted."

It took a moment for the reality of that to sink in. Then, he said, "What!"

"The Big Guy's decided that Heaven could use a little of your financial know-how. Consider yourself kind of on retainer, pending further assignment."

He fell back into the pillows and stared at the ceiling. "What does that mean? Do I have to go to . . . to Heaven?"

"Oh no. You'll be working out of your home office, here on Earth."

That didn't seem to reassure him much. "So what am I supposed to do?"

I glanced at the spot of ceiling he stared at. If he'd been scarred by his premature trip to Heaven, he showed no outward signs of it. "I guess you'll find out soon. We've both been assigned to Michael. Well, I've been transferred to Michael's division and your soul has been placed back under my care."

He wrenched his gaze from the patterned ceiling. "You're kidding, right?"

"No." I stared into his soft dark eyes and felt more incompetent that I had in my life. "I promise I'll do a better job than I did last time."

"I sure hope so!" Again that guarded look, quickly disguised. But I'd seen it. And there was no denying the many ways I'd changed his life forever. If it weren't for me, Alex would still be in his Bay Street office trading stocks instead of trying to win back Heaven's share.

Which brought us to the painful part of the discussion.

"Alex – " I didn't want to ask that question. "Do you want me to leave?"

I hoped he'd blurt out a fervent "No, of course not!" But instead, he pondered the question. While my heart sank.

"No," he said after a time.

I should have accepted his answer, but I pressed for more.

"Are you sure?" Before he could say anything, I added, "Because I saw the way you looked at me when we were in my apartment in Heaven. You never did tell me how you came to be in Naamah's custody. And – " I added the final damning piece of evidence, "you've been sculpting she-devils!"

A guilty blush stained his face.

"It was sitting on your desk," I added, feeling a little guilty myself for snooping through his private things. I pounded in the last nail. "So, if Naamah's really more to your taste, you should just say so!"

"Naamah! How can you think that, even for one minute?" His face darkened from embarrassment to fury. "Besides, if you're really my Guardian Angel again, you should know the answer!"

Oh! Now he was using my own professionalism, or lack thereof, against me. My own face coloured with anger. "That's not fair, they haven't transferred the files yet. And besides, that sculpture sure looked like her!"

We stared at each other, faces red and hands clenched.

"Just answer the question, Alex. I don't care what's in your dossier. I want to know what's in your heart. And no, that's not in the database!"

His expression softened a little then, but not much. Alex was a man used to toeing the hard line. "Naamah knocked on the door. I knew I shouldn't have answered it, but I thought it might be you. When I opened the door, she had that flamethrower pointed at me. So I went with her," he admitted a little sheepishly. "I knew you'd know what to do."

That sounded plausible. "And the sculpture of the she-devil?" I prompted.

"I always sculpt things that are bothering me. I work out my angst through my art." He shot me a hot stare nearly as penetrating as Lucifer's. "If you must know."

"Okay . . . " I wasn't an artist. He could be telling the truth. And then I thought of the angel in his bedroom. "So when you sculpted that angel – "

"It was because a certain Guardian Angel kept showing up in my nightmares."

Touché!

I had to admit, it hurt just a little to hear that the sculpture that had touched me so deeply with its beauty had been Alex's attempt to banish a nightmare about me.

Hardly worthy behaviour for an angel, but I struck back. "Well, it didn't work, did it? You didn't get me out of your mind. Or out of your life."

Alex laughed, that rare belly laugh I so seldom heard. "No." He deflected the barb. "But I'll say this for you, Porsche, you're good to have in my corner in a fight."

It sounded like a compliment. It felt gratifying to have my combat skill appreciated. But I'd been hoping for something a bit more personal, a little bit more about me. Like *please stay, Porsche, I can't live without you.*

Okay, I know that sounds hokey. But then he dealt me a fatal blow to the heart.

"I like you."

I recoiled from his words as though he'd struck me.

He liked me? *Liked me!*

I'd gone to Hell and back to save his soul. I'd fought Heaven and Hell to save his life and he . . . *liked* me?

"Yeah?" Some demon seized control of my tongue. "Well, I like . . . pizza!"

His eyebrows drew together. "What's that supposed to mean?"

I stood up, walked to the bedroom doorway. "You figure it out."

And yeah, I know I'm about the worst bet since selling your soul for a gold coin, and if I were Alex I'd be running as fast as I could in the opposite direction. But I still wanted to hear the words. I wanted to believe I was loveable. At least a little.

"Wait! Porsche!" Alex vaulted off the bed. Hitting the floor running, he pursued me down the hall.

I stopped at the door to his apartment. He put his hand against it. I resisted the urge to pop the hinges by hauling it open.

"What?" he demanded. "What did I say?"

Damnation, I thought. The man really didn't know. And I refused to humiliate myself by explaining it to him.

You're his Guardian Angel, a voice inside squeaked, *you shouldn't be pursuing this relationship.* And then again, The Big Guy had sent me back here. Who knew what he intended?

Gently, I placed a finger in the centre of his forehead. "Think about it, Alex."

He leaned against the door, like that could stop me from leaving. "Are you breaking up with me?" he asked incredulously.

I answered with another question. "Do we have anything to break up here?"

Just answer the question, Alex and get it over with.

But instead he said, "Maybe you need some time to think it over."

"Fine." I undid the deadbolt. Despite Alex's considerable resistance, I wrenched the door open without doing property damage. "A hundred years ought to do it."

His eyes widened in genuine fear. "I don't have a hundred years."

Well, neither did I, but he didn't need to know that. I shrugged.

He shut the door and threw the bolt. I let him do it. It made no difference. I could take a quick locator jaunt out of there any time I chose. Just as I could break the door down. If I chose.

Alex seized my arm and tried to drag me back toward the living room. I dug in my heels. He let me go.

"I don't understand. Why are you so mad? What did I say?"

I hissed at him, sounding more like an over-grown version of Cupid than myself. "For the second time, Alex, think about it."

Poor guy truly looked dumbfounded. I should have taken pity on him.

"I said I liked you. I said . . . oh!" Realisation dawned. "Okay," he said slowly. "I got it." He glanced at the living room behind us and the sun setting through the panoramic windows. The evening looked calm, ripe for a stroll along the boardwalk. Except that I'd got myself into yet another fight.

"Come on, Porsche. Let's sit down and . . . " he gulped like it was the last thing he wanted to do, "talk."

I followed him toward the couch wondering how I was going to get out of this one with some of my dignity intact.

We sat on his leather couch. Where did you start the kind of conversation we needed to have?

Finally, Alex said, "That wasn't what you wanted to hear, was it?"

"I had hoped for something a little . . . " I shook my head. "I don't know . . . "

"Stronger?"

"Something like that."

"Porsche – " He reached out, encased my hand in his larger one. "I know Cupid calls me A Bad Idea."

"Very Bad Idea," I supplied automatically.

Annoyance crossed his face, but he let it go, showing far more restraint than I did. "Whatever. And technically we're not even the same . . . species."

"But?" I spat the word at him.

"But I still want you to stay."

"Even though having me in your life opens a whole universe too scary to contemplate?" I shoved the truth at him. If he intended to wiggle out of it later, I wanted to know now.

"Not so scary," he said, and then winced. "Okay, really, really scary. But whatever happens . . . I love you Porsche."

There. Once he'd said the L-word, I didn't feel quite so righteous. Were I Alex, I'd think twice, too. Probably more than twice. "Alex, I am sorry. For . . . well, for everything."

We sat in silence for a few moments, neither of us knowing what to say. The sun lingered on the horizon bathing both our faces in crimson light. Finally Alex smiled. "Looks nice outside," he said.

"It probably won't hail tonight," I agreed, thankful for a new topic of conversation.

The smile broadened. I refused to look at those dimples. "One night without a drum beating over my head would be nice."

I walked to the window and squinted against the last of the sunlight at the pier below. "Looks like the boardwalk is still in one piece. Want to go for a walk?"

"Sure," Alex said. "We could have a drink on the patio. Heck, we can probably expense it. After all, we're supposed to be watching for she-devils, aren't we?"

"Let's hope we don't see any."

As I turned away from the sunset something caught my eye. Clouds drifted lazily across the lake. Patterns formed, broke and reformed.

But as the sun dipped below the horizon, it shone one last beam through a heart-shaped ring of cloud.

I grabbed Alex's shoulder, turning him in the direction of the spectacle.

"Looks like Cupid's changed his mind about you."

EPILOGUE

IN WHICH OLD FRIENDSHIPS ARE RENEWED

CUPID DREW A SILVER ARROW FROM HIS quiver. Placing it against his bow, he checked his aim. I followed the line of his arm to the mark sitting in the café. The target looked about twenty-seven. Blond straight hair hung down to his collar. The ends of his hair had been dyed black in an earlier attempt at the Goth look. His vivid blue eyes stared into a giant cup of black coffee. In spite of the hot summer sun, the guy didn't look like he'd spent a day outside. Pale skin and downcast eyes gave him a fragile, artistic look. Brooding, he took a long drag on his cigarette and contemplated his coffee's dark depths.

I didn't want to startle Cupid and throw off his aim. That could have disastrous results. I know. I'd seen it happen. They say opposites attract for a reason. So, I hovered above the ground in the shadows cast by an ugly bronze sculpture and scoured the pavement for the starving artist's intended mate.

A trio of elderly ladies were the only females in the patio smoking section. They couldn't possibly be what Cupid had in mind. Unless he'd completely lost his mind since we'd last talked. The only person inside the café was a bicycle courier buying a bottle of water. I squinted. Well, maybe.

Cupid let the arrow fly. The tiny silver arrow glinted in the sunlight before burying itself in the brooding artist's heart. He jumped and clutched at his chest. The arrow glimmered, then vanished. Cupid cocked another arrow.

I looked wildly around, but couldn't see anyone else. Cupid couldn't possibly have the smoking grannies on the patio in mind. Could he? Maybe the bicycle courier was more his style. Risking discovery, I drifted closer, happier to be moving about in my angel body.

Just then a brunette jogged along the path winding through the courtyard. A sports bra and a pair of tiny spandex shorts left little of her bronzed body to the imagination. The artist's head swivelled in her direction, his coffee forgotten.

Cupid released the arrow. The brunette stumbled and fell. The artist leapt from his seat. Coffee spilled across the white wrought iron table, but he was too busy running to her rescue to notice.

I drifted down until my feet touched grass. Cupid hovered at shoulder level, but facing the two in the café, he couldn't see me.

"Wouldn't have put those two together," I said aloud.

Cupid yelped. Seizing another arrow, he set it against his bow and prepared to use it in self-defence.

"Hey!" I protested. "Put that away!"

Cupid cast a quick glance back at the artist and the athlete. The brunette now sat at his table. He'd run inside to get her a bottle of water and was now dabbing at his spilled coffee with a wad of napkins. The brunette didn't seem to mind the attention. She sipped her water and stared at her saviour in wonder.

"Are you trying to scare me to death?" Cupid demanded. He summoned a pretty menacing glare.

"Oh, don't be so dramatic!" I studied the world's newest couple. The brunette didn't look like she was going anywhere. She'd clearly found something more interesting to do with her afternoon than jog. I shook my head.

"Are you questioning my judgement?" Cupid was still trying his best to admonish me.

"No," I said quickly. "They just don't look like they have much in common."

Giving up on the glare, Cupid finally smiled. "That's the idea." He pointed a chubby finger at the artist, who now was showing more life than he'd probably had all year. He'd already captured the jogger's hand and was staring deeply into her eyes. "The first thing she'll do is to convince him to give up that tobacco habit of his. That way he won't die like he's otherwise going to when he's forty-five. She just moved to the city and doesn't know anyone. He's going to take her to gallery openings and introduce her to a whole new group of friends." Cupid studied his handiwork wistfully, then looked back at me. "Speaking of couples who don't have much in common."

I held up my hands in surrender. "Okay, okay, I'm sorry! Besides, I thought you'd changed your mind about Alex."

"Well . . ." Cupid really hated to admit he'd been mistaken. Ever. "I was wrong about Alex. The guy's got guts, and he clearly cares for you."

That was as close as poor Alex would ever get to an apology. But even my dad seemed to like Alex, so my best friend was just going to have to deal.

Cupid pulled a scroll from a pouch on his quiver. Today's log. By the silver check marks against the list of names, I could tell he was running behind. He put another silver check against two more names, and then thrust it back in its pouch. Cruising up beside me, he hovered impatiently.

I should have let him get back to work, but there was one more thing I just had to know. I pointed a finger at his chest. "You've been holding out on me."

Surprise crossed the cherub's face, followed quickly by a wariness that confirmed my suspicions.

"Out with it, Cupid."

He had the audacity to ask, "Out with what?" Flapping his wings, he prepared to take off. I snagged him by one chubby toe.

"Wait a minute! You have to tell me about Percy and Naamah." We were eye to eye now. Damned if I'd let him get away and keep a deliciously juicy piece of gossip to himself. "And don't pretend you don't know what I mean."

"That was a mistake." Sighing, Cupid perched on my shoulder. The arrows in his quiver clanked noisily against my ear.

"Not your mistake?" I asked, horrified. Not even on the worst of days could I imagine my buddy putting those two together.

"Of course not!" The cherub sounded truly wounded.

I tried to appease him. "Well, I didn't think so."

"Turns out you're not the only angel ever to stray to the dark side."

Turning my head, I studied him with one eye. "Don't think I'm going to let you get away with that cryptic half-answer."

Cupid flapped his wings, threatening another takeoff and messing up my hair. "Some of us have work to do today, Porsche."

I resisted the urge to create some turbulence of my own by swatting at him. "So hurry up and tell me." Truth was my own work was waiting. But I wouldn't leave without that one last riddle solved. "If it wasn't your work, whose was it?"

"A college prank gone wrong."

"Wynn Jarrett," I said, hazarding the only logical guess.

"Oh I'm sure Wynn was the ring leader."

"Let me guess," I said, getting more of the picture than I wanted. "Wynn took Percy drinking at Purgatory."

Cupid only nodded.

"Hasn't changed his modus operandi much, has he?"

The cherub shrugged. "Why would he, when it worked so well?" Then realising what he said, he leaned against my head. "No offence."

"None taken."

"And poor Percy wanted so badly to be accepted, he went along with it all."

"Don't tell me Wynn set him up with Naamah?" Why didn't it surprise me that Wynn and Naamah were buddies? Oh well, I thought grimly.

"Barely got out with his hide intact." Cupid looked oddly embarrassed. "Sad thing is, I think he liked her."

"She'd eat him for breakfast."

To that the cherub let out a hearty belly laugh. I slapped a hand over his mouth. "Shh!"

The huge bronze sculpture hid us from view. But with the trees still stripped of their foliage, there wasn't much cover to be found.

I shook my head. "Poor Percy. No wonder he's been so strait-laced ever since."

Glancing at the jogger and the artist I found them engrossed in a meaningful conversation on the coffee shop patio. The couple had just met, but they were gazing into each other's eyes like they'd known each other all their lives.

"He wouldn't be the first soul she ruined to satisfy her sordid tastes."

I nudged Cupid with one finger. "I can't believe you've been keeping this from me all this time!" Thinking back to our conversation in Cupid's living room, I realised I'd been had. "You even tried to throw me off the trail!"

"I wouldn't even have known about it if I hadn't been on a training session that night. So lips sealed."

"I won't breathe a word," I agreed. "But that sure explains a lot of things."

Behind us in the courtyard, the brunette and the artist were walking down the path arm in arm. Well, at least Cupid had done his good deed for the day. I should get back to work myself, I thought.

Cupid pulled out his log, glanced again at it with dismay. He unclipped the locator from the tie of his loincloth and dialled in coordinates. "Drinks Friday night after work?" he asked. Poor guy, I think he really missed me.

"Sure," I said. "Somewhere Alex can go." Which meant somewhere nearby on Earth.

"Okay." The air crackled with energy as Cupid winked out.

I stared after his departing shimmer. If Cupid was willingly drinking with Alex the Very Bad Idea and Percival Thor was Naamah's ex, then things were definitely not the way I'd thought they were.

Not at all.

STEPHANIE BEDWELL-GRIME HAS HAD careers as a television producer, medical photographer and teacher. She is the author of three previous novels and over fifty short stories, and is a four-time finalist for the Aurora, the national Canadian award for speculative fiction.

DON'T MISS THE FIRST INCREDIBLE INSTALLMENT . . .

GUARDIAN ANGEL by STEPHANIE BEDWELL-GRIME

Porsche Winter has a problem . . . as a fully fledged guardian angel, she is charged with the safety of her clients at all times. But you take your eye off the monitor for just one moment, and the Devil is in there with a demon snatching the soul from one of your clients. But not just any client: dreamboat and all round lust object Alex Chalmers.

With the soul lost to the Devil, Porsche realises that this is just a part of a plan for the Dark One to assert his authority over the Netherworld and to take control of Heaven. It doesn't help that Porsche too is the object of the Devil's lust, or that she's been set up for a fall by office slimeball Wynn Jarrett.

With all that's going on, Porsche's day has started badly and is set to get even worse . . .

'*Guardian Angel* is a wickedly inventive supernatural tale of modern business and all its devilish wheelings and dealings. Both clever and imaginative, it's also invested with enough humour to make it a blue-chip novel. I'm calling my broker and telling him to invest in Stephanie Bedwell-Grime'

– Edo van Belkom, author of *Scream Queen*

'The story ticks along at a fair pace; quicker than an express train drop into the fiery pits of Hell'

– Vector

'A nice change of pace fantasy with likeable characters and a devilishly clever villain'

– Chronicle

'A Tom Holtish comedy . . . Bedwell-Grime limns Porsche and the cosmic setup deftly, producing something akin to the film *Wings of Desire* (1987) as rewritten by Mel Brooks'

– Paul di Filippo, *Asimov's Science Fiction*

Available from Telos Publishing Ltd.
£9.99 (+ £2.50 UK p&p) Standard p/b ISBN: 1-903889-62-6

OTHER TITLES FROM TELOS PUBLISHING

TIME HUNTER

A range of high-quality, original paperback and limited edition hardback novellas featuring the adventures in time of Honoré Lechasseur. Part mystery, part detective story, part dark fantasy, part science fiction . . . these books are guaranteed to enthral fans of good fiction everywhere, and are in the spirit of our acclaimed range of *Doctor Who* Novellas.

THE WINNING SIDE by LANCE PARKIN
Emily is dead! Killed by an unknown assailant. Honoré and Emily find themselves caught up in a plot reaching from the future to their past, and with their very existence, not to mention the future of the entire world, at stake, can they unravel the mystery before it is too late?
An adventure in time and space.
£7.99 (+ £1.50 UK p&p) Standard p/b ISBN 1-903889-35-9 (pb)

THE TUNNEL AT THE END OF THE LIGHT by STEFAN PETRUCHA
In the heart of post-war London, a bomb is discovered lodged at a disused station between Green Park and Hyde Park Corner. The bomb detonates, and as the dust clears, it becomes apparent that *something* has been awakened. Strange half-human creatures attack the workers at the site, hungrily searching for anything containing sugar . . . Meanwhile, Honoré and Emily are contacted by eccentric poet Randolph Crest, who believes himself to be the target of these subterranean creatures. The ensuing investigation brings Honoré and Emily up against a terrifying force from deep beneath the earth, and one which even with their combined powers, they may have trouble stopping.
An adventure in time and space.
£7.99 (+ £1.50 UK p&p) Standard p/b ISBN 1-903889-37-5 (pb)
£25.00 (+ £1.50 UK p&p) Deluxe h/b ISBN 1-903889-38-3 (hb)

THE CLOCKWORK WOMAN by CLAIRE BOTT
Honoré and Emily find themselves imprisoned in the 19th Century by a celebrated inventor . . . but help comes from an unexpected source – a humanoid automaton created by and to give pleasure to its owner. As the trio escape to London, they are unprepared for what awaits them, and at every turn it seems impossible to avert what fate may have in store for the Clockwork Woman.
An adventure in time and space.

£7.99 (+ £1.50 UK p&p) Standard p/b ISBN 1-903889-39-1 (pb)
£25.00 (+ £1.50 UK p&p) Deluxe h/b ISBN 1-903889-40-5 (hb)

KITSUNE by JOHN PAUL CATTON

In the year 2020, Honoré Lechasseur and Emily Blandish find themselves thrown into a mystery as an ice spirit wreaks havoc during the Kyoto's Gion Festival, and a haunted funhouse proves to contain more than just paper lanterns and wax dummies. But what does all this have to do with the elegant owner of the Hide and Chic fashion chain . . . and to the legendary Japanese fox-spirits, the Kitsune?
An adventure in time and space.
£7.99 (+ £1.50 UK p&p) Standard p/b ISBN 1-903889-41-3 (pb)
£25.00 (+ £1.50 UK p&p) Deluxe h/b ISBN 1-903889-42-1 (hb)

THE SEVERED MAN by GEORGE MANN

What links a clutch of sinister murders in Victorian London, an angel appearing in a Staffordshire village in the 1920s and a small boy running loose around the capital in 1950? When Honoré and Emily encounter a man who appears to have been cut out of time, they think they have the answer. But soon enough they discover that the mystery is only just beginning and that nightmares can turn into reality.
An adventure in time and space.
£7.99 (+ £1.50 UK p&p) Standard p/b ISBN 1-903889-43-X (pb)
£25.00 (+ £1.50 UK p&p) Deluxe h/b ISBN 1-903889-44-8 (hb)
PUB: DECEMBER 2004 (UK)

TIME HUNTER FILM

DAEMOS RISING by DAVID J HOWE, DIRECTED by KEITH BARNFATHER

Daemos Rising is a sequel to both the *Doctor Who* adventure *The Daemons* and to *Downtime*, an earlier drama featuring the Yeti. It is also a prequel of sorts to Telos Publishing's *Time Hunter* series. It stars Miles Richardson as ex-UNIT operative Douglas Cavendish, and Beverley Cressman as Brigadier Lethbridge-Stewart's daughter Kate. Trapped in an isolated cottage, Cavendish thinks he is seeing ghosts. The only person who might understand and help is Kate Lethbridge-Stewart . . . but when she arrives, she realises that Cavendish is key in a plot to summon the Daemons back to the Earth. With time running out, Kate discovers that sometimes even the familiar can turn out to be your worst nightmare. Also starring Andrew Wisher, and featuring Ian Richardson as the Narrator.
An adventure in time and space on DVD.
£14.00 (+ £2.50 UK p&p) • Reeltime Pictures, PO Box 23435, London SE26 5WU

HORROR/FANTASY

CAPE WRATH by PAUL FINCH

Death and horror on a deserted Scottish island as an ancient Viking warrior chief returns to life.

£8.00 (+ £1.50 UK p&p) Standard p/b ISBN: 1-903889-60-X

KING OF ALL THE DEAD by STEVE LOCKLEY & PAUL LEWIS

The king of all the dead will have what is his.

£8.00 (+ £1.50 UK p&p) Standard p/b ISBN: 1-903889-61-8

GUARDIAN ANGEL by STEPHANIE BEDWELL-GRIME

Devilish fun as Guardian Angel Porsche Winter loses a soul to the devil . . .

£9.99 (+ £2.50 UK p&p) Standard p/b ISBN: 1-903889-62-6

ASPECTS OF A PSYCHOPATH by ALISTAIR LANGSTON

Goes deeper than ever before into the twisted psyche of a serial killer. Horrific, graphic and gripping, this book is not for the squeamish.

£8.00 (+ £1.50 UK p&p) Standard p/b ISBN: 1-903889-63-4

SPECTRE by STEPHEN LAWS

The inseparable Byker Chapter: six boys, one girl, growing up together in the back streets of Newcastle. Now memories are all that Richard Eden has left, and one treasured photograph. But suddenly, inexplicably, the images of his companions start to fade, and as they vanish, so his friends are found dead and mutilated. Something is stalking the Chapter, picking them off one by one, something connected with their past, and with the girl they used to know.

£9.99 (+ £2.50 UK p&p) Standard p/b ISBN: 1-903889-72-3

THE HUMAN ABSTRACT by GEORGE MANN

A future tale of private detectives, AIs, Nanobots, love and death.

£7.99 (+ £1.50 UK p&p) Standard p/b ISBN: 1-903889-65-0

BREATHE by CHRISTOPHER FOWLER

The Office meets *Night of the Living Dead.*

£7.99 (+ £1.50 UK p&p) Standard p/b ISBN: 1-903889-67-7

£25.00 (+ £1.50 UK p&p) Deluxe h/b ISBN: 1-903889-68-5

HOUDINI'S LAST ILLUSION by STEVE SAVILE

Can the master illusionist Harry Houdini outwit the dead shades of his past?
£7.99 (+ £1.50 UK p&p) Standard p/b ISBN: 1-903889-66-9

ALICE'S JOURNEY BEYOND THE MOON by RJ CARTER
A sequel to the classic Lewis Carroll tales.
£6.99 (+ £1.50 UK p&p) Standard p/b ISBN: 1-903889-76-6
£30.00 (+ £1.50 UK p&p) Deluxe h/b ISBN: 1-903889-77-4

TV/FILM GUIDES

A DAY IN THE LIFE: THE UNOFFICIAL AND UNAUTHORISED GUIDE TO 24 by KEITH TOPPING
Complete episode guide to the first season of the popular TV show.
£9.99 (+ £2.50 p&p) Standard p/b ISBN: 1-903889-53-7

THE TELEVISION COMPANION: THE UNOFFICIAL AND UNAUTHORISED GUIDE TO DOCTOR WHO by DAVID J HOWE & STEPHEN JAMES WALKER
Complete episode guide to the popular TV show.
£14.99 (+ £4.75 UK p&p) Standard p/b ISBN: 1-903889-51-0

LIBERATION: THE UNOFFICIAL AND UNAUTHORISED GUIDE TO BLAKE'S 7 by ALAN STEVENS & FIONA MOORE
Complete episode guide to the popular TV show.
Featuring a foreword by David Maloney.
£9.99 (+ £2.50 UK p&p) Standard p/b ISBN: 1-903889-54-5

HOWE'S TRANSCENDENTAL TOYBOX: SECOND EDITION by DAVID J HOWE & ARNOLD T BLUMBERG
Complete guide to *Doctor Who* Merchandise.
£25.00 (+ £4.75 UK p&p) Standard p/b ISBN: 1-903889-56-1

HOWE'S TRANSCENDENTAL TOYBOX: UPDATE No.1: 2003 by DAVID J HOWE & ARNOLD T BLUMBERG
Complete guide to *Doctor Who* Merchandise released in 2003.
£7.99 (+ £1.50 UK p&p) Standard p/b ISBN: 1-903889-57-X

A VAULT OF HORROR by KEITH TOPPING
A Guide to 80 Classic (and not so classic) British Horror Films.
£12.99 (+ £4.75 UK p&p) Standard p/b ISBN: 1-903889-58-8